The Stone M

MW01230599

A VAMPIRE'S BOHEMIAN

BOOK IV

USA Today Bestselling Author

Vanessa Fewings

Vanessa Fewings

Bohemian

Cover design by Najla Qamber

Cover photo credit Shutterstock:
Greta Gabaglio and Volodymyr Tverdokhlib

Book edited by Louise Bohmer

ISBN: 9781492798767

The Stone Masters Vampire Series

A Vampire's Rise

A Vampires Reckoning

A Vampire's Dominion

A Vampire's Bohemian

Mortal Veil (short story)

PROLOGUE

A wave of vertigo.

I stared dead ahead, averting my gaze from the sheer drop twenty stories down. Balancing precariously on the uppermost outside ledge of the Bainard Building with my back pressed against the cold brick, I regretted hiding out here. It had seemed reasonable fifteen minutes ago. My usual nerves of steel were failing.

Without a search warrant I had no right to be here, or rather in there, snooping around Lord Rupert Hauville's office. Whoever had entered the room had almost caught me red-handed, hacking into his desktop computer and a few clicks away from getting what I'd come for.

Evidence.

In any other circumstance, I might have enjoyed the view of Knightsbridge. In fact if I crooked my neck far enough I'd be able to see as far as Harrods. Chilled by the night air, goose bumps prickled along my forearms. This was easily the most irresponsible risk I'd ever taken and there were plenty to compare it to. Pursuing vampires for one.

A raindrop splotched on my forearm and then another. Rain struck the ledge, making it slippery beneath my inappropriate strappy high-heeled shoes, which were not my usual choice of footwear when scaling buildings. This evening had been going so well. I'd infiltrated Hauville's fundraising party, mingling amongst the city's elite charity goers while extracting intelligence on the man from the guests. This black evening gown I'd chosen to wear was far too flimsy for one of London's coldest evenings. I'd not exactly foreseen this.

Maybe it would have been safer to take on whoever had entered. After all, I was trained in self-defense. Although not on police time, this could be considered police work. My unusual brand of investigating always delivered results, and I'd often overstepped protocols proving my willingness to go out on a limb.

Or even a ledge.

The window frame slammed shut.

Damn.

Taking several deep breaths calmed me, despite the adrenaline surging through my veins and making my heart race. Blood pounded in my ears. An ill-timed wave of dizziness swept over me.

I knelt and turned awkwardly to peer through the window at a now empty room. Dreading what I already knew, I grabbed the sides of the window frame and tried to ease them up. My fingers slipped off. I gave it another go.

Stealing precious seconds to think my way out of this, I held panic at bay. Or tried too. Going left wasn't an option. The wall ended there and I wasn't ready to explore what lay around the corner. Not that it was even possible to climb around it. To my right was another window, but what led to it was a rain soaked ledge.

Take off your shoes, came that quiet inner voice offering reassurance. With fumbling fingers, I undid the straps on each shoe and removed them. Now barefoot, I felt more stable, though shockwaves of cold bored into my soles. Clutching my heels, I edged to my right, careful not to drop a shoe and knock out a pedestrian.

I faced the wall and knelt close to the window. I didn't even try and open it. From here I could see the catch was locked. Several strikes on the glass with my spiked heel proved breaking it wasn't possible. The rubber merely bounced off the window pane.

Standing again, I hugged the wall and rested my forehead against it. Silently, I invited a Zen-like trance to find me, taking deep steadying breaths while reassuring myself I'd get to live through this. There came that old familiar vow, the one where I pledged I'd never put myself in this kind of danger ever again.

A promise I intended to keep this time.

CHAPTER 1

A click, and the window frame flew up.

Raising my eyes to the starlit sky, I thanked God for this miracle and edged back along the ledge, weak from those twenty minutes or so since I'd first stepped out here. My legs were numb from the cold. With my hands grasping either side of the window frame, I used the leverage to jump back in, landing firmly on the Persian rug.

I froze—

And seriously considered climbing back out. I couldn't move. Couldn't speak. The chill sunk deep into my bones. A razor sharp fear caught my last breath and held it hostage.

"Well that was reckless," Orpheus said with a wry smile.

London's most notorious vampire stood a few feet away, his arms casually folded across his chest and his piercing hazel eyes locked on mine.

Frozen in time at thirty-years-old, he was tall and breathtakingly handsome, with inky black hair that framed a perfect face. That heart-stopping beauty concealed a cold-blooded nature, as did his aristocratic air. That tailored tux, with his bowtie hanging loose, oozed old money and lots of it. From his mussed up locks, he'd probably flown here or leaped across the rooftops at speed. Shadows danced over his chiseled features and his stillness exuded a supernatural eeriness. His eyes reflecting worldliness. Those four hundred years he'd lived were an unfair advantage to anyone, including one of his own. He held that stunning smile he used so well to intimidate, knowing its effect and reveling in it.

Those who didn't know Orpheus might mistake all this intensity for serenity. Until his bite met your neck.

Judging by his black-tie tux, he'd been to the theatre, or opera maybe. His well polished shoes hinted he'd not walked far, leaving me to deduce he'd come from the West End. His dangling bowtie gave the impression of frustration, or even an attempt at casual, which didn't suit him.

Orpheus' silence gave away that he'd zeroed in on my thoughts, aiming to extract them for his own amusement. I eased my shoes back on, taking my time to secure the straps and wondering how he'd gotten in.

He shrugged out of his jacket. "Like you, through the front door."

"What are you doing here?"

He tut-tutted. "Whatever happened to manners?" He neared me and wrapped his jacket around my shoulders. "Where is my thank you?"

"What for?" I said.

"Saving your life."

There came a welcome warmth soaking into my chilled bones. "I'd have been fine." When his heady cologne reached me, it pushed all the wrong buttons and made it hard to think straight. I feigned he had no effect. His smile didn't exactly help.

Hauville could return any second, and knowing Orpheus he'd fly out the window and leave me to face him. I scanned the office again, taking in the dark wood paneled walls, the neatly lined books upon a single shelf, many of them classics. Dante's *Inferno* caught my eye, mainly because it was in Italian. Other than that the space was simple. One leather well-worn armchair, and beside it a tall lamp with tassels hanging from the shade. Upon the maple desk sat a few scattered files, but none of them had contents relevant to my case. Though that computer probably did.

"Don't mind me." He tilted his head toward it.

"Are you following me?"

"Don't be ridiculous. What were you thinking climbing out there?"

"Great view. You should check it out."

So I can bolt through the door.

Despite my five inch heels, he still looked down on me. That glare of his effortlessly formed cracks in the wall I'd thrown up. "I really should get back to the party," I said.

My self-defense skills were useless on him, and if he focused his supernatural seduction on me I might be forced to surrender my dignity.

"What do you want, Orpheus?"

"For you to stop putting yourself in harm's way so I can enjoy the rest of my evening."

"You've done your heroic deed for the day."

"A friend of yours called in a favor."

"Jadeon?" Saying his name sent a flurry of emotion through me.

"I love you," Jadeon Artimas, my once lover, had told me the last time I'd seen him. *"I'm letting you go so you can have the life you deserve."* He'd left me at Trafalgar Square beside the fountain, disallowing me the chance to tell him what I wanted, what I needed. Him. My beloved vampire. That had been two months, six days, seven hours ago, and if I glanced at my watch I'd be able to calculate the minutes. My thoughts drifted back to all that had unfolded. Enough craziness to keep my mind spinning twenty-four hours a day trying to make sense of it all.

"Have you seen him?" I asked.

"Jadeon has your best interests at heart, Ingrid."

"Why should I believe anything you say?" My thoughts drifted...*you tried to kill me.*

"Turn you," he said. "Evidently I changed my mind."

How cruel of nature to bestow upon a nightwalker such charm, a talent for seduction with merely their presence. Even his voice was primed to lure and render his victim powerless.

"I could say the same about you," he said. "You look stunning."

A shiver ran up my spine, though not from the cold. Getting in here had been no small feat, and the precious seconds I had to finish the job were being stolen by him. Even if Orpheus had saved my life.

"Jadeon would never have sent you," I said.

Orpheus didn't react, which was his way of letting me know

he didn't care what I believed. Ironic that balancing precariously on a ledge was less perilous then staying in here with him.

"I'm offended," he said, having read my thoughts again.

"Jadeon would never put me in harm's way."

"You don't need any help as far as that's concerned."

"Where is he?"

"Usual haunts."

And yet he eluded me.

"I was having a lovely evening with Lucas," Orpheus said. "We were at a play in the West End."

I remembered Lucas Azir fondly. Though having only briefly spent time with this Egyptian archeologist, I knew he'd be a good influence on Orpheus. Something told me they were old friends going way back.

"I first met Lucas in the Valley of the Kings," he said. "Lucas was like a kid at Christmas. Though instead of toys it was bones."

"Where's Lucas now?"

"Back at the theatre. We were enjoying Les Miserables. Right up until I got a message you were up to your old tricks."

"You mean working?'

He gave a disarming look. "You would have frozen to death. Or a pedestrian might have seen you and called the police. I'm sure Scotland Yard wouldn't appreciate one of their inspectors being featured on the nine o'clock news."

"Thank you for opening the window." I pointed to the door. "Say hello to Lucas for me."

Orpheus slid his hands into his pockets and he even managed to make that simple gesture look sexy. "The truth is Jadeon asked me to keep an eye on you. Or, rather, Dominion did."

Dominion, the title Jadeon now held having been destined to since birth, decreed to reign over the immortals and keep order. The very position I'd helped him secure and the one that now ironically kept us apart.

"Take me to him," I said.

Orpheus strolled toward the window and peered out. "Jadeon wants you to stop searching for him. It's a dreadful waste of time. His words."

My chest ached with the idea Jadeon really had sent Orpheus to deliver this message.

The door creaked open and I froze, ready to greet whomever came in, my excuse ready, my heart racing from being caught in here.

There was no one there.

"You can leave anytime," he said, having opened it telepathically.

"That's unlike you to be so considerate," I said.

"It's complicated, Ingrid."

I shut the door.

He leaned back against the windowsill. "Trust me."

"Impossible."

"I have something you want."

"And what might that be?"

"Information."

"I'm listening."

"Lord Hauville is one of the most influential peers in the House of Lords."

A jolt of excitement shot up my spine. "Go on."

"Hauville has friends in high places."

"So I heard."

"He plays golf with the Prime Minister," Orpheus added. "But you already know that."

Hence my need for precision. Hauville's connections made my superiors nervous, and getting a search warrant had been a challenge. They'd advised me to get them more to go on first, and though this wasn't what they'd had in mind my gut told me the answers were here.

"You're always one step ahead, Ingrid," he said. "You make those you work with antsy. No one likes being left behind."

"You seem to know an awful lot about me."

"Oh, I know more about you then you do." His lips curled into a smile.

Despite being on high alert, there was a heady dose of intrigue forging through my veins. The last thing I'd expected tonight was a brush with the underworld. It felt good, even if I hated to admit it. I wasn't willing to let Orpheus disappear into the night. Not yet. He was my only connection to Jadeon and a tenuous link at that.

"You're here tonight to ensure the evidence is accessible before requesting a search warrant." Orpheus neared me. "Heaven forbid you piss off your superiors back at the station. Again."

"What else do you know about Hauville?" I grazed my lip with my teeth in anticipation.

"He's a philanthropist. But it's not his charitableness that's drawn you here."

I tried to focus on the conversation, but it was hard, considering Orpheus was using his dark gift to make me tingle exquisitely in all the wrong places. It wasn't only a violation, it was distracting.

He raised his hands in defense. "I'm not doing anything. Though I have to admit, if it wasn't for the promise I'd made to Jadeon I'd be the one biting your lip right now."

I raised my chin in defiance. "What else do you know?"

"Seems you know everything."

"I beg to differ."

"You've never begged for anything."

"I begged for my life when you tried to take it."

He gave me a long lingering look, proving he knew exactly what I was thinking, feeling even. Pretending he had no effect on me was naive.

"Hauville heads up a counterfeit business," he said.

I already knew this, but I needed to know how Orpheus did. "Why would a man with such a grand reputation threaten it?"

"When Hauville's father died, the inheritance tax threatened his castle in Scotland," he said. "Maybe that had something to do with it."

I looked away, seeing in my mind's eye the pieces of the case coming together. There were numerous gaps in my investigation that I still needed to fill. "You believe that Hauville turned to crime to save his family home?" I said.

"Perhaps."

"And you'd know all about crime."

Orpheus folded his arms. "Careful, or you'll end up leaning over the desk with me behind you teaching you a lesson in respect."

I let out a slow, calming breath.

"Not happy with that fake Chanel purse you bought?" he said.

"Counterfeits are not limited to fake handbags," I said. "And anyway, I prefer Marks and Spencer."

"Oh, you working class girl you."

"What else do you know?"

"Hauville's dealing in drugs."

"Medicine. Counterfeit tablets. Gullible Americans are buying medication off his website and the stuff they're getting has no benefit." I stepped closer to him. "People have died."

He gestured to the computer. "The profits are transferred to an off shore account."

I was sharing way too much, but for what I sensed I'd get out of this conversation it seemed worth it. Maybe he'd even tell me where to find Jadeon.

"You were hoping to access those accounts from here?" he said.

I refused to comment. Instead I read him with the same laser-sharp intensity he held me with.

"You checked the building's schematics, I take it?" he said.

"Orpheus, if you know something..."

"You're asking for my help?"

I knitted my brow. "Yes."

"Yes, what?"

"Please."

"Good girl. Right answer. Keep up the courtesy and we'll do fine."

"We're not working together."

"Care to amend that statement?"

"Fine. Thank you for your assistance."

"That'll do for now."

After a furtive glance either way down the corridor, I followed Orpheus, questioning the sanity of trusting him. I prided myself on reading a person's face as well as their body language and gleaning the things they didn't say. When reading him there came an uncanny feeling I could trust him, though pinpointing the exact reason evaded me. Orpheus took my hand in his with an ironclad hold, impossible to escape, as he led me on. His skin felt warm and it made me wonder if he'd just fed, and on whom. *Shouldn't I question him on that? Arrest him?*

Squeezing his hand back was my way of letting him know that my decision to follow him was for the sole purpose of solving my case. There came a haunting thought I could very well be his next victim, though you'd never have guessed it from the way I trotted willingly beside him. Being near him again was exhilarating, and I cursed the part of me that wanted, no, needed this. A desire to throw myself into the worst kind of danger. The lure of the underworld was an intoxicating adventure that I found impossible to resist, and from the way he grinned at me he knew it too. We turned the corner and trekked onwards, passing room after room.

"Here we are." He let go of my hand.

I wondered if I was about to regret this.

There was something different about him, a subtle change in his eye color. His irises were an iridescent hazel encircled with a deep brown halo.

"Although I'm flattered by the attention," he said, having caught my stare. "How about getting your mind back on why you're here."

Orpheus' hand reached for me, removing a starched white handkerchief from the top pocket of his jacket, which was still around my shoulders. He placed it over the doorknob.

My mind raced with all the possibilities of what lay hidden on the other side. Though more intriguing still was how Orpheus knew about it.

"You know an awful lot about my investigation." I grabbed his wrist. "None of this is in the news so either you're spying on me or—"

"We could of course stay out here and risk getting caught." His hand tightened on the handle. "With no search warrant, you're trespassing. Which is a crime." He held an expression of mock surprise. "We have something in common at last."

"What interest do you have in Hauville?"

"That's classified."

"Since when do vampires hold classified information?"

"Since Dominion." His hand found its way to my lower spine and rested there.

"I'm listening." I was also weakening from his touch.

"My directive was to get you out alive. Knowing you as well as I do, if you don't get what you want, you'll be back. We can't have that now, can we?" He cocked his head. "Someone's coming."

When these moments with Orpheus were over, what then? Would he tell me where to find Jadeon? Perhaps I really could persuade Orpheus to take me to him.

"That part of your life is over," he said. "You've pushed the limits of morality as far as you're prepared to go."

"I've already crossed the line into the underworld."

"You've merely glimpsed inside. Ingrid, you're not prepared for the person you'll become."

"What do you mean?"

"You have to be prepared to move beyond your self-imposed limitations of what you brand normality." He opened the door and nudged me in.

I breathed in the dusty air, ready to turn around and leave if necessary. Despite the risk of getting caught, my initial reaction stirred my curiosity. Orpheus raised his eyebrows playfully.

Furniture lay all over the place, as though we'd stepped into a storeroom. A dining table had been tipped on its side, and close by rested several discarded mahogany chairs stacked on top of each other. Paintings were strewn here and there as were candle holders. There was a disturbing taxidermy collection including a stuffed fox, a tatty black cat, and even a boar's head. Their glassy eyes stared at us disapprovingly.

"My first instinct was to leave," I whispered. "That's on purpose."

"Good girl," he said.

Footsteps traced outside the room; a heavy gait that soon passed.

"How do you know about this?" I said.

"Jadeon called me on the way here. His office has been tracking Hauville's movements." He brought a fingertip to his lips. "Don't tell him I shared that with you."

"What's Jadeon's interest in Hauville?"

"Your interests are evidently Dominion's."

This sounded wrong on so many levels. "Are you telling me

you and Jadeon are friends now?"

"Our paths did intertwine in the most dramatic of ways," he said. "As did ours, Ingrid."

He was right of course. Orpheus had stalked me for the last few months, and though I found his face pretty to look at he was fucking scary. The turn you into a vampire on a whim kind of scary.

I looked away.

"Let's not talk about that now," he said.

I tried to shake off this powerlessness. "You had something you wanted to show me?"

"This."

I scanned the mess. "Where the hell am I meant to start exactly?"

"You've come a long way. But you still have a long way to go."

"Until what?"

"The underworld is ready to trust you."

"I've kept my knowledge of your kind secret." I frowned. "To the detriment of my work. My investigations."

"You're a loose cannon. With you it could go either way."

"I'd never betray Jadeon."

"That remains to be seen."

"Never."

"Time will tell. It always does."

There lay a heavy dose of truth in his words. I had once threatened to reveal their kind to the world, sought out clues to be used as evidence to expose them. My love for Jadeon had changed all that. Instead of wanting to bring him to justice I'd fought to protect him. Though my heart ached for him even now, and this sense of betrayal still ravaged my soul, my loyalty had never wavered. Surely Orpheus knew that?

"Orpheus, if you can read my mind you can read my heart."

"What happens when you truly grasp that he's not coming back to you?" he said. "What then?"

"Love always finds a way."

"Until it doesn't."

"You know more than anyone about lost loves and second chances."

He looked thoughtful. "This is not about me. Dominion's life has changed beyond all recognition. He's facing new dangers. He must know you are safe. There can be no distractions."

"I can protect myself."

His attention drifted to the window and beyond.

"I'm not ready to be turned," I said.

"Let there be no misunderstanding," he said fiercely. "This is not what he is asking of you."

"Then what?"

"Ingrid, let him go."

"If I were to talk with him—"

"Nothing would change." He brushed a strand of hair out of my face.

This conversation was leading nowhere. I'd more than tipped my hand at how much I yearned for Jadeon, revealing my weakness, and I hated myself for it.

"Me being here for you is my peace offering," he said.

"It's not enough."

"Maybe this will help." He set off for the other side, heading for a heavy oak door.

Using his handkerchief again to cover the handle, he found it locked. A click announced he'd released the catch with merely a thought, a trick of his telekinetic powers. He beamed a mega-watt smile my way as he opened the door.

The windowless room was larger than the one we'd left behind and reflected an organized mind. A table was positioned in the center. Upon it rested two computers, one at either end. File cabinets were stacked high with folders, all neatly marked with names, and on closer inspection also with years going back to 1999. Four clocks hung at the back, reflecting the time zones of New York, London, Paris, and Hong Kong.

Orpheus rubbed his hands together. "Evidence."

A cupboard sat flush against the right wall. I made my way over to it, borrowing Orpheus' handkerchief to ease it open. Stacked high on shelves were what appeared to be counterfeit samples of numerous items, among them handbags, perfumes, obscure velvet pouches, and transparent bottles of pharmaceuticals.

I looked at Orpheus, my expression incredulous.

"Another case solved," he said, wrapping an arm around my waist.

"What's your interest in all this?"

He pressed a fingertip to my lips. "A thank you will suffice."

My eyelids fluttered with the headiness of being so close to him. "How did Jadeon know about this room?"

"He has a knack for secrets."

"That stirs my curiosity."

"Suppress it," he said with a hint of amusement. "I have to go. Lucas is waiting for me."

"I'll have to come up with a reason why the police need to search this building. They can't know I've been in here."

"Sounds like a plan," he said. "Now let's get you out of here."

"Wait, please." I clutched Orpheus' shirt. "Take me to him."

Orpheus pulled his jacket farther around my shoulders in an uncommon gesture of kindness. And though he didn't say the word, his eyes told me *no*.

CHAPTER 2

New Scotland Yard buzzed with its usual frenetic energy.

Escaping the heap of paperwork waiting for me on my desk, I carried my mug of coffee as I walked along the endless white-washed, starkly lit corridors to the evidence room. It amazed me how quickly I'd gotten used to the noises in this place: phones ringing off the hook, people talking over each other, and the usual hustle and bustle of *The Yard*. What looked like chaos to any visitor was really the tireless focus of behind the scenes officers in the metropolitan police, serving London's entire population. Having been transferred in from Salisbury a few months ago, I'd gotten used to this intense working environment. A far cry from the small city station I'd come from.

Even here, in the heart of the city, they had no idea about the vast underworld of supernatural beings living amongst them. Though from a few unsolved case files I'd rifled through in the records department, investigators had come across nightwalkers. They just hadn't realized it. In one file I'd read the report of a man jumping off a speeding train, landing on his feet, and surviving only to run off and evade the pursuing officers. Another case reported a woman pronounced dead following a pub brawl stabbing, but soon after she leapt to her feet and flew from the bar, leaving behind the gob smacked coroner who had pronounced her dead fifteen minutes before. Yet another file contained the on duty policewoman's report of what appeared to be a series of vampire-style attacks, where drunken party goers complained a mysterious woman had gate-crashed their event and literarily sucked blood from their necks. All their blood samples came back clean. Drug free. Still, no one believed them, least of all the police.

London was rife with vampire activity and an even dose of denial.

Two nights ago, while standing in Hauville's office, Orpheus had doubted my ability to keep silent on what I knew about the immortals. I'd sworn yet again to honor their code of secrecy. Yet here were my people. Living, breathing mortals who held the highest moral codes and who strived to maintain peace and uphold the law. Could I really keep such a profound secret? I really believed I could. Was I being naive?

"Time will tell," Orpheus had warned me.

I would never betray Jadeon's trust, despite the contradiction of my vocation clashing with my knowledge of those with a penchant for blood. Even though Jadeon had reassured me his kind had long given up causing harm, my moral compass was spinning. As Dominion, could he really honor his promise and rule his kind? Ensure they lived within our rules as well as the underworld's? Surely Orpheus' words 'time will tell' were more relevant when applied to them and how far they dared to go to protect our world from theirs.

Even if I decided to share what I'd discovered, who'd believe me anyway? My sanity, not to mention my reputation, would be questioned. All the evidence I'd managed to collate over the last few months was now gone. *Stolen.* And I suspected Jadeon had been the one who had swiped it. I had, after all, threatened to release it to the public.

Maybe Jadeon was right. The world wasn't t ready.

Passing a vast network of cubicles, and the men and women tirelessly working away within them, made me question if I belonged anywhere. I felt stuck in some kind of halfway land between the ordinary and a preternatural realm.

This melancholy wasn't getting me anywhere. It was time to ignore this aching for Jadeon that devoured my insides. This misery of heartbreak for which there was only one cure; throw myself into work.

Leaning on the doorjamb, I took in the evidence room and sipped my coffee.

Beneath the glare of florescent bulbs worked my small team of three officers. They were busy collating evidence. Twenty-eight-year old Nick Greene was one of the Yard's many civilian technicians, and right now his face was far too close to a computer screen. I'd have to talk to him about that. Though Nick would probably shrug off his answer in that boyishly-charming way of his. From his disheveled appearance, he'd been up late playing video games and drinking far too much diet soda.

Standing behind him and peering over a pair of bifocals was Sergeant Gerald Miller. A man with over fifteen years experience in the Met and a wisdom to match the time he'd spent on the beat. From his casual attire of navy-blue trousers and brown suede jacket, he was slowly getting used to being out of uniform, and the dapper looking handkerchief tucked into his upper right pocket revealed his desire for promotion. I'd have to work on that for him.

Beside him stood Constable Helena Noble, new to the force, and to prove it the creases in her uniform were all in the right places. Helena easily reminded me of how I'd been when I first joined—overly enthusiastic and consistently bubbly. This was a team I could trust.

Helena caught my stare and her back stiffened. "Hello, ma'am."

"Good morning." I headed on in. "Mr. Greene, you're sitting far too close to the screen."

"I've told him," Sergeant Miller said. "He thinks he's too young for glasses."

"I am." Nick kept his focus on the screen.

At the far end of the room, stacked upon a long table, sat the collection of evidence gathered from Hauville's office. I approached, taking in the perfume bottles, medicine pots, and fake purses. All samples of Hauville's counterfeit goods. Staring back at me through beady eyes was that boar's head and beside it the stuffed black cat.

"Where's the fox?" I said.

"What fox?" Nick said, joining me.

My gaze swept the table, still not seeing it. I'd tipped my hand I'd viewed this evidence before. "Good work everyone."

Had Hauville really used these garish objects as a distraction to his storage room? It certainly seemed that way. And where the hell was the fox? And why was it missing?

"What's the appeal with having stuffed animals in your house?" Helena asked.

I examined the boar's head. "It's a trophy. Maybe Hauville hunted and killed the boar himself. He's into the sport, apparently. The cat could have been a pet."

Helena cringed. "Nasty."

"They made it here with the rest of the stuff," Miller said. "Though why, we have no idea. They were found in the room next to it."

"I wanted to make sure we didn't miss anything," I said. "Hauville's lawyers are working on getting all this back to him, so we don't have much time."

We made our way over to the table where Hauville's computer sat.

"How did you know about all this?" Helena asked.

"Nick tracked Hauville's website IP address," I explained. "A brief search of the Bainard Building turned up this."

"Hauville's an idiot," Miller said. "Surely he should have known we'd track his website?"

"It's certainly baffling," I said. "But I'm not complaining."

"When are we going to arrest him?" Helena asked.

"Still waiting on the commissioner's nod," I said. "Chief Inspector Brooks reassured me it's imminent. Until then we continue to build our case." I took the seat beside Nick.

He reached for the mouse. "The software's working away at cracking Hauville's access code in the background, but it takes so damn long."

From having attempted to hack into Hauville's computer back in his office, I knew the issue Nick was having. "Wife's date of birth?" I suggested.

"Tried it," Nick said.

"Didn't he have a daughter who died? Olivia, wasn't that her name?" I glanced back up at Miller.

Nick clicked away on the keyboard. "No." He capitalized Olivia. "And no."

I caressed my forehead, traveling back in my mind's eye to Hauville's fundraising party, strolling once again along those carpeted corridors while trying to get a sense of the man from the decor. The Bainard served as the headquarters for his philanthropic activities. His portraits of military officers dressed in their finest regalia, with their cavalry emblems, revealed his time served in the Household Cavalry Mounted Regiment. During my brief visit I'd also caught his love of Italy, revealed by his private collection of Italian painters.

I'd admired the lavishly decorated ballroom where I'd nibbled on canapés and sipped the finest champagne, all the while mixing with Hauville's guests, many of whom were socialites. I'd soon extracted from the party goers information about Hauville that could very well be utilized later, like his obsession with pomp and ceremony, his desire for social climbing, his interest in politics, and his heavy focus upon himself.

"Id, ego and super ego," I muttered.

"Sigmund Freud fan are you?"' Nick said.

"Shush," said Miller.

My thoughts delved deeper, remembering what I knew about Hauville and cross referencing it with Freud's structural model of the psyche. I placed myself in Hauville's shoes, his love of luxury, the pleasure he garnered from playing golf with the Prime Minister, and him making sure everyone knew of this. His belief he could get away with a crime. His arrogance of not even attending his own fundraising party.

When I opened my eyes again, Nick's stare was locked on me.

"Steele, Hauville's middle name, and his date birth." I gestured for him to try that.

"Why his middle name?" Helena said.

"It's the same as his only daughter who died," I said. "Olivia Steele Hauville."

Nick clicked away on the keyboard. "Bloody hell. That worked."

"Inspector!" Helena said, astonished. "How did you do that?"

"It's like there's a part of my brain that gets it before me." I raised my hand. "Don't ask."

"Some people do it with math problems," Nick said. "I had a

friend in school who could figure out these complex algebra calculations, but had trouble explaining how he'd worked them out. The teachers believed he was cheating but he wasn't."

"Hauville's egotistical," I said. "I started from there."

"That's why we're calling you, ma'am," Miller said.

"Lucky guess." I leaned in to better view the screen.

"You beat the software," Nick said. "That's some gift."

"Emotions lead decisions," I said. "Which computers lack. Unless of course we're dealing with a psychopath. And we're not, apparently. Let's take a look at what Hauville's been up to." There came a thrill of excitement that we might have more on him.

"And we are in." Nick clicked away, entering the labyrinth of Hauville's computer files.

"Try that." I gestured to an icon titled accounts.

"Surely it can't be this easy?" Miller said. "It's not even assigned an access code."

"His arrogance is front and center," I said.

Within Quick Books software, page after page of accounting documentations flashed on the screen. Records of online transactions from overseas.

"We have him," Miller said. "Look at that."

Nick clicked print. "Two years ago I got into a computer and its default was set to fry the hard drive. I'm not kidding. From then on I print every page."

"Was that the Ribaldi case?" Miller asked.

"The very same," Nick said. "He literally got away with murder. I still have nightmares over that one." He glanced over at me. "Ma'am, maybe you'd take it on as a cold case?"

"Maybe," I said. "Let's check Hauville's emails."

Nick clicked the mouse, taking us back to the main screen.

"Gothique?" Helena pointed to an icon. "What do you think that is?"

"Click on it," I said to Nick. "Gothique is French for gothic."

"Fuck!" Nick sat back. "What is that?"

We stared at the photo of the young pretty girl. A brunette, twenty-ish. Her arms were spread out at either side and secured in shackles to a brick wall. She was dressed in gothic attire—

corset and black pants. Her dazed stare was captured in a dusky hue of poor lighting. Nothing gave away her whereabouts, or whether her consent had been given. It reeked of sinister.

My throat tightened. "The girl's left arm. Can you zero in on it?"

Nick coughed. "Fucked up freaky."

"Nick," I said firmly. "I need you to close in"

"Her arm?"

"Her inner forearm," I said. "That tattoo."

With several clicks of the mouse, Nick zeroed in on the image. There, upon the girl's left inner forearm, was a small, round circle. The mark of a Gothica. The brand of a vampire's servant. My gut churned with the realization—

She had the exact same mark I'd been branded with.

CHAPTER 3

Cornwall's most beloved castle, Saint Michael's Mount, rose majestically out of the granite rock it had been built upon.

I was finding its far eastern wall not as easy to scale as I'd first anticipated.

Although only halfway up, the above turrets were now in sight, and if I kept this pace I'd be standing on top of St. Michael's roof by nightfall. The brickwork was solid granite, making it impenetrable, but the surrounding plaster and whitewash were malleable, allowing for the hammering in of my climbing blade. I attached my metal D-shaped carabiner through it and my rope through that, tugging it tight. If I lost my footing, I'd only fall as far as the last blade.

Considering I'd been trained to climb with a partner, I was excelling on my own, and though I'd tackled vertical climbs less than a handful of times I'd not forgotten the technique of maintaining my balance and using the strength in my legs to hoist myself. Taking short breaks when needed, I recalled my instructor's warning not to ignore the body's symptoms of stress: first shaking legs, followed by calf pain and, if ignored, immobilizing cramps, which at seventy-five feet up wasn't good.

Below, a blue-green ocean shimmered hypnotically. A crisp orange and yellow sunset burst forth shards of light over the water and glistened on tumbling waves. A cool breeze blew in from the east, causing the fine hairs on my forearms to prickle. I closed my eyes to let it wash over me, refresh me. Resting my face against the cold brick, I took a few moments to gather my thoughts.

This morning, what had seemed like a routine case of counterfeit activity had quite possibly turned into a kidnapping case. That one image of a restrained female had been the catalyst for Hauville's computer being transferred over to S C & O, Scotland Yard's Homicide and Serious Crime command. My team had been left with a few folders, some fake samples, and that old boar's head. Protocol had been followed, satisfying everyone except my team.

Risking my life to get inside this castle was no longer about me needing to see Jadeon. That girl in the photo may very well need rescuing. That symbol on her left inner forearm had marked her as a Gothica. The exact same circle brand that was given to young men and women when they took up the life of a vampire servant, with the promise of one day being transformed into a vampire themselves. The same symbol that had been forced upon me not so long ago to protect me from a rogue immortal's attack. Apparently no one would dare harm a Gothica belonging to Orpheus. Though I was never his servant, and had never belonged to him. Perhaps that was why my circle had been placed around a birthmark, which transformed the symbol into a circumpunct. A circle with a dot in the middle was the most ancient of symbols, representing balance. I'd actually become rather fond of this lasting proof of all that had happened. Or perhaps it was all that I had to prove it really did happen.

I rammed another blade into the rock, scattering dust. Hammering the blade felt cathartic, my right bicep feeling the tension of each strike. After getting into the rhythm of the climb, it didn't take long to arrive at the turrets. Reaching up, I pulled myself through one of them, twisting on its ledge and landing firmly on the castle roof.

'Usual haunts,' Orpheus had told me when I'd asked him where Jadeon was, and this castle had been Jadeon's family home for centuries. The thought of seeing him made me shiver with excitement. My flesh tingled with the memory of his touch. His embrace. If I could just make him see reason.

I climbed out of my harness and shoved it into my backpack, and then placed it against the wall where I'd easily find it should I need to make a quick escape. After the long climb, it was a relief to find the roof door unlocked. Though I'd brought my pick with me just in case.

Once inside, I ascended the thin stone stairwell and soon found myself standing in one of the castle's uppermost corridors. I breathed in the scent of history. It reminded me of the smell of candle wax and oak. A thrill of anticipation shot up my spine at the prospect I was here again. I tucked my flashlight into my jacket pocket, not needing it as my eyes adjusted to the dimness. Continuing on, I cautiously strolled along the corridor of the second floor.

From the upper balcony, I overlooked the enormous foyer. The low hanging chandelier was free from cobwebs, its sconces holding new candles, though the wicks had been untouched by flames. The marble flooring sparkled. The two suits of armor guarding either side of the stairwell had been polished. Running my fingertips along the banister, I found no dust.

A series of chimes from a grandfather clock announced it was ten o'clock.

How ironic I mused, the mysteries of this place were nothing compared to those who lived within its walls. My memories drifted back to the first time I'd visited. I'd accepted the invitation from Lord Jadeon Artimas to spend the weekend here. I'd been so naive, having no idea immortals even existed. Of course I'd heard of Bram Stoker's Dracula, but never considered they really existed. Never.

Yet those first few hours here when I'd explored the castle alone, accepting Jadeon's offer to look around, I'd uncovered objects dating back two hundred years, and more alarming still they pertained to him. Like the goblet engraved with his name and dated 1798.

Blushing wildly, my cheeks burned like fire as those moments found their way back to me. I pressed my fingertips against my lips, remembering how he'd seduced me, guiding me into the dungeons and laying me on that central table. He'd taken me there, taken my breath away, entrancing me completely, his touch alighting my senses and awakening my desires. I'd given myself over to him and allowed myself to truly love and be loved for the first time in my life.

My hands eased up on their grip of the banister. Even here,

surrounded by all that was his, the vastness of how much I missed him still wrenched at me.

As I headed in an easterly direction, all my senses were on edge.

I'd discovered there was far more to this place, with its hidden rooms leading to breathtaking revelations. Others very likely waited to be discovered. I'd sworn never to share what we'd found in the lowest room. Even now, I remembered seeing it for the first time, that towering five ton, twenty-foot rock. The centerpiece within a cathedral-styled chamber. The rock matched its brothers that stood tall at Stonehenge. Just what the men who'd dragged that lone rock here had intended it for remained uncertain.

I'd helped decipher the clues that led us to this remarkable find. Jadeon had lived here for over two hundred years and only now discovered it beneath the castle, using the most secret of staircases to reach it. I'd been the one to solve the clues which led us to it, proving once again my worthiness to mingle amongst them.

Hadn't I?

I rested my forehead against Jadeon's bedroom door.

Braving my first step, my heart pounding with anticipation, I pushed it open. He wasn't here. Perhaps I'd find him reading in the study? Or in the highest tower painting a nightscape? I swallowed my disappointment.

Running my fingertips along his neatly lined suits hanging in his closet, I hoped he was here. I headed to the top of the stairwell and down.

Lingering in the center of the foyer, I considered which way next. Jadeon had told me that having been born here he'd gotten used to the enormity of the place. He much preferred the cozier rooms, like the library with its collection of well-stocked books, or even the drawing room with its leather couches and open fire, along with the grand piano.

Above my head, the chandelier swung wide.

"Bloody hell!" I dropped to my knees, my heart thundering, my throat too tight to scream.

An enormous bat-like creature hung upside-down from the chandelier, his wrinkled face human enough, but not his leathery flesh or widespread wings. He peered down at me with curiosity, his black beady eyes locked on mine.

"Paradom?" I screeched, remembering him from Bodium castle when I'd been trapped in a cell with him. He had sucked the life out of one of the other captors in the prison with us, and yet I'd remain unharmed. That circled brand had indeed kept me safe. Pushing those frantic memories away, I bolted onward across the foyer—

And ran right into Sebastian Price and almost knocked him backwards.

"Whoa," he said, sidestepping. "Ingrid?" His Welsh lilt echoed.

I glanced back.

"He won't hurt you," Sebastian said, offering his hand to steady me.

I flung myself into Sebastian's embrace and wrapped my arms around him.

"Hey, you," he said, hugging me back.

I broke away and took a good look at him, daring to see how he'd changed with the kind of transformation brought on by being turned. Sebastian looked well. His black complexion was healthy with no sign of translucence, and his chocolate brown irises were rich in color but not fluorescent. He wore jeans and a shirt, perfectly molded to his dancer's body. He looked fitter than ever, his eyes twinkling with a happiness I'd not seen before.

"How did you get in?" he said.

"This is how," came a clipped English accent.

There, halfway up the central staircase, stood Alex Artimas, and he was holding my backpack. He looked ethereal, his blond curls and blue eyes radiating the illusion he wasn't a vampire but merely a twenty-something young man. He was dressed in ripped jeans, the designer kind, and a crisp white shirt open at the collar. His beauty was startling even now. High cheekbones, furrowed brow, and an intense glare that went for the jugular. *Mine.*

Turning my gaze from him, I faced Sebastian again, finding his smile a safe haven. There came a glint of hope that if Jadeon's younger brother Alex was here maybe Jadeon would be too.

"What did you do to my wall?" Alex snapped, holding out a

palm in which lay several climbing blades.

"You've placed locks on all the doors," I said. "You gave me no choice but to be a little inventive."

"Those locks are meant to keep people out." Alex dropped the rucksack and it tumbled down the stairs.

I glanced back up to see Paradom sucking his thumb.

"Paradom doesn't like arguing," Sebastian said.

"We're not really arguing," I called up.

"We are," Alex said.

I gestured my sincerity. "Sorry."

Alex looked incredulous. "You've done more damage than when the Spanish raided the castle."

"The Spanish didn't actually attack though, did they?" Sebastian said.

"Jadeon's not here," Alex said. "So you fucked up my wall for nothing."

"After all we've been through." I took a step toward him. "Surely you've come to trust me."

Alex vanished and I blinked several times at where he'd been standing.

The chandelier creaked its disapproval at having both Alex and Paradom now hanging upside down from it. Though unlike Paradom, who used his clawed feet to grip a rung, Alex wrapped his legs over an arched arm.

"Welcome to my world," Sebastian said, smiling.

"You should try it, Seb," Alex shouted down. "It's actually rather comfortable."

Sebastian's attention fell back on me. "I'm sorry. Jadeon really isn't here."

"Do you know where I can find him?" I said.

His expression was consolatory. "I don't. He never tells us where he is."

"What if you need to contact him?"

"Alex can always send Jadeon a mind message," Sebastian said, cringing at giving that away.

I faced Alex, ready to beg him.

He merely rolled his eyes and said, "No."

"How have you been?" Sebastian asked, pulling my attention back to him.

"Fine, and you?" I said, running through the words that would change Alex's mind.

"Still no," Alex shouted at me.

Seb chuckled. "I'm fine too."

"You look well," I said. "Really good, Seb. You look happy."

"I'm training again."

"Ballet?" I asked, and on his nod, "Oh Seb, that's wonderful."

"Jadeon made it a condition of me staying here."

I held back my tears at seeing Sebastian again, at being near the friend I'd shared so much with. I'd not realized how much I needed this.

"Tea?" Sebastian offered.

"Tea would be lovely."

I could see why Jadeon was so fond of him. He had a way of accepting the moment for what it was, not pushing back, not needing for it to be anything other than what it was.

Paradom leaped off the chandelier, leaving it rocking with Alex still hanging from it. He hopped toward me, his toenails scratching the marble flooring. Paradom's head tilted as though he was as equally fascinated with me. Jadeon had told me that Paradom had been burned literally to ash, and those remains had been joined with another vampire's ashes. After being resurrected, Paradom had lived as one vampire with two personalities, until those individuals with good intentions had tried to separate him. During this experiment, the other vampire had apparently died. What was left of their union was Paradom, a winged creature, his thoughts as muddled as his words, though his sweetness never wavered.

Although doubt flooded my belief in this fanciful story, it was hard to come up with another explanation for what created this unique being. This winged miracle.

My thoughts scattered into a thousand unreasonable images as those awful memories of the same thing happening to Jadeon and Orpheus found its way back to me. They had been joined as one. Though they had survived the ordeal and were now back to their separate and very different selves. That was a long time ago, I reassured myself. Three months, my muse kindly reminded me. Though it felt like yesterday.

Madness.

Impossible.

Don't go there and put that kind of strain on yourself again. The kind that almost led to a breakdown.

"Did you bring cat food?" Paradom asked.

"What?" I was shaken from these nightmarish thoughts.

"We have a ton of it in the kitchen, remember?" Sebastian said. "Ingrid and I will bring you some. Go start your painting."

Paradom trotted up the stairs like a well-behaved child.

"Painting keeps him happy," Sebastian said. "He's actually rather good at it." He led me off to the kitchen.

"Sorry about the wall," I said, walking beside Sebastian.

"I'll plaster it up," he said. "Correction, I'll get Alex to. He's comfortable with heights." His face changed as though remembering something. "I haven't spoken with another mortal for months. I'm glad you came. Not that I don't enjoy Alex's company. He comes over a little brash at times but he's is really very sweet."

"We have a history," I said. "I arrested him once. It nearly got him killed."

Sebastian scratched the back of his head. "He appreciates what you did for his brother. For saving Jadeon's life."

"He trusts you, Seb. I can see that."

Sebastian guided me into the kitchen.

I sensed there lay a deeper friendship between him and Alex, a love that I had no right to pry about. Sebastian looked content, and after years of homelessness when his ballet career came crashing down after a car accident, he deserved this. They both did.

"We have the best selection of teas." He rummaged inside a cupboard. "I've been truly spoiled since I came here."

The kitchen had been refurbished. The red stove was probably never used, and above the center isle the hanging dark green pots and pans were secured by brass hooks. Even the fridge looked new.

"You're living here permanently?" I said.

He curled his lips nervously. "Tell me you're not wearing a wire."

"Of course not. And I'm sure Alex would have detected it if I were." My gaze swept the room. "Isn't it strange how all this becomes normal and everything else in life appears foreign."

Sebastian flicked on the kettle. "You and I, we have something remarkable in common."

"We really do."

"We get to hang out with scholars."

A wave of uneasiness came over me that this visit could very well be my last. I missed all this. Missed my friends, even if they were quirky.

"With Alex, I feel like I'm living with a history professor." Sebastian waved his hands with enthusiasm. "What we read in history books is a diluted version of what really happened. Alex remembers it all. The finest details. Like how dark everything was without electricity, and the fear of even the smallest infection."

"No antibiotics back then," I said. "We're so lucky."

"We take so much for granted."

"It's nice to have someone else to talk to about it," I said. "For so long I thought—"

"You we're going crazy?"

There was a flash of movement in the doorway. It was Paradom.

"Hey there," Sebastian greeted him.

Paradom hopped toward me and soon closed the gap between us. He reached his clawed hand out and placed something into my palm. His brows raised and his eyes reflected kindness. He hopped off and was gone.

"He likes you." Sebastian removed two mugs from a cupboard.

"So the locks on all the doors are to keep him in?" I said.

"A bit of both."

"If he ever got out—"

"Paradom comes over as eccentric, but he knows he's safe here. He'd never leave. It took Alex and I weeks to lure him out of the dungeon." Sebastian opened a tin of Harrods tea and reached in.

Discreetly, I unraveled the piece of paper and read the scratchy handwriting. "*Jadeon teaches Paradom to paint.*"

Sebastian set two mugs on the countertop.

"Will Jadeon be here tonight?" I asked.

He dropped a teabag into each mug. "Let me show you something." He strolled over to the pantry door and opened it.

Inside were neatly stacked cans of cat food.

He took one of them out and placed it on the countertop. "We don't have any cats."

"Paradom seems alert," I said. "Conscious of his surroundings."

Sebastian held out his hand for the note and I handed it to him.

He read it and looked back up at me. "Jadeon showed Paradom a few brush strokes. That was a while back."

"I need to speak with him."

"It's a delicate situation." Sebastian poured boiling water into the two mugs.

"I appreciate that."

Sebastian caressed his chin thoughtfully. "Jadeon spends most of his time trying to keep the peace. Sounds like an impossible job to me."

"Dominion, lord of the vampires." I swept my hand dramatically. "How about he not forget his friends who got him there?"

Sebastian gave me a long, hard stare.

"I miss him," I sounded defeated.

"Next time he visits I'll tell him he needs to see you. I promise."

"Thank you." I accepted the mug of tea. The warmth soaked into my fingers and it felt good. "I'm working on a case. At first it seemed rudimentary, but something's come up. Evidence pertaining to the underworld."

"What kind?"

"We're not sure what we have yet."

"Well, if we can help in any way." He blew on his tea.

"I'll keep that in mind."

Sebastian gave me a reassuring smile and slid open a drawer. He removed a tin opener and set about peeling open the cat food. He scooped the contents into a bowl.

"Shouldn't Paradom be drinking blood?" I said. "He is a

vampire after all."

"Alex takes care of that. He lets Paradom drink from him. In-between that, Paradom craves this stuff." He sniffed the bowl and made a face. "Still, he likes it." Sebastian led the way out of the kitchen.

We were back in the foyer again and heading up the main stairwell.

"Does Orpheus ever visit?" I asked.

Sebastian picked up his speed and we turned the corner, heading fast along the corridor.

"You wouldn't tell me if he did, would you?" I said.

"Ingrid, you're a policewoman."

"That makes you nervous?"

"Both worlds are a contradiction."

"I wrestle with that every day," I said. "Has Jadeon said something to you? Be honest with me."

He stopped before a door. "You go first."

I pursed my lips, my stubbornness rising.

"First through the door, I meant. I know you're not willing to compromise." He reached out and opened it.

Paradom glanced our way when we entered, though quickly resumed his brushstrokes upon a canvas resting on a wooden stand. He delicately held the brush, balancing it between his claws. Discarded paintings were everywhere, most of them of nightscapes, their frames resting against the wall. This had once been Jadeon's artistic sanctuary and I hoped it still was. I looked around for any sign he'd been here, any painting that had his touch, any hint of a wet canvas. Other than the one Paradom was working on, the others seemed to have been ignored. Some were left unfinished. My heart ached with the evidence of Jadeon's abandonment.

"I forgot his spoon." Sebastian headed out. "I'll be right back." He closed the door behind him.

Though wisdom told me to leave with him, there came serenity in watching Paradom sweep that fine brush over the canvas, the delicate hues forming the image of a lush garden. The way Paradom painted water lilies floating on a deep blue pond reminded me of a Monet.

"Paradom, that note you gave me?"

His brush paused.

"When did you last see Jadeon?" I said.

Paradom resumed with gentle strokes. "Two."

"Two nights ago?"

"Weeks." He spun round, his brush poised in the air.

"When is he due back here?"

He hesitated. "She isn't dead."

"What?"

"That girl...in your head."

"Oh." I took a deep breath, realizing. "Okay." I humored him.

He rested a claw on his forehead. "All the answers are in here." He pushed a claw into his temple.

"I need more evidence."

"Look deeper." He raised his eyebrows. "Deeper than that."

"Do you know where Jadeon is?"

"London." Paradom looked worried. "He wants what you want."

"To save that girl?"

"To save you."

"I can look after myself, Paradom." I stepped closer. "Where in London is he?"

"We all save each other in the end."

I rubbed my brow to ease the tension. "I suppose."

"Your heart is saying goodbye."

He really was inside my mind, extracting the truth and saying it back to me. Had I hoped Jadeon was in London? Had Paradom merely mirrored my thoughts?

"If you survive their attempt to turn you, they'll bow at your feet." he said.

"Who?"

He peered over my shoulder. "Spoon."

"Please, tell me exactly where Jadeon is? Do you have an address?"

"Dominion?"

"Yes, where's Dominion?"

He raised a claw.

Sebastian entered carrying the bowl and a spoon. "Here you go." He handed it over to Paradom.

I begged Paradom with my eyes while sending a mind message that I hoped he'd hear.

"He's with the inventors." Paradom's gaze widened. "Protected by the elders."

"What was that?" Sebastian's attention hopped between me and Paradom. "What did I miss?"

"That's where you'll find him." Paradom scooped a spoonful of mushy cat food.

Sebastian stared at me questioningly.

I ignored him and stared at Paradom. "I'm listening."

The pungent aroma of processed cat food reached my nostrils and caused a wave of nausea. "I need you to tell me more."

Sadness flashed over his face. "This bridge you cross crumbles beneath your feet."

A jolt of fear slithered up my spine and I stood straighter, readying for what came next.

Paradom smacked his lips together. "Tastes like cat food."

"It is cat food," Sebastian said, looking amused.

"Don't take another step." Paradom pressed a claw against his lips. "Or there will be no way back."

"What year is it?" Sebastian asked him casually.

"Huh?"

"Okay," Sebastian said. "What century are we in?"

Paradom frowned. "Have cars been invented yet?"

Sebastian gave a thin, reassuring smile. "See, nothing to worry about."

"You brought me in here on purpose," I said. "You knew Paradom would confuse me."

"That's very cunning of you," Paradom said, frowning his displeasure at Sebastian.

"Eat your cat food." Sebastian stared at the floor.

"Seb, you know I'll find out the truth in the end," I said.

"That's what he's afraid of," Paradom said. "That's what they're all afraid of."

CHAPTER 4

It felt good to be holding an arrest warrant.

It also felt good to be back in my world of tracking down criminals and putting them away. Here, in the sitting room of Hauville's Windsor residence, I was ready to apprehend our suspect. Helena stood a little way behind me and she oozed nervousness. Despite my reassurance, she still fiddled with her necklace.

"Limit your body language," I warned her.

Helena lowered her hand to her side.

"Remember, we read them," I said. "Limit their ability to do the same to us."

"Got it," she said.

Studying the room, my mind wandered back to last night.

Although fond of puzzles, crosswords, and conundrums, the conversation with Paradom yesterday evening had left my head spinning. Those last haunting words were distracting.

"Don't take another step," Paradom had said. *"Or there will be no way back."*

My mind struggled to fathom what he meant. Though Sebastian had demonstrated Paradom's confusion, it was only slightly reassuring, considering the threat of disaster Sebastian himself had warned me of if I dared to continue searching for Jadeon. Maybe Paradom really was delirious and Sebastian had used him to scare me off.

I needed to refocus on the task at hand, which was apprehending Lord Hauville.

Beige walls reflected a soft yellow from the fancy light fixtures positioned around the room. Sweeping drapes were pulled back on either side of tall windows to allow sunlight to flood in. A rose patterned couch matched the armchairs on either side. In the center, a soft pastel rug looked antique and yet remained pristine. Upon the corner table sat a vase of fresh daisies, and right before that sat a silver framed photo of Lord Hauville and his wife, along with their twelve-year-old daughter Olivia. Their only child, now dead. Life really could be cruel. Despite Hauville's illegal activity, I still felt terrible for him. Other than the photo, nothing in this room hinted at a child's presence. If she'd once played in here, there were no stray dolls to account for that.

This room revealed not only a feminine touch but a room hardly used. The Hauvilles were loners. Private people, preferring to entertain in their London residence and not here in this Windsor country estate.

"Thank goodness you're here," came an upper class accent.

Lady Hauville entered with exuberance. She looked around fortyish, her blonde hair up in a chignon, and her minimal makeup gave off an earthy-country style. She wore clean jodhpurs, a fresh riding jacket and unsoiled boots, all hinting she'd not yet ridden.

I offered my hand. "Inspector Jansen. Good morning, ma'am. This is Constable Noble."

Lady Hauville gave a thin-lipped smile. "Tea?"

"No, thank you," I said. "We understand this is a difficult time for you. What with the investigation—"

"My daughter's death." She raised her chin. "She died three weeks ago and it still feels like yesterday."

"I'm so sorry," I said. "May I ask how—"

"A rare blood disorder." Lady Hauville pressed her lips together, this conversation evidently still not easy for her.

"Hemophilia, wasn't it?" Helena asked.

Lady Hauville looked shaken.

I threw Helena a warning glare to indicate I'd handle this.

Lady Hauville caught it though didn't react. "Hemophilia is more common in males. So you can understand our surprise when our baby girl was diagnosed with it."

"You're a doctor?" I said. "You recognized her symptoms?"

"Inspector, I was under the impression you were here to discuss my husband?"

"We want to share our condolences," I said. "Let you know we understand how difficult this is for you."

"To answer your question," Lady Hauville said sourly, "I'm a trauma surgeon. I work at The Royal London Hospital."

"You commute from here to London?" I asked.

"During the week I used to stay at our London residence."

"The Bainard Building?"

"Until your men raided the place. I'm now staying at my sisters, near St. James' Park. Until we get all this sorted out. This is a terrible ordeal, as you can imagine. Rupert hasn't taken it well. And now all this. These lies. Someone is setting him up. But we have no idea who."

"My job is to get to the truth, Lady Hauville," I said. "If your husband is innocent we'll clear his name."

"That's such a relief to hear," she said. "Please, feel free to call me Imogen."

"Imogen, I'd very much like to speak with your husband," I said. "Your lawyer informed us that he and Lord Hauville would be here today."

"You didn't get the message?" she said.

"Message?"

"Yes." Imogen glanced over at Helena. "Really? It doesn't exactly inspire confidence."

"What message, Lady Hauville?" I said.

"I called Scotland Yard this morning."

My fingers tightened around the warrant.

"That's not why you're here?" She knitted her brow. "My husband's gone missing."

"When was the last time you saw him?" I tried to keep my tone low, calm.

"Two days ago."

Damn.

He'd evaded us. I imagined Hauville had made it to Europe by now. Perhaps Italy, if his Dante's *Inferno* was a hint at a foreign language. Perhaps one of his many moneyed friends had flown him over in a private jet and smuggled him into the country. Interpol would now be needed to track him down.

"Where and when exactly did you last see your husband?" I asked.

"We had dinner at the Ritz," she said. "Two nights ago."

"Did he say anything to you that might have hinted at his disappearance?"

"He was upset with this intrusion." She pursued her lips. "Other than that he seemed fine."

"Did he mention going away?"

"No, he did not," she snapped. "Remember, I reported him missing."

I hid my suspicion. "Of course. Did he leave any personal belongings behind? His phone? Wallet?"

"No."

"Does he have a diary or a scheduler?" I said.

"Ms. Lawrence, his secretary, takes care of all of his appointments. She hasn't seen Rupert or heard from him either."

"May I have Ms. Lawrence's contact information?"

"I'll see you get it."

"I don't want to alarm you, but it's standard procedure to call all the hospitals in a situation like this," I said. "My department will take care of that."

She turned to the window and stared through it.

The lawn was perfectly manicured, and beyond that lay tall Bay trees leading into a dense wood. I wondered if Hauville could be camping out there somewhere.

"What am I going to do?" she whispered.

"We'll find him," I said softly.

And then we'll arrest him.

Her focus fell on the window again, her thoughts seemingly wandering.

"You're going riding?" I asked.

"The horses still need to be exercised."

"Who takes care of them when you're away?"

"A local stable."

"You have quite a bit of land."

"Ten acres." She looked annoyed. "He's not here, inspector, if that's what you're insinuating."

"Lady Hauville," I said, "it would never be my intention to

cause you any more distress than you're already going through."

She relaxed a little.

Still, if she wasn't here during the week I might take a hike around the grounds later, explore the property for any sign that Hauville might still be here.

"Will there be anything else?" she asked.

"No," I said. "Thank you for your time. If you do hear from your husband, please call us immediately."

"Inspector," she said. "As both my husband and our attorneys have told you, you have our full cooperation. I want to put this behind us."

I gave a nod of acknowledgment.

And I want to know more about that girl.

CHAPTER 5

I flipped through the files in my in-tray.

The first was a domestic abuse case, the wife having withdrawn her complaint against her husband who'd threatened her life. Despite me spending over an hour in the interview room with her, trying to persuade her he'd do it again, Mrs. Summers had insisted she was the one in the wrong. Next, the case of Regency High School's vandalism, where the school's security system had caught our culprit, thirteen-year-old Bryce Arnold, red handed. The parents had lawyered up and the trial was set for the end of the month. The next file made the last two look interesting: a family in Highgate had placed a complaint against their neighbor's Chihuahua, who allegedly kept digging up their flower beds.

I shoved a Malteser in my mouth to soothe the irksomeness of that one. The calming taste of chocolate melting on my tongue delivered on its promise and eased up my tension a notch. My hand went for another malt ball when there was a knock at the door. I hid the packet back in the drawer.

Sgt. Miller entered. "Hey, ma'am."

I gestured for him to sit and he took the seat opposite.

"Ingrid, are you comfortable with merely tracking the counterfeit activity?" he said.

His use of my first name hinted his need for the conversation to leave formality behind.

"We don't seem to have much choice."

He let out a sigh. "No ping on his BlackBerry yet?"

"Not yet. The crime lab is tracking the footage from the CCTV cameras. Hopefully they'll find evidence of him leaving the Ritz."

"That photo of that young girl. What do you make of it?"

"As you know, the internet is strewn with photos like that," I said. "It's hard to decipher what we're really looking at. Still, it certainly deserves our attention. S C & O have his computer now. Hopefully their analysts will turn up more. They should have a report for us soon."

"Well, we have all the counterfeit evidence tagged and documented, so our end of the investigation is pretty much wrapped up."

My attention fell on the in-tray and its threat of dissolving precious time I didn't have. A duck quacked from Miller's left jacket pocket.

He cringed and pulled out his cell. "Sorry, ma'am. Teenage daughters. They must have changed my ringtone at breakfast."

I gave a smile at their mischievousness and wondered if they looked like him.

"They may be teenagers," he said, shoving it back in. "But they're still my little girls. That photo was disturbing. She just looked so young, so..."

"Haunting," I said. "I've got a gut feeling about her too."

He looked reassured. "My leave pass. I left it in your bottom left drawer."

I slid open the drawer and froze, seeing a print out of the photograph from Hauville's computer. The shocking image of the girl I thought I'd lost to S C & O. Miller had printed it out and by doing so he'd breached protocol.

He pushed himself to his feet. "Thank you, ma'am. I knew I could count on you." He headed for the door. "Constable Nobel wants to accompany me when I interview Hauville's secretary. That okay?"

"Sure."

"I'll hopefully have something more for you."

Constable Nobel appeared in the doorway. "Ma'am, do you have a minute?" Helena was carrying a velvet wrapped box.

"Of course. We were just talking about you accompanying Sgt. Miller to interview Lord Hauville's secretary."

"Thank you, ma'am," she said. "I'd like that."

With Miller's exit, she closed the door and sat opposite. She placed the box on my desk. "How did the meeting with Chief Inspector Brooks go?"

"Considering our counterfeit case has been upgraded to a possible kidnapping, he was a little distracted. These type of cases tend to be high profile."

What Helena couldn't know was that a Gothica would have no one to report her missing, other than the vampire whom she served, and the underworld would never use law enforcement to find her. It made me wonder if that was why Orpheus was at Hauville's. Perhaps he too was trying to find that girl from the photo. Orpheus certainly seemed to know an awful lot about my case.

"So we're waiting on Interpol to do its thing?" Helena said, snapping me back into the room.

"Yes, but we're bearing in mind Hauville could still be in the U.K.," I said. "Which would mean an awful waste of time for ICPO. He owns Ballumbie Castle, so he could be hiding out there. Scottish police are checking on that."

"And the photo of that girl? We don't know if it's recent or whether Hauville even took it himself?"

"Not yet. We merely have the date the file appeared on his hard drive. Which was three weeks ago."

"Ma'am, why didn't you mention the photo to his wife?"

"Imogen's been through so much already. Once we know for sure it's not just a file Hauville saved from the internet that he uses to get off..."

"She had an interesting tattoo," she said. "The one on her inner arm. It looked so simple. I googled it."

"Oh?"

Helena nibbled on a fingernail. "A circle represents infinity."

My mind drifted to when I'd been marked with mine.

That dark chamber at Belshazzar's, Orpheus' club. The reassurance from the one who'd branded me with that red hot poker that this mark would keep me safe. Whispers telling me what it meant. That I now belonged to Orpheus. And no vampire dared to defy Orpheus.

Yet he'd kept his distance from me. Had it been Jadeon's influence that had prevented Orpheus' advances? His once obsession to make me his. His ability to let me leave his presence unscathed.

"Ma'am?"

"Yes?" I said, shaken from my musing.

"What do you make of it?"

"Huh? Oh, I'm just encouraged that both you and Miller have picked up on this new detail on our case. I feel it too. Helena, are any of your friends working in S C & O?"

She looked thoughtful. "Kevin Simmons. We graduated together." She realized what I was insinuating. "I'll check in with him and see if he can keep us updated."

"Discreetly."

"Of course, ma'am. Aren't you going to open it?"

That gift wrapped box was intriguing. Dangerously so.

"It's addressed to you," she said. "Want me to open it?"

"Who's it from?"

"Someone dropped it off at reception for you."

"Let me get some gloves."

Helena already had the bow off, quickly followed by the velvet wrapping, then she breached the seal of the hardwood box.

"You're contaminating evidence," I scolded her playfully.

She giggled. "If it's chocolates can I have one?"

"As long as you don't mind being poisoned."

She looked horrified.

"I assume the worst."

"I'm taking a leaf out of your book, ma'am." She reached in and raised a small metal object out, turning it around in her hands. "You have a reputation for taking risks and getting things done."

"Not sure that's a good thing."

She peered closer at it. "What is it?"

"I have no idea."

The orange-sized object was intricately designed, but was unlike anything I'd ever seen before. It had no obvious purpose. I whisked a tissue out of its box and covered my forefinger with it before giving one of the spikes a prod. The metal rod gave slightly. This thing had moving parts. My fingers itched for time alone with it.

The door opened wider and Dr. Riley Russell appeared—our resident coroner. When I'd first met him I'd guessed his age at around thirty, but he dressed older and acted even older than that. He had a kind, intelligent face—one you could trust. When he saw Helena his face wrinkled into a smile.

"Dr. Russell." I motioned for him to come in. "How are you?"

"Very well," he said in a crisp Oxford accent.

"They let you out of the lab then?" I grinned.

"I escaped." Riley sat on the edge of the desk. "Got your message, Ingrid. I've reviewed our records of deceased females that came through over the last year. All aged sixteen to thirty. None of them had a circular tattoo."

"More likely a brand," I said.

He shook his head. "No markings like that on any of them."

"Are you saying that girl was branded like a cow?" Helena asked, astonished.

"I'm considering every possibility," I said.

"You've seen it before haven't you, ma'am?" Helena said.

I resisted the urge to caress my shirt over my own brand.

"Ma'am?" Helena said.

"It's vaguely familiar."

Helena scrunched up her nose. Clearly my attempt to throw her off the scent wasn't working.

"Constable Nobel," Dr. Russell said. "Bridge? My office at lunch time?"

Her face lit up. "Dr. Russell's teaching me how to play bridge."

"Really," I said, pointing upward. "Have you cleared this extra-curricular activity with the brass?"

Dr. Russell smiled as he put on his metal-rimmed spectacles. He peered down at my desk. "An object de art?"

"You recognize it?" I said.

"No, but it looks antique. What is it?"

"We don't know." Helena's eyes widened with intrigue.

"Constable Nobel, please get it finger printed." I rolled my eyes. "Don't forget to tell the lab yours will be on it."

"What do you think it is?" she asked.

"Well if anyone can work it out it's the inspector," Dr. Russell said.

"Ma'am, open the card," she said. "Look, it came in this beautifully wrapped box with Inspector Jansen's name on it."

I peered down at the pristine envelope.

Dr. Russell chuckled. "Watch the inspector's process. She starts like this and then, wham, she has it."

"What does the card say?" Helena tore the seal.

"Helena!" I said. "There could be ricin in there, for goodness sake."

"Statistically it's unlikely," Dr. Russell said.

"Don't encourage her," I said. "You know protocol."

He shrugged. "Still."

I caressed my brow, sensing Helena had been around me too long. She removed the note card from the envelope and turned it around for me to read. Beneath my name and written in an italic hand was a cuneiform script.

"It's written in Sumerian," I said, unable to interpret the pictographs.

"Now that is impressive," Dr. Russell said.

"What does it mean?" Helena said.

"The note's written in an ancient language," I said. "From an ancient civilization." I peered up at Helena. "Fourth millennium B.C."

Dr. Russell added, "Someone's been watching too much history channel. Someone needs to get out more and have a life." He raised his hands in defense. "Just saying."

"Someone needs to stop being such a cheeky bugger and climb back into their hole in the basement." I raised my hands in defense, mimicking him. "Just saying."

Dr. Russell chuckled, his attention falling once more onto Helena.

Studying the illegible note, and then the metal object, I knew they came from an immortal. The pressing question was from whom? I'd been rebuffed by those within the underworld and was no longer welcome. So why this and why now?

"Do you know what it says?" Helena said.

I gave her my answer with a smile.

"Looks like a clue." Dr. Russell headed for the door.

"Someone knows you very well, inspector."

I sat back. "How do you mean?"

"If there's one thing that does it for you, Ingrid, it's a clue." He closed the door behind him.

"Who'd be able to read that?" Helena said.

"Oh, you'd be surprised."

CHAPTER 6

The British Museum was even creepier at night.

Particularly the Egyptian exhibition. It didn't take a lot to heighten the spookiness of its vast collection of mummies showcased in glass coffins. Numerous smaller cases held the shriveled body parts of birds, cats, and dogs. These animals were mummified by their masters to ensure their entrance into the afterlife, much like humans.

The elaborately wrapped kittens caught my eye, reminding me of the time I'd spent with Professor Lucas Azir, renowned Egyptologist and close friend of Orpheus. Lucas had shared with me that kittens were associated with the goddess Bastet, and during their time on earth had been worshiped. His level of knowledge had even impressed the curators here. A result of him having personally lived through the ages, I assumed. Lucas was a vampire. Though unlike Orpheus, he was sweet and kind and oozed an old world charm. Our friendship had gone the same way as the others; a recent casualty of my ban from all things immortal.

Being back in this fabulous museum brought back memories of adventures Lucas and I had shared. I yearned for those days when I'd naively believed these friendships would endure. Would I ever get used to not having them around?

On my way home from the Yard, I'd had a flash of inspiration to visit here, despite my gnawing hunger. I couldn't resist taking a detour on the tube and coming to the only place I knew that housed experts who might be able to determine what this metal object was. My curiosity was at a fever pitch, and no doubt whoever had given it to me knew it too. Just as Dr. Russell had suggested, the one who gifted this probably knew me.

Having been escorted by the bored looking security guard to Dr. Amy Hanson's office, I now waited patiently for her to appear. I'd called on ahead and she'd agreed to give me a few minutes of her time.

Despite her title as senior curator, her office was small, tucked away in the lower recesses of the building. I wondered how she could bare its stuffiness. Still, she'd made the space homey with several photographs of her family. In one, she smiled beside her studious looking husband, and before them posed their two young children. All so normal. A far cry from the surrounding books on ancient cities and their artifacts. Beyond this room sat a collection numbering eight million works, which crowned this museum as one of the largest in the world.

The last time I'd been here was a few months ago and I'd promised myself I'd return and soak in all this culture. Yet work had encroached on my life as it so often did, stealing precious time and forcing me to break that vow.

It felt good to be here now, even if this visit was brief.

Dr. Amy Hanson appeared in the doorway in a flurry of scholarly focus and dust covered white shirt and khakis, which no doubt matched what she'd wear on a dig. Salt and pepper hair and spectacles aged her forty-something years. Her tall, slim frame gave away that she, like me, often got sidetracked and forgot to eat.

"Inspector Jansen," she warmly greeted me.

I held out my hand and felt the firm grip of hers. "Always a pleasure, Dr. Hanson."

"You must excuse this." She gestured to her stained shirt and khakis "A new exhibit arrived this morning from Iraq and I'm knee deep in artifacts." She flashed her smile, hinting that her exhilaration broke through her exhaustion.

"How are you?" I asked.

"I'm well," she said. "Tired, but everything's fine."

"How's the family?"

"Children are growing fast." She raised her brows. "Too fast. Eating us out of house and home." She gave my arm a pat.

"You look well since the last time I saw you."

"I'm fine too, thank you. I won't take up too much of your time. There's something I'd like you to take a look at." I removed the metal object from my handbag. "Maybe you have a colleague here who might be able to identify it?"

She peered down at the object in my hands. "Medieval period. Where did you find it?"

"It was sent to me anonymously. It came with this." I rummaged inside my bag for the note and handed it to her. "Both came with no fingerprints. I had forensics sweep it before I left work."

"Forensics?" She looked puzzled.

"I'm overly cautious. There's no crime associated with it."

"A gift?"

"Yes, I suppose."

"It was your astuteness that proved invaluable in helping us with the museum's theft." She smiled. "You'll be happy to hear no more excitement on that front."

The thought of anyone violating what felt like a sacred place wrenched deeper than most crimes.

"Cuneiform?" She studied the note. "This doesn't match the date of the artifact. The note's 30th century BC, and that," she peered at the object, "late middle ages."

"So few people read cuneiform, apparently."

"Why don't you ask Professor Azir?" she said. "Surely he's more suited to deciphering this?"

"We've lost touch."

She looked surprised.

"My schedule's pretty crazy." I hoped to sound convincing and not give away my sadness.

I recalled Dr. Hanson's excitement when she'd first met Lucas. Their animated discussion on Egyptology and his father's work. Which was really *his* work. A game of smoke and mirrors Lucas played to hide his immortality, even from me at first. His eccentric professorial demeanor leant itself to such a ruse.

"He does love his secrets," Dr. Hanson said.

I held her stare. "He's here?"

"Dr. Azir agreed to come on board as a consultant." She motioned right. "His office is down the corridor."

"He was monumental in solving one of my most difficult cases." I failed to subdue my excited tone. "He's a hard man to find."

She gestured to the door.

A jolt of excitement shuddered up my spine, rendering my claustrophobia almost ineffective. It had been brought on by the closed in walls of the passageway that we headed down.

"The staff are quite taken with Dr. Azir." She gave a wry smile. "They secretly refer to him as Mr. Eye-candy."

That was, of course, an understatement. I recalled meeting Lucas that first time atop Leiden's art gallery. He'd strolled out of the shadows, hands in his pockets, tall, dashing. His striking features revealed an uncommon beauty from his Middle Eastern descent. Despite his thirty-something appearance, he oozed the confidence of an immortal and emanated a stark sensuality. There was no doubt what had drawn Orpheus to him. Not to mention Lucas' passion for history, and his intelligence was as sharp as his stare.

The very same one that now held mine.

Lucas peered up from his desk with a flash of recognition, his subtle cringe causing me to feel one too.

"Hey," I said, trying to lessen the tension.

Dr. Hanson hadn't caught his reaction. She merely gestured for me to enter and threw a wave goodbye to us both before withdrawing.

"May I?" I said, entering.

Lucas made his way around his desk toward me.

"I had no idea you worked here," I said, taking in his office, which was only slightly larger than Hanson's.

"I have permission to consult here."

"Orpheus gave it?" I asked.

"Dominion," he said, infusing the name with pride and revealing his admiration for him.

There came a flurry of hope he might tell me where Jadeon was, but I suppressed it, not ready to burn that bridge just yet. "You need permission to work here?"

"I'm in the public eye. All such activity must be sanctioned by the elders."

The elders? Hadn't Paradom mentioned them? I refocused,

making a mental note to return to that subject later.

"You always have a way of getting me to say too much," he said.

"How can knowing you work here be an issue?"

"The new rule of law means everything is locked down. No communication with mortals unless sanctioned by the elders."

"Is Sebastian sanctioned to live at The Mount?"

"We shouldn't be having this conversation."

"Lucas," I said, hurt by his avoidance. "Have I not earned your trust?" I stepped toward him. "Proven I'm an advocate."

"I can't risk my position here."

I really was being locked out and kept at arm's length. "Please, don't turn your back on me," I said, missing Lucas terribly even though he was right here. This distance between us wrenched my stomach.

"Oh, Ingrid." He closed the gap between us and wrapped his arms around me and pulled me into a hug. "Forgive me."

I melted in his embrace, needing this kindness to banish my feeling of being considered the enemy.

"It's good to see you. Really it is. Forgive my paranoia." He took my hand and kissed it. "There, see? Nothing has changed between us."

"I'm not here and I never saw you."

He relaxed a little, yet his eyes hinted at uncertainty. "You're on police business?"

"Well I wasn't originally." I motioned to clarify. "I'd love to show you something. Then you'll never see me again." The words brought pain.

"I don't want that. I mean, never to see you again. It's complicated."

"That's the word Orpheus used the night he left you at Les Miserables and came to visit me in Knightsbridge."

He gave a nod, validating Orpheus' alibi. Seeing Lucas again reminded me why I'd fallen for his old world charisma. I'd fooled myself we were friends.

"We are friends," he said.

"Stop reading my mind."

He gave a bashful smile. "Eye-candy. I can live with that."

"Those were not my words. You have quite the reputation."

"My head's in a book most of the time. Or rummaging around the mummy collection." He saw the metal object in my hand and his gaze shot up to meet mine.

"That's a promising response," I said.

"Where did you get it?"

"Do you know what it is?" I peered down at it.

"It's a Scirpus."

"Scirpus?" I handed it over to him.

"Latin for puzzle. Also known as an enigma." He turned it over. "Did you move the parts? Or did it come like this?"

"Haven't touched it."

"Who gave it to you?"

"It was sent anonymously to me at the Yard."

He looked up.

Great, I reminded him I'm a policewoman.

"It came with this." I showed him the card.

He read the cuneiform. "Interesting."

"What does it say?"

"It's an invitation."

"To where?"

"Solve the enigma and it will lead to the invitation." He waved the card. "Exact interpretation."

"Are those Fabian Snowstrom's words?" My mind reached back to those hours I'd spent in his presence. The most ancient of all vampires, and luckily for me a seeming ally. "You wouldn't tell me if it was from Fabian, would you?"

"Tea?

In the far corner sat a table, and atop that a kettle. Two mugs rested beside it and a tin of Typhoo tea. A fresh orange waiting to be peeled and eaten, along with a packet of salt and vinegar crisps, plus a box of Jaffa Cakes. These few items served their purpose of conveying the usual comforts of an office—delicate touches of normality. Even Lucas working through the night would be construed as passion for his vocation.

"Take a seat." He sat on the edge of the desk. "Would you like that orange? A biscuit?"

"No, thank you." I popped the metal object back in my bag. "I'll grab something later. Do you know what it is? The puzzle?"

"Think of it as a modern day Rubik's Cube." He scrunched

up his nose. "Only without the colors."

"Thanks for that." I caressed my forehead, not sure if I had the energy for the challenge. "So explain this, why am I being coaxed back to the underworld? And by whom?"

"Ah, a conundrum."

"Can you hear the screaming in my head?" I made it a joke, trying to shake off my frustration.

"Let me make you some tea."

"It's too late for caffeine. I'll never sleep." I sat back. "Don't take this the wrong way, but you're such a kind man, Lucas, it really surprises me you're friends with Orpheus."

He gave a wry smile. "He sired me."

"He turned you? So that forces you to remain loyal?"

"There's a connection. A bond. But I also enjoy Orpheus' company."

"But he's such a rogue."

"You judge him on modern day morals," he said. "Before the Victorian Era, England was merciless. The 19th century brought with it values of social, economic, and sexual restraint."

I widened my eyes.

"You just have to get to know him."

"How did you two meet? Did he attack you?"

"Goodness, no. He saved me." Lucas pushed himself farther up the desk. "I was on a dig in the Valley of the Kings."

"Tutankhamen's tomb?"

Lucas looked surprised.

"Orpheus told me he met you there in the 1920s. That's all he told me."

"Huh." Lucas gave a ghost of a smile. "I was Howard Carter's assistant. I was an annoying archeologist in the making."

"Howard Carter discovered Tutankhamun's tomb?"

"Along with his friend and colleague George Herbert," Lucas said. "Did you know that Tutankhamun was crowned Pharaoh at nine years old?"

"No. That's very young."

"He reigned for ten years before he died. Probably from a fracture that became infected. Of course we only found that out recently. Our science was limited back then."

"And Orpheus' involvement?"

"He was visiting Egypt. He happened to stumble on the tomb I was working in. Luckily for me."

"What happened?"

"The senior archeologists had left for the day and only a skeleton crew remained. There were five of us, two junior archeologists and three guards. We were working in shifts. Public pressure was on for us to present our findings quickly. This was an unprecedented discovery, as you can imagine. It was late, around 2 A.M. I'd taken a break from dusting off a pair of beaded sandals I'd found that were close to disintegrating." Lucas stared off as though transported back to that time and place. "The first thing I noticed was the quiet. Then I saw them. Three tomb robbers had entered the cave. Their knives were stained with blood. I knew immediately they'd killed our guards. Alan, my colleague, panicked and ran for the exit, but he never made it. They stabbed him to death."

"Horrible," I whispered.

He looked tense. "They were after gold. I watched them gather what they could carry from where they'd left me in the corner, half dead. There came a blur of movement and one by one they fell. At first I assumed the man who'd entered behind them was with them, until he broke the necks of two of the thieves and then tied up the last one, keeping him alive."

"Orpheus?"

"Yes. All I could think of was how angry Howard Carter was going to be when he realized we'd failed to protect the tomb. Even though I lay dying. Silly, I suppose."

"I'm so sorry." Though these words weren't enough.

"Orpheus knelt beside me and asked if he could get me anything." Lucas ran his fingers through his hair, showing this wasn't easy for him. "I was bleeding to death. They'd stabbed me at least twenty times. The agony was blinding. There's nothing quite like fear and pain. Nothing. Orpheus told me I was dying. He seemed so calm. I asked him to stay with me. I didn't want to die alone."

There came laughter from somewhere down the corridor, and it made me cringe from how inappropriately it clashed with Lucas' narrative.

"Orpheus told me he was waiting for me to near the veil. I

begged him to let them find my body. 'I can offer you something better,' Orpheus said. 'Immortality.'"

"Did you understand what he was asking you?"

"I was in and out of consciousness. But he seemed to want me to want this. There's a vampire code, you see. Before anyone is turned, their permission must be granted."

"Is that always the case?"

"Not always, but it's the most civilized way to proceed before turning someone. Sense doubt, and you put them through hell. I mean, imagine finding out you're immortal. Some individuals just aren't suited to it."

I grimaced, having never actually given it much consideration. Though the idea of asking permission brought some reassurance. I motioned for Lucas to continue.

"My thirst was overwhelming," he said. "The body's way of trying to save itself." His face flushed with emotion. "I believed I was drinking wine."

"You were drinking Orpheus' blood?"

Lucas let out a long sigh. "When I came round I realized why he'd kept the last thief alive. It all felt so natural."

The stillness of the room closed in and his words hung heavy. The flicker of his eyelashes told me he'd shared the truth.

"Was the attack on you and your men ever documented?" I asked. "I don't remember reading anything about it."

"For the sake of public relations it was covered up."

"And Orpheus?"

"He spent a few months with me. Teaching me all the skills needed to survive. That was the new way. The old way was to let the fledgling fend for themselves."

"Where was Sunaria during all this?"

"Orpheus believed her to be dead." He shrugged. "I don't think I'd have made it without Orpheus by my side."

"Did you hate him for transforming you?"

"I love him for it. I'm not your average vampire who questions his immortality. I'm grateful. My work consumes my every waking hour."

"Have you seen Sunaria since…that awful evening when she attacked us?"

It was a delicate subject. The last time we'd both seen

Sunaria, Orpheus' lover, she'd held me at knife point and slit Lucas' throat while he was trying to protect me. I shivered with the thought of it.

His face softened thoughtfully. "Orpheus protects me too."

"So Sunaria hasn't attempted to hurt you again?"

"Orpheus can be very persuasive." Lucas twisted his mouth into a mischievous smile. "One day you'll come to love him as much as I do."

"Let's not go that far."

"I'd be happy to look at it for you."

"Huh?"

"You have a photocopy you'd like to show me?"

My shoulders dropped. "I'll never get used to that."

"Sorry, if I could turn it off I would." He shrugged. "We learn to shut down our own thoughts, but when a mortal thinks they might as well be speaking."

"The funny thing is the more I try to control what I'm thinking the more embarrassing my thoughts become." I reached into my handbag.

"Yeah, like don't think of a red tree, right?"

"Exactly. Oh Lucas, it really is wonderful to see you." I handed him the photocopy.

"Likewise." He stared down at the image of the captured girl.

"We found this on a computer. Forensics are trying to ascertain when it might have been taken and, if we're lucky, where. With no missing girl fitting this description reported, it's a low priority for them, I'm afraid."

"Mark of a Gothica," he said, reaching across his desk for the round magnifying glass. He used it to study the image more closely. "She's restrained against her will."

"I thought that too. Belshazzar's was a place where people could live out their S & M fantasies. This looks different."

"I agree. This girl used to be Gothica."

"She's a vampire?"

"Look at her irises." He handed over both the photocopy and the magnifier. "And a vampire could break from these restraints."

I studied the image through the glass. "Someone's sedating

her?"

"Perhaps with a chemical straightjacket. Like laudanum."

"Opium?"

"It's the only substance that would sedate a vampire." He raised his hand with caution. "That's actually a well kept secret. Share that with no one."

"Of course. I appreciate your frankness." I looked back down at the girl's picture. "Orpheus knows about her, doesn't he?"

Lucas raised his chin and his eyes burned with certainty. "If there's one thing you can count on, Ingrid, it's that we always look after our own."

CHAPTER 7

I hardly remembered getting home from the museum.

Seeing Lucas had been wonderful, though I was left with more questions than answers. I decided to let my subconscious mull over all I'd learned tonight. Very often answers presented themselves when I distracted myself. The shower was a particularly good place for these kinds of revelations. All that hot water and white noise did something to my brain. Still, right now I needed to eat.

Peering into my fridge, I acknowledged what I already knew. Inside sat a carton of soymilk, a can of tuna fish, and an old cheese stick that would probably kill me if I ate it. I'd had no time to go shopping, or more truthfully the drudgery of it had put me off. A bowl of Special K was in my future.

The chardonnay I'd just uncorked tasted of aged vanilla and it hit the spot. It wasn't the best I'd ever drunk but it would do.

It was good to be home.

I carried the bottle into the living room, grateful to back in my London flat. This three bedroom luxury residence was tucked away in Chelsea, situated east of Redelsdale Street, and had served as one of the many safe houses belonging to Lord Jadeon Artimas. Over decades, he'd procured properties scattered around the country, should a haven be needed. Or so he'd once told me.

Though it wasn't officially my home, it had come to feel like it. I'd only planned on staying here for a few weeks until I'd found my own place. This location allowed for a quick commute to Scotland Yard and my busy schedule hindered looking for somewhere else. Or maybe that was the lie I told myself and I'd come to believe it. The more likely explanation was I drew comfort from being around *his* stuff. Like the large selection of impressive paintings of nightscapes he'd collected. I'd gotten used to these simple but luxurious furnishings. All this dark wood and leather leant a cozy air. Though the Edward III sword hanging behind his desk in his empty office gave me nightmares, its ownership being illegal. I much preferred spending time in Jadeon's bathroom with its enormous tub and marble tiled shower, which was presently calling my name.

For now though, I needed to sit and decompress.

Seeing Lucas tonight had been a lovely surprise. Though before I left I'd promised not to bother him again. A vow I doubted I'd keep. I missed him, missed all of them, and most of all I missed Jadeon.

Despite prolonging my withdrawal from a world now lost to me, the visit had proven invaluable. Lucas had confirmed my fear about that girl, validating the photo was real. Adding to this revelation that she was in fact a vampire. My only dilemma was whether to focus my full attention onto this investigation or, as Lucas had suggested, allow the underworld to take care of it. As far as I could tell they were already investigating this. Orpheus' appearance at the Bainard Building hadn't only been about protecting me, it seemed.

The mystery of the metal object would have to wait.

After setting the wine bottle on the coffee table, I sank into the leather sofa, sipping away and mulling over tonight's visit to the museum. My gaze drifted over to the antique bookcase with its collection of history and travel books, none of them mine. Over to my left sat a writing desk, and straight ahead a 64 inch television I was too tired to watch.

I jolted upright.

Upon the dining room table rested a stuffed fox staring back with beady glass eyes. It had come from Hauville's taxidermy collection and was the very same one I'd seen in his storage room. The same one that never made it to our evidence room. I set my glass on the coffee table.

And began the search for an intruder, moving slowly,

guardedly, making my way to the bedroom and finding it untouched. Next, onto the guest bedroom, also finding it empty and undisturbed. All the cupboards I searched were clear. Kitchen: clear. I opened the bathroom door—

My heart tried to escape through my chest.

"Hey Ingrid," Anaïs said.

She lay naked in the bathtub, bubbles of white foam frothing around her. The aroma of sandalwood filled the room.

"Anaïs?" I screeched, resisting the urge to run, which my adrenaline insisted I still do.

Anaïs' exotic Asian eyes held mine. Her beauty was hauntingly familiar; her long, black mane was wet and slicked back and her white skin bathed in the soft yellow lighting, emphasizing her supernatural aura. Her small breasts peeked above the bubbles, revealing pierced rings through pert nipples.

I flipped down the toilet seat and sat on it. "You nearly gave me a heart attack."

"Sorry," she said. "I dozed off."

"How long have you been here?"

"An hour."

Before Anaïs had been transformed she'd been a Gothica, a servant of the undead, and like me she had the circled brand to prove it. The only thing we had in common.

"What do you want, Anaïs?"

"How have you been?"

"I've had better days."

"It only hurt a bit," she said.

"What did?"

"Getting them pierced."

My jaw fell open.

She stared down at her nipples. "You were wondering how much it hurt." She raised a finger. "To answer your other unspoken question, I got them done before I was turned."

"Why are you in my bath?"

"Killing time," she said. "You're usually home by eight."

"I stopped off somewhere."

"How's Lucas?"

Damn, I have to avert my thoughts.

"How did you know what time I'd be home?" I said sternly.

"It's good to see you too, Ingrid."

I considered going back into the living room for my wine. Then remembered the fox.

"Inside it is a camera," she said.

I swallowed hard, feeling a painful twisting in my abdomen working its way into my throat.

"Don't panic," she said. "Orpheus removed the fox before anyone saw it."

By *it,* Anaïs was referring to footage filmed through the fox's glass eyes, capturing both Orpheus and I contaminating the evidence and rendering it inadmissible in court.

Bloody hell.

I covered my face, annoyed I'd messed up. The future of my career now rested firmly in Orpheus' hands.

"The footage is in a safe place," Anaïs said.

Fuck.

My throat tightened. "Any chance I can see it?"

And destroy it. Of course, they could always make a copy. I rubbed my eyes in frustration.

"A friend of mine has gone missing." Anaïs said.

"Have you filed a missing person report?"

She cocked her head.

"She's a vampire?" I said.

"Turned three months ago."

"So reporting her would be an issue?"

"You've got it."

"When did you last see her?"

"Two weeks ago."

I arched an eyebrow.

Anaïs frowned at me. "We were happy."

"I understand." A wave of empathy came over me. "Anaïs, of course I'll help you. You don't need to blackmail me."

She slid down the tub and water whooshed toward her feet. Like her fingernails, her toenails were painted black. A tattooed fleur-de-lis marked her delicate ankle. It was like having a wild animal in my bathtub. Anaïs was breathtaking, graceful and oh so feminine, and her eyes mesmerized their prey. All this served as subterfuge for her unpredictability.

"I thought we'd learned to trust each other?" she said.

With a shaky inhalation I said, "Of course we have."

I hoped Anaïs' friend wasn't the one in that photo we'd found on Hauville's computer. I pushed that thought far away, not wanting to alarm her.

"I'll make it worth your while," she said.

"Excuse me?"

"I'll help you find Jadeon."

I reacted and immediately regretted it.

"See, I can help you too."

I forced a smile. "Why don't you dry off? Meet me in the sitting room."

"I thought you wanted to see him?"

"Some doors are not meant to be walked through again."

"You still love him, though."

"This is kind of private."

"And he still loves you."

I liked Anaïs, really I did, but her ability to read me left me vulnerable, and despite being the one fully clothed she made me feel naked. "Apparently you need permission from the elders to speak with me? Did you get it?"

She looked away.

"Didn't think so." I pushed myself to my feet and strolled back into the sitting room and went straight for the fox. Sure enough, there was a camera inside. I placed the fox on the coffee table so its beady eyes could punish me with their glare. Then I took a swig of wine from my glass, but it tasted bitter now.

I'd been so naive to think Orpheus had helped me wrap up my case. He'd set a trap, and like an idiot I'd walked right in having believed Jadeon had sent him. Orpheus saving my life from my escapade on that ledge had been a strike of luck on his part and he'd taken advantage of it, like he was taking advantage of me now.

Was that why Anaïs was here? To deliver his threat?

Within a few minutes, she reappeared, having dressed in black leather trousers, her skimpy T-shirt damp since she barely dried herself, her wet hair pulled back in a ponytail. She looked edgy in laced boots with spiked heels and oozed gothic chic.

She sat beside me on the couch. "Orpheus doesn't know I'm here."

"Huh." Even if it were true it didn't help ease my paranoia. "I would offer you one." I raised my glass.

"I've upgraded to blood." Her attention settled on my throat and she clenched her teeth, her fangs sharp and ready.

"Not exactly reassuring." I leaned back.

"I bet your blood tastes amazing."

"Look, it's been a really long day. I have to be up early." And that fox's beady-eyed stare hadn't left me.

"You're going too slow on this case."

"Lord Hauville's counterfeit case?" I asked, surprised.

"Yes. Only it's not just a counterfeit case, is it?"

"What do you know about it?"

"You conducted a preliminary investigation before all your findings were handed over to another department."

"How do you know that?"

She shrugged. "Everything you saw before the evidence was taken from you is all in here." She pointed to her head.

Hadn't Paradom intimated the same thing?

Anaïs looked excited. "What if I were to tell you that you can increase your ability to solve this crime a thousand times quicker?"

Leaning forward, I placed my drink down next to the fox.

"I know it sounds freaky," she said.

"Okay, you've lost me. What are you saying?"

"Look, there's this stuff you can drink. It'll have you firing off on all cylinders."

"What is it? Coke?"

"No, nothing like that."

"Anaïs, I'm a police inspector, and even if I wasn't I'd still never dabble in drugs."

"It's not a drug. It's blue illuminate."

I felt a headache coming on "What is that?"

"The spell that you drink."

What the fuck!

What the hell had driven her to believe such crap? "Listen to me—"

"Ingrid, you've had the privilege of spending time with vampires. Your doubt about the possibilities of the supernatural surprises me."

I assumed all this had something to do with the photo of that young Gothica. Anaïs after all had been one before she'd served out her time as a vampire servant and taken the leap into immortality. She probably knew the girl. It really wasn't that much of a stretch.

I caressed the tension out of my forehead. "Shouldn't we talk about your friend? Let's make a list of everywhere she might go. Other friends too. Let's work methodically."

"I've been everywhere and spoken to everyone." She gave a nod. "I've exhausted every possibility."

"What's her name?"

"Beatrice Shaw."

"I'll check our records. Why don't you ask Orpheus to help you find her? I have a sneaky suspicion his resources are as good as mine if not better."

Her eyes widened. "Blue illuminate will help you see things you don't know."

"You're trying to tell me this concoction can make you smarter?"

"Yes."

"Then why don't *you* drink it?"

"I did. But you can only do it once. It's pretty potent. The effects last for about forty-eight hours. Apparently the next time you take it the spell blows your brain cells to smithereens."

I stared at her for the longest time. "And you want me to drink it?"

"It's safe the first time." She looked sincere. "I don't blame you for not believing me."

"I'm trying to hold on to rationality." I raised my hand. "I've had a really long day. My workload is exhausting—"

"Show it to me then. The metal object you went to Lucas with." She pointed to my handbag.

Damn, my thoughts betrayed me.

Reluctantly I pulled the metal object out of my bag and handed it to her. "Please be careful with it."

"What did Lucas tell you it was?"

"A puzzle. But he didn't know how to unravel it."

She snorted. "Yeah, right."

"You think Lucas lied?"

65

"I think he's scared of whoever sent it to you." Her pale, long fingers examined it and she twisted the object's small parts round and around until it changed shape. She transformed what had appeared as metal chaos into what was forming a more prominent shape. She placed the object into my hands. "There you go."

I peered down at the metal circle with three sturdy hooks protruding from its center. I held it up reverently. "A key?"

She looked triumphant. "Though what for is a mystery."

I placed it on the coffee table. "Why would anyone give me a key?"

She shrugged. "I need to look at Lord Hauville's computer."

I dragged my gaze away from the key and back to her. "We have specialists examining it right now."

"They don't know what to look for."

"What should they look for?"

She turned her head away, evidently not willing to share that.

"If you know something," I said.

"Maybe you can get me into Scotland Yard? I'll be discreet."

"I'm afraid that's out of the question." I held her stare.

"I know about the photo found on Hauville's computer."

"That's why you're here?" My shoulders slumped. "How do you know?"

"Orpheus told me about it."

"Was it Lucas who told him?" Yet I'd only just left Lucas at the museum, so the timeline didn't match. Still vampires moved at lightning speed. Nothing was ever as it seemed with them.

Just as it wasn't with Anaïs now. She was up to something. And from that small flutter of her eyelids, she knew I knew.

"I haven't seen Lucas in months," she said.

"Then how does Orpheus know about the photo?"

"He's been tracking the investigation. When you moved the computer over to S C & O—"

I sat back, realizing. "Orpheus has a contact at Scotland Yard."

"So can I see it? The photo?"

"Please tell me Orpheus isn't interfering in this

investigation."

"If he were you should be grateful."

Even though there was no room for egos when it came to getting the best results, the idea of Orpheus meddling made me antsy.

"Well?" she said.

"What I have is a photocopy." I reached into my handbag and brought it out. "Are you sure you want to see it?" I leaned over to her and held her hand.

"Yes."

"The girl appears to be constrained against her will."

Anaïs found the courage to look at the photo.

"Is it Beatrice?"

Her lips trembled.

"Oh, Anaïs, I'm so sorry. If I find any evidence pertaining to where she might be I'll tell you right away. I promise."

"Her car was totaled," she said. "But there was no sign of her afterward. She just vanished."

"Two weeks ago?"

"Yes, that was the last time I heard from her."

"She'd make a full recovery if she was injured. As a vampire, right?"

"Of course. We traced her cell phone to the Bainard Building. The phone turned up in a dumpster hours later in SoHo. We lost track after that."

"I'll see if any traffic cameras caught the incident," I said. "I need the location, date, and time it happened."

"On the 8th, at Oxford Circus, around 10 P.M. The other car was totaled too."

"Okay. Now we have to find out if this photo was taken before or after her accident," I said. "What happened to her car?"

"It got towed."

"Where is it now?"

"Waiting to be crushed. Trust me, we examined it for any evidence of where she might have gone."

"We being Orpheus?" I said.

"Yes. We found nothing."

"Hauville's missing, presumed on the run," I said. "Did you know that?"

"Yes." Her attention stayed on the photo. "There's nothing on the news about this. Something tells me your colleagues at Scotland Yard aren't taking this seriously."

"We don't have a lot to go on."

"Well at least she might still be alive."

I remembered what Lucas had told me about laudanum, which would explain Beatrice's inability to send a mind message to Anaïs. The drug apparently incapacitated both body and mind, if given enough. A sinister crime by someone who knew they were dealing with a vampire. There were more questions than answers and it made my head ache.

I squeezed her hand again. "Anaïs, what are you not telling me?"

"None of us killed Hauville if that's what you're asking."

"At least let me look at the evidence you've gathered."

"That's why I'm here. We have nothing."

"We've identified the girl as your friend," I said. "It's a start."

"There may be someone who knows more."

"Who?"

"Dominion."

"Jadeon Artimas?" I said.

"Yes. Would you like to see him again?"

"Um. Well..."

"I can make it happen."

"When?"

She looked surprised. "Tonight."

I swallowed hard, not sure if I was ready to face Jadeon again so soon. Not after his insistence that it was better all round if we were apart.

"Well?" She offered her hand to shake. "Do we have an agreement?" She leaned forward. "Come with me to see Jadeon and I'll give you all the footage shot through the fox."

Absurd. Seriously, what was I agreeing to? Was I really going along with her blackmail?

Her hand slid into mine. "And I promise no more interference with your investigation."

"And I promise to do everything in my power to find Beatrice."

We shook on it.

Anaïs pushed herself to her feet. "Let's get you changed into something more appropriate."

"Why?"

"We'll be entering the domain of the elders. I hope you don't mind but I've brought a couple of outfits that are more suitable. We have to mingle in."

"Elders?"

"They dress elaborately. Our gowns are in the car. I'll go get them."

"You knew I'd say yes."

"I suspected you wouldn't pass up the chance to see Jadeon again. Once a week our hierocracy convenes in Pall Mall. And that's where we'll find him."

"What is this place?"

"The Athenaeum. It's heavily guarded, but with me you'll get in."

"Sounds risky."

"Some risks are worth taking," she said.

Paradom's words found me again. Something about a warning not to take another step. Something about a bridge crumbling beneath my feet.

This doesn't feel right.

But Anaïs had already gone.

CHAPTER 8

Anaïs drove the black Lamborghini way too fast.

We sped across London, weaving between the chaotic traffic, and despite my insistence that police officers were just as likely to get a speeding ticket Anaïs reassured me she could talk herself out of one.

She looked stunning, dressed in a sleek Oscar de la Renta gown, her high-heeled shoes balancing both the clutch and accelerator with ease. Anaïs had insisted I wear a Stella McCartney black evening dress with a plunging neckline. To compliment it, she'd given me a faux diamond encrusted gold bracelet, which she'd strategically placed upon my left forearm to conceal my Gothica circled brand.

"Gothicas are forbidden from entering the Athenaeum." Anaïs raised her hand to make her point. "I know you were never one, but they don't know that. And if they see it," she glanced at my arm, "we're in trouble."

Fear slithered up my spine. "Are mortals permitted?"

"Rarely, but stick by my side." She glanced over. "Dominion would never let anything happen to you and we are there on vampire business."

Adrenaline forged through my veins, dissolving my previous exhaustion. I found it so easy to drift into this nocturnal world and heed the call of the dark. It was easy to heed the call to adventure, effortlessly finding my way back to *him*.

I tried to relax and trust Anaïs to handle this thoroughbred car.

An edgy soundtrack blared through surround speakers, the dramatic music a perfect backdrop.

"Massive Attack," Anaïs said. "Angel."

"Is this your car?"

Anaïs snapped a glance my way. "Why?"

"Just a feeling."

"Maybe it belongs to Orpheus."

I lowered the window to let in some air. "Please tell me Orpheus won't be there."

"It's a big place, so even if he is we probably won't see him."

"You're sure?"

"Look, once Jadeon sees you everything will be fine."

I wanted to believe that, really I did, but Jadeon had been pretty insistent about us going our separate ways. I hoped he'd not be too pissed off when he saw me.

Although I'd spent time with Anaïs before I'd not really gotten to know her. So much could be drawn from studying her tattoos, though the Tinkerbelle on her left shoulder looked out of place. She got that one as a teenager, perhaps. I mused further, wondering if the red rose on her chest or the fleur de lis fleur-de-lis on her ankle had come from a traumatic childhood. Maybe her feistiness was what led Orpheus to mark her as his.

"You do that a lot, you know," Anaïs said. "Make up an opinion on someone before you've gotten to know them."

"It's my job to read people."

"And then place a label on them?"

"I don't exactly have a vampire's mind gift to rely on."

I'd always prided myself on my ability to scrutinize a face, decipher the meaning of the smallest movement or twitch, and come to a conclusion that would serve the law.

"Take Orpheus, for example," Anaïs broke the quiet.

I shot her a look.

"See?" she said. "Assumption is plastered all over your face and you know nothing about him."

"I know enough."

"You assume he's evil because he doesn't play by your rules."

"He does very bad things to people." I understated the

obvious.

"Orpheus took me in." Her expression softened, becoming dream-like. "He found me begging in Convent Garden. He handed me a turkey sandwich and a chocolate milkshake. For the first time in my life I knew what it felt like to be cherished."

"He was seducing you."

"I hadn't eaten in days." Anaïs shuffled in her seat. "Ingrid, you follow your own train of thought like it's sacred."

"I admit to being conservative."

She pressed her foot on the accelerator and the Lamborghini responded effortlessly. The gravity pushed us back in our seats.

"At sixteen, I got in with the wrong crowd," she admitted. "My boyfriend introduced me to hard drugs. I was strung out and circling the drain. Orpheus took me in and made me a Gothica."

This was the first time anyone had talked about Orpheus in this way and I was riveted.

"Panthea, my mistress, was always travelling," Anaïs said. "So I was left to my own devices. I had money and the freedom to really explore London. Later, I realized Orpheus gave me to Panthea so I could remain independent because she was never around."

"Are Gothicas ever taken advantage of by their masters?" I asked. "It's an interesting relationship."

Anaïs slowed the car and we stopped at a red light.

She looked at me. "During the five years we serve our master or mistress, there can be no intimacy between us."

"No sex?"

The light went green. Anaïs pressed the accelerator again and we took off.

"A gesture of affection, but that's all. It's an edict Orpheus put in place to protect us."

I barely noticed we'd turned onto Bromptom Road. I was too engrossed in what she was saying.

"What about dating other Gothicas?" I said.

"Again, not allowed. We're only permitted to date vampires."

"That's how you met Beatrice?"

Her face lit up. "Yes. Orpheus introduced us. He knew we'd click."

"Does Orpheus treat you well?"

"Like family. Every Gothica is like his child."

"What happens if you change your mind after five years and no longer want to be transformed into a vampire?" I said, remembering Jadeon had once told me that the gift of immortality was the reward for serving as a loyal Gothica.

The idea of it still blew my mind.

"It's only ever happened a few times," she said. "In those rare cases, the individual has their mind wiped and they're given a sum of money to restart their lives in the mortal world. They are cut off from us. Mind-wiping ensures they forget our world exists. We do have a choice. Most of us are begging our masters to turn us sooner. Doesn't happen though. Five year rule."

"Why five years?"

"Orpheus believes it gives Gothicas a chance to see what it's really like to be a vampire. They are an intrinsic part of vampire culture. They protect their masters when they sleep. They run errands for them during daylight hours. Whatever they want, really."

"Like an elaborate internship." I gave a nod, realizing there was so much more to a vampire's lifestyle. "Do you have a Gothica?"

"Not yet."

Something told me Orpheus would be taking care of that detail for her too. "You were never scared? Before you were turned?"

"Sometimes, but mostly excited." She flashed a smile. "Orpheus is amazing to be around."

She'd gone from enlightening me to making me a liability. All I now knew weighed heavily. My oath to uphold the law had been broken so many times. Retrospectively, my vow had become a lie. Merely words with no substance. Yet this guilt was lifting and I reflected on the reason. This underworld had always been around, hidden for centuries, and with Dominion as its overlord there came the promise of order.

"You're thinking of Jadeon again." Anaïs slid the gearstick with verve. "Everything I've shared with you is my way of proving you can trust me. Trust Orpheus."

"Unfortunately it's going to be hard to change my mind

about him."

Anaïs parked the car curbside on Pall Mall. She turned off the engine.

"Even though Jadeon rules, we still takes orders from Orpheus."

"How does Jadeon feel about that?"

"He approves."

"How can that be?"

"If you want more answers, they're in there."

Pillars rose majestically before a cream colored building. Tall windows with a dramatic brass balcony ran the full length of the upper floor. It emanated grandness. Was a vampire lair really smack bang in the center of London?

"Come on." Anaïs got out.

We soon reached the front step of the Athenaeum.

Anaïs rang the doorbell. "I'll do the talking."

Although I knew the elders were the most ancient of vampires, there were so many other unanswered questions, like how old were they? What kind of power did they wield? More importantly, what kind of danger was I stepping into?

"Think of them like a vampire council," Anaïs said. "With Dominion as the most senior of the assembly."

"Will I live through this?" I asked, not quite sure why, though something in the way Anaïs' voice had lowered to a whisper made me nervous.

"Of course."

On the double door, unfamiliar symbols were inscribed; a chaotic arrangement of carvings impossible to decipher.

"Bit prominent, isn't it? I mean we are right in the center of Pall Mall."

"Best place to hide anything."

I was about to step into the center of a hive more perilous than Belshazzar's, Orpheus' old club. My thoughts raced with how Jadeon might receive me. With him holding this new title of Dominion, was there etiquette?

Anaïs grabbed my arm. "If I can smell your fear, so will they."

CHAPTER 9

An elderly butler greeted us.

His age of seventy or so made me doubt this man was a vampire, and his welcoming smile calmed me a little.

Anaïs bowed her head. "Fonctionnaire." She placed both her index and middle fingers to her forehead and then lowered them to her lips, and then her heart.

The butler side stepped, allowing us to enter.

She'd just given him the password. A large double doorway opened, the wood so thick it could only mean one thing. Daylight was heavily controlled here.

An immense room unfurled before us. An imperial grandeur unlike anything I'd ever seen before. The walls were decorated with Egyptian frescos as was the low ceiling. There were no windows, not in this room anyway. Black marble flooring spread out like a cloud of perfection beneath our feet. The dim lighting threw shadows. A trick of the light made time stand still, or perhaps it was the graceful movement of the other guests. I could see why Anaïs had insisted we dress like this.

There, mingling in the center of the grand foyer, were fifty or so extraordinarily well-dressed men and women, all of them deep in conversation. Most of them were so breathtakingly beautiful they didn't look real. It wasn't only their unworldly paleness; it was their striking features, which went beyond beautiful. All of their irises were startlingly vivid: some as blue as the ocean, others were deep chocolate browns, some had rich turquoise, even the occasional speckled amber eyes fell upon us...

Reassuringly, they soon turned away.

Although I'd enjoyed attending glamorous events in the past, nothing compared to this. Perfect looking women were everywhere, their dresses going beyond any haute couture I'd ever seen. Even the men dressed decadently in luxurious rich silks, velvets, and some donned a form of armor.

My attention drifted back to the women. A few wore elaborate headdresses made from rare metals, some bejeweled, while others had their long hair interwoven with crowns. A few women bared their breasts and others seemed not to care that their attire was see-through. This glamorous collection of multi-cultural nightwalkers was intimidating.

I drew in a deep calming breath as I took them all in.

A scantily-clad, twenty-something blonde waitress offered us drinks balanced upon a tray. Beside a tall flute of what looked like champagne was another glass containing a blood red mixture. Anaïs reached for them both and handed me one. Soon after, Anaïs took her first sip. Her eyelids fluttered shut and from her look of contentment she was drinking blood.

I questioned what I was doing here. I felt so small, so insignificant, amongst this impressive collection of socialites. These gods and goddesses of the underworld.

"Still your thoughts." Anaïs' hand reached for mine. "Follow me."

We walked around the large gathering and I tried to look dead-ahead, to not catch anyone's eye or stir their intrigue. Remembering I was meant to be stilling my thoughts, or at least keeping them at bay, I turned my mind onto something more passive. The knowledge I was considered sustenance for this grand gathering made me more than a little panicked.

Anaïs' incredulous stare locked on mine.

We headed down an easterly corridor stretching out before us and much to my relief placed some distance between us and the highfaluting crowd. I wondered how much I'd hate myself if I turned around and went for the exit. Though letting Anaïs down felt unfair, and the thought of Beatrice being in danger kept me moving forward. I couldn't bear to think of her in harm's way.

I glanced over at Anaïs, coveting this gothic siren's

confidence as she strolled onward, oozing her usual self-assurance. She again picked up on my rambling thoughts and threw me a reassuring glance.

"How come they let us just walk right in?" I said.

"Because you're with me." Anaïs twisted her mouth to the side.

The gesture made me doubt this was the whole truth. Turning the corner, the space opened up to a small, simple room with leather furniture neatly positioned here and there. Just ahead, we saw a gentleman with shocking white hair, dressed sharply in a black suit, lingering before a marble fireplace. His hand reached out for the head of a lion carved into the mantel. He gave it a pull and the fireplace scraped open, gaping like an angry mouth. He disappeared through it.

Anaïs headed after him.

Peering into the opening, I made out the first few steps of a stairwell and Anaïs raised her eyebrows in expectation. Apparently we were going through, daring to see what lay on the other side. Hesitating, though not wanting to be left behind, I followed. The fireplace began its journey back, quickly closing and nudging me forward into the dark.

It was too late to turn around.

Anaïs' hand took mine, her pull insisting I stay close. My heart raced all over again, my doubt devouring the last of my confidence. Descending, using my right hand out against the wall to feel my way, I took my time, willing myself not fall.

The temperature dropped, causing the fine hairs on my forearms to prickle.

This reminded me of St. Michael's Mount. My mind found refuge in the memory of the adventures I'd had there with Jadeon, descending a stairwell very much like this one. I willed him to be at the end of this quest.

Straight ahead, shards of light burst up from beneath the bottom of a door and, with caution, Anaïs nudged it open. We entered what appeared to be a small foyer, and beyond that more steps waited. We followed the silver inlaid pattern onwards, downwards, both of us eager to see more.

Standing before an enormous doorway were the inscribed words: *"The only true wisdom is in knowing you know nothing."*

Anaïs pointed to it. "Socrates." She pushed open the door, which creaked on its hinges.

My eyes adjusted to the dimness, trying to understand what I was looking at. The vastness was drenched in a soft golden hue of artificial light. We'd stepped inside an enormous library. A one hundred foot high ceiling loomed above. Stretching out to either side of us were miles upon miles of dark wooden arched shelves holding an immense collection of books.

"Wow," Anaïs' whisper carried into the void.

My words fell away, never to be spoken, the awe and splendor stealing them, silencing my scattered thoughts. The urge to investigate got the better of me and I headed off in the direction of the closest shelf and reached for one of the heavily bound books.

"Impressive, isn't it?" a man's voice came out of the dark.

My hands left the book where it sat. Slowly, I turned to face the man with the white flock of hair. He looked ethereal bathed beneath this golden-yellow light.

I wanted to run, and from Anaïs' expression so did she.

"Beautiful library," I said, making it sound casual, acting as though we were meant to be in here.

"Do you know what Libricide is?" he said calmly.

I tried to pick up on his true reaction to us discovering one of London's most well kept secrets.

"Libricide is the burning of books," he said, his gaze sweeping left and right as though admiring children he'd fathered and not the endless books amassed. "What you see is a victory of extraordinary accomplishment."

"It's breathtaking," I said.

"You helped to save all these?" Anaïs said.

"Some, yes. Over time, those of us who considered ourselves guardians of knowledge ensured the unadulterated collection of historical documentation."

I recalled seeing footage of piles of books burned in protest, either by religious fanatics or evil dictators such as Hitler. It had been hard to watch and impossible to understand.

As though picking up on my thoughts, he said, "The attempt to decimate knowledge goes all the way back to AD 367, when Athanasius, Bishop of Alexandria, demanded all writings which he deemed unacceptable to be eradicated. Later, zealots attacked the world's largest library in Alexandria in Egypt. They burned it to the ground." He sighed. "The list goes on."

There came the realization of what we'd actually stumbled upon and the understanding that lives had been risked, perhaps even lost, to ensure the protection of such a collection.

"Indeed," he said, having read my thoughts. "Whatever it takes." And with those words came his threat. "Come with me."

We followed, Anaïs and I swapping cautious glances.

Running wasn't an option. Anaïs could very well make it out, but I'd not escape this vampire or even the others. I only hoped now more than ever that Jadeon was here.

We entered a smaller and yet just as impressive library. Hundreds of votives surrounded us, all of them throwing off shadows that danced over dusky walls. Flickering flames sparkled with a mystical illumination.

There was an enormous dark wooden table in the center, and sitting around it were ten or so men and women.

Vampires.

Several languages were being spoken at the same time. I caught a few words of French and something that sounded Gaelic. A man's crisp English accent with a soft Spanish lilt rose above the others, and sent a wave of panic through me.

And then I saw him—

Orpheus.

My heart flinched in my chest. "Anaïs, you didn't?"

Her betrayal snatched my breath.

"I didn't know he'd be here, I promise," she whispered.

"They found the library," the white-haired man announced to them.

Orpheus rose and in a split-second he stood close, dangerously so. His black velvet waistcoat and tie and his tailored double-breasted jacket matched his fine trousers, making him look all business. Easily intimidating. His jaw tensed, the small muscles twitching.

His hazel glare held mine then fixed on Anaïs. "What have you done?"

"We need to speak with Dominion," she said shakily.

"Do you have any idea what this means?" He pointed. "To

bring her?"

"Beatrice is in danger," I said. "I believe I can help—"

"Please," Anaïs snapped. "It's taking too long to find her."

"Silence, both of you." Orpheus faced the others. "This breech is unacceptable."

"I'll take care of them?" The palest female stepped closer.

"Anaïs is mine to punish," Orpheus said. "I'll handle her."

"The mortal?" the pale female said. "Shall I—"

"Not yet," Orpheus said. "Anaïs, go home."

"I won't leave Ingrid," she said.

Orpheus folded his arms across his chest, and from the way Anaïs reacted I knew they were still talking but privately, silently, using the mind gift to communicate. Her face was flushed with anguish and I tried to read her. Her confidence fell away and she appeared to crumble, her hands out in front, pleading.

"Anaïs?" I moved closer to her.

"Ingrid, I'm sorry…" She lowered her head.

"Go," I said. "It's okay. I'll be fine." Though something told me that might not be the case, but I wanted her out of here. I needed her safe.

"I won't go," she said.

Orpheus closed his eyes and Anaïs yelped in pain.

"Point made, I believe?" he said.

"Stop it," I said. "Don't you hurt her."

Anaïs flew out of room, and I felt relief she'd gotten the chance to put distance between herself and this place. I balled my hands into fists, readying for whatever came next as my throat tightened.

One of the council members closed the gap between me and him. His grey locks contradicted his twenty-something years. I side-stepped away but his hand found my back, his icy touch reaching through the material of my dress. He nudged me closer to Orpheus. He was a vampire, they all were, their fluorescent irises caught in the sparkling lights of the votives.

"I need to speak with Dominion," I said shakily. "Beatrice could be in danger."

"I'm more worried about you right now," Orpheus said. "If I wipe your mind again it will probably kill you." He caressed his chin as though thinking it through.

"We have no choice," the pale female said.

She held an air of superiority. Arrogance born from having faced off with mortality and won. For them, death's sting had been just that—an annoyance long forgotten. I'd been close to vampires before, spent endless nights alongside the undead, but these nightwalkers were different, their air of authority so intense and their preternatural natures so glaring that they emanated an uncommon vitality. A deadly threat.

Regret for coming here seeped into my bones, or poured out of my pores. It was hard to tell my thoughts were so addled. Orpheus remained still and it felt like he was using this silence to torture me.

"Did Anaïs deliver me into your trap?" I said, still unsure.

"No." His stare swept over my dress—

Lingering on where the material plunged between my breasts, showing more flesh than was wise considering Orpheus' sexual appetite. He drew back his lips, baring white fangs, and I could swear he'd focused on my throat. Somewhere, at some time, though I couldn't recall where, I'd heard that when a vampire bared his fangs it meant either two things: sex or feeding. My legs felt unsteady. Orpheus' eyelids lowered. He was hypnotizing.

He continued to undress me merely with his stare. "Laws are there for a reason." His voice was low, calm, precise. "You of all people know that."

"This place—"

"Doesn't exist."

I went to speak, but something in his demeanor changed and I closed my mouth, fearing my words might set him off. His fury was legendary. His ability to follow an impulse without regret was infamous.

"We have to punish you," he said. "For coming here."

My focus locked onto the door Anaïs had minutes before fled through. I wouldn't get far, though my heart was racing so fast it was telling me I should at least try. Yet my feet remained rigid, failing my chance to flee. Orpheus turned away and he ran his fingers through his dark locks, his stare searching the room.

His glare found me again. "What the fuck were you

thinking?"

"I'm not here for me."

"She's seen too much," one of the others said.

There came a stirring in the room, as though each and every one of them had picked up on something at the same time and they all shifted nervously. Whispers carried, hushed words spoken in foreign languages. A doorway burst open and there came a breeze, a whirling as a burst of cold swept the room. Several of the candles went out.

A jolt of exhilaration shot up my spine.

Jadeon stood a few feet away.

His expression was taut. His stare focused on me with a startling intensity. Relief swept over me, and for the first time since arriving I felt safe. The others bowed their heads in respect. Even Orpheus offered a gesture of greeting. Though the way in which Orpheus regarded Jadeon with admiration caused my uneasiness to return. Something was wrong. Orpheus and Jadeon were mortal enemies, yet from this interaction between them there was no sign of it.

Jadeon's back stiffened as his eyes wandered over my face and body then rested on the bracelet covering my circled brand. I'd never seen him dressed so dashing. Of course he'd always looked stylish, but this was extraordinarily masculine. So commanding. His long black coat hung over his broad shoulders. Wisps of dark hair fell over his eyes. Jadeon was heart-stopping handsome, his height equaling Orpheus', but the way he held himself made him look taller. His brown iridescent irises were easy to disappear into, like I'd done so many times before. His chiseled jawline was only slightly more striking than those full lips. A mouth that had kissed mine so many times before and spoken promises of love.

Yet now he regarded me critically, chastely.

"Dominion." The pale female slashed through the silence. "Forgive our failure."

I needed air, needed to be out of here and away from all this intensity.

Jadeon regarded me sternly just as Orpheus had done. An ill-timed arousal lingered low in my belly. Was this intentional on his part? Was he wooing me into submission?

"Hi," I said breathlessly.

Jadeon closed his mouth and hid his fangs.

I stepped forward. "I can explain."

"Shut up," said Orpheus.

Jadeon's gaze slid over to him. "What is this?"

"I'm as surprised as you," Orpheus said.

"Anaïs brought her," said the pale female.

Jadeon threw her a sideways glance. "I see."

"We've decided her fate," she told him.

Jadeon nodded, as though considering her comment. "Who let them in?"

"Please," I said. "I'm here to talk to you about Beatrice."

Jadeon motioned to the pale female. "Ensure this never happens again."

She vanished so quickly that several papers whirled from the table and fanned out onto the floor around us. One of them landed near my feet, yet my usual curiosity to try and read what was on it was lost.

My heart wrenched from Jadeon's indifference and I sucked in a sob, pained that this wasn't the romantic reunion I'd envisioned. He made me feel like a stranger.

"Orpheus," Jadeon said through clenched teeth. "Get her out of here and wipe her mind."

"You understand the risk?" Orpheus said. "Having had her mind wiped before?"

Jadeon looked thoughtful. "Then turn her." He headed back the way he'd come and soon reached the doorway.

"That's it?" I called after him. "After all I've done for you? This is how I'm treated?"

Jadeon spun round to look at me. "You were warned." His stare shot to Orpheus.

"Consider it done," Orpheus told him.

Jadeon gave a quick nod of approval and was gone. The door slammed behind him.

CHAPTER 10

Orpheus' ironclad grip dragged me back up the winding stone stairwell. Despite the discomfort of being forcibly removed from the Athenaeum, there was relief. Though my heart broke into a thousand pieces as the memory of Jadeon's icy stare haunted my every thought. He'd acted as though nothing had ever been shared between us. This wasn't the man I remembered.

Oh, but he wasn't a man.

Had he really just ordered Orpheus to turn me?

Orpheus pulled me into an unfamiliar room, making me doubt we were heading outside. He was going to turn me right here. I resisted his pull and tried to wriggle free from his grip. My flesh was clammy and my throat disallowed a scream. But a cry for help would be futile.

"We're not going through the front door," he said tightening his hold.

The endless trek through the hallway was too much. It felt like a lifetime before we stepped out into the night. I took a deep, cleansing breath of cold air.

I was going to bolt.

"Now that would be annoying," he said.

"Please let me go. I won't tell anyone about this place. I promise."

Orpheus looked harried, and it was a look I wasn't used to seeing on him. His expression lifted only slightly when he saw a Rolls Royce turn the corner.

"Did Anaïs get out okay?" I said.

"She's safe now."

The Rolls pulled up and Orpheus opened the rear passenger door and nudged me inside. I slid across the leather seat. It was disconcerting to see my handbag waiting for me, especially as I'd slid it under the Lamborghini's passenger seat. Still, my keys were in it, along with my phone. Pushing that thought away, not wanting Orpheus to pick up on it, I hid it beside me.

As Orpheus slid in next to me, a gentle waft of his cologne reached my nose. A heady, crisp combination of something familiar with a hint of incense. If midnight had a scent, this would be it.

I went for the door handle, pulling on it frantically and getting nowhere.

Orpheus frowned his disapproval. "Quite finished?"

Turning sharply away, I tried to calm my racing heart and get my mind to a place where I could think straight. Despite needing to shut down my thoughts, the truth was glaring. Orpheus heard every single idea.

The chauffeur eased away from the curb and took a sharp turn onto Kensington Street. The speed forced my head back. Orpheus leaned over so damn close, his chest against mine, his hand stretching across me.

I braced for his bite.

I held my breath...

He pulled the seatbelt over my body and clipped me in before sliding effortlessly back to the other side. He returned his attention to the window and beyond, focusing on the passing scenery.

My hands trembled and I choked back tears but they came nevertheless, soaking my cheeks. He handed me a crisp, white handkerchief. Dabbing my face with the soft linen, I willed my tears to stop.

His dark stare settled on me. "It's over now."

"Is it?" I begged him with my eyes to tell me it really was.

Jadeon hates me.

Orpheus' expression hadn't changed from when I'd first laid eyes on him. He was annoyed. Harrowed. Pissed off.

"Stop the car," I snapped.

"I'm taking you home."

"No, you're not. I want to walk."

A blue flash reflected in the rearview mirror. I spun round to see the police car trailing behind us, its light flashing.

Oh no.

"We have to pull over," I said.

"Henry, can we have some music, please?" Orpheus said.

I leaned forward and shouted to the driver, "Sir, you need to pull over."

Orpheus glared at me and it felt like he'd reached inside my chest and scolded me with merely a look. I slumped back in my seat, stunned by his fierceness.

When I saw another police car in front, lights flashing, I let out a moan.

"They're escorting us," Orpheus said. "So calm down."

My head snapped round to peer out of the back window. Then out the front window again to comprehend what he was telling me. The front police car was indeed picking up a good pace and clearing the road ahead for us. Our journey was not going to be derailed apparently, and I had no choice but to let the vista distract me. Orpheus evidently had friends in high places and it irked me he had this kind of power.

Mozart burst through the sound system, the notes falling and rising and doing nothing to calm me.

"Please stop staring," Orpheus said.

"I'm trying to work you out."

He threw an amused glance. "Good luck with that."

"What was that place?"

"Will we be making idle conversation the entire way there?"

My anger welled and I spun round to face him.

"I could always turn you in here." He glanced at his watch. "Should be done by the time we get you home."

I flinched and slid farther into the corner.

Orpheus held all the power. Beneath the surface, he was breaking me down. Though I tried to hide it from him that it was working. Couldn't let him see he'd gotten to me. That I was weakening. This day had spiraled out of controlled.

I am out of control.

Glancing over to see if he'd calmed, I braved to say,

"Promise me you won't hurt Anaïs."

"Henry," Orpheus said. "Can we have some air."

"You need my help to find Beatrice," I said.

He scolded me with a look.

"At least tell me what you have so far?"

"Henry, something else," Orpheus said. "Opera. Puccini."

The sound system went quiet and within a few moments there came the elegant vocals of a tenor lyrically interwoven with that of a soprano.

We drove the rest of the way in silence, the police escort making easy work of the route through the traffic. Within half an hour we were met with the usual hustle and bustle of Chelsea. I had mixed feelings when I saw my flat. A mixture of fear that Orpheus knew where I lived and relief I was home.

Outside the car, I was glad to see the police had driven off. I hoped to God they didn't know it was me in the Rolls. From their number plates, those boys worked at Scotland Yard. The blackout windows had provided some advantage.

How many times had I warned women never to go with their abductor? Don't get in their car and whatever you do don't ever go into a building with them.

Yet here I stood beside Orpheus at my front door. There came a flurry of activity to my right. It was Debra, my next door neighbor. Her jaw gaped when she saw Orpheus and she raised a subtle brow to let me know she approved. This split-second offered a chance to cry out for help. I returned a polite smile to Debra. Refusing to put her in jeopardy, my fingers fumbled for my keys.

Orpheus and I left the coldness behind and stepped into the living room.

Would we talk before he turned me? Would there be a chance for a last meal? A drink perhaps? Something strong, something numbing, like that bottle of wine from earlier that I'd sipped on while chatting with Anaïs.

That seemed like a million light years away now.

I wanted to open the window. Needed more air. Maybe it was worth the risk of diving out. Despite the fall, I'd stand a better chance of surviving it then staying in here with *him*.

It was impossible to outrun him. Impossible to fight him off.

Futile to believe that this vampire could be manipulated into letting me live.

Lips trembling, throat tightening, I conveyed with all my will I didn't want this. "Please, I want to live."

Orpheus frowned. "What did I say to you back at the Bainard Building?"

"I can't remember."

"I asked you to trust me."

"Then do something to inspire my trust."

He held me with his calculating eyes. "How does this work for you?"

I spun round—

It was Jadeon.

He leaned casually back against the wall with both his hands in his pockets. "After thinking it through," he said calmly, "turning you is my privilege."

I snapped my head back round to look at Orpheus, but he'd gone. Though something told me the danger wasn't over.

"What you did tonight was worse than reckless," Jadeon said, pulling my attention back to him. "Had Orpheus not been there you'd be dead."

"The way you spoke to me—"

"Was deserved."

The pain of that moment found its way back to me. Jadeon's denial that he even knew me. The way he'd acted with such disregard.

"Are you still mad at me?" I asked nervously.

"All indicators point to yes."

"Why the hell are you encouraging Orpheus to be anywhere near me?"

"Because other than me no one else can protect you as well."

"Then why not you?" I said. "Why can't you be with me?"

"There are things I have to do—"

"I don't want Orpheus anywhere near me. Understand?"

"Then you shouldn't have visited the Athenaeum."

"I didn't expect him to be there. I went there looking for you."

His face remained serene. "Take a shower. It'll help you relax."

"What? Before you turn me?" The words tumbled out with my fear.

"Ingrid." He came closer and grasped my shoulders. "Shower. Now."

He took my hand and led me through my flat. *No, his flat.* The one I'd stayed in believing I was safe, yet all I'd done was delay the inevitable. I couldn't believe this was happening. Not now. Not after I'd survived so much for so long.

Inside the bathroom he eased up my dress, pulling it over my head. Then he threw it onto the tiled floor. I wrapped my arms around myself, shielding my bra, blushing wildly.

"Take them off." He gestured to my underwear.

I refused, remaining still and defiant.

Even though he'd seen me naked before, made love to me, there was something about his aloofness that made me question being so vulnerable. Unfazed, he calmly slid open the glass door and leaned in to turn on the faucet. Water poured from the showerhead.

"Get in," he said.

"You had no right to treat me that way."

"In." He slid the door farther open.

His glare convinced me. I stood beneath the pounding hot water, gaining some comfort from the way it caressed my scalp and warmed my flesh. My bra and panties were soaked and clinging.

"I'm waiting for your apology," he said, peeling his shirt off his body, up and over his head, then making quick work of the rest.

He joined me in the shower.

I averted my eyes from his nakedness, his swelling manhood, the beauty that was Jadeon Artimas. Two-hundred years ago he'd been turned in his prime and at his fittest. A twenty-five-year-old sculptured to perfection. Tall and lean and oh so strong. A body primed for fencing with the most agile of opponents and easily winning.

And I was in the shower with him.

Jadeon's lips curled in amusement, having read my thoughts. He neared me, reaching around my back. I felt the clasp of my bra give. He threw it over the shower door. Next, his fingers were on my hips, hooking through the string of my panties, and he knelt to slide them down my legs.

I stepped out of them. "Is this how it's done? How you turn someone? You strip them first to humiliate them?"

He rose with the grace of a hunter and towered over me, placing a fingertip on my lips. "Shush."

Jadeon threw my panties next to where my bra lay. It was impossible to drag my gaze from his gorgeousness. That intense stare locked on me with a startling blaze.

I took in his beautiful kind face, his supernatural grace, his jaw tensing and relaxing and tensing again as though he was thinking this through.

My breathing became ragged and I closed my eyes, wanting it to be over, allowing the inevitable to find me. "What are you waiting for?"

"For you to hand me that." He glanced at the sponge.

Hand shaking, I reached up and handed it to him.

"And that." He pointed to the bath gel.

I gave him that too and watched him pour the soapy liquid onto the sponge. The scent of vanilla mixed with sandalwood filled the air. He reached past me to place the bottle down. That tuft of hair on his chest made him look so human, so virile. I turned my back on him, overcome with having him so close, dazzled by his domination of every nuance. His every gesture mastered each moment.

Mastering me.

Rising steam enveloped us both.

The sponge caressed my shoulders, sliding down my spine and lower still over my buttocks, sending quivers. I allowed myself to savor this time with him, these moments I'd yearned for every night since the last time I'd seen him. I'd imagined this, prayed for this, and now he was with me again, his fingers lifting my wet hair from my nape and massaging my neck with the sponge, gentle, slow strokes lulling me.

"Turn around," he said.

The sponge slid from my throat, moving languidly, caressing my breasts, lingering over my nipples and encircling each one, sending spasms of pleasure low into my belly. My hardening buds begged for more of this languishing friction. Jadeon's cologne wafted through the steam, the darkest invitation of him, and it calmed me. Reaching out, my hands met his chest and I dug my fingernails into his flesh.

"Did I give you permission to touch me?" he said.

I let go and watched him lift the shower faucet off its hook and use it to wash off the soap suds covering my body, sweeping the spray across my front and teasing it over my stomach.

"You need to do as you're told," he said, directing the water between my thighs and holding it there, forcing the pressure over my clitoris.

My hands shot out to either side and I scraped my fingernails across the tile, my sex rippling in response to the water pounding me there. My thighs weakened and the softest gasps escaped, leaving me breathless. The rawness of his power, his fierceness, brought me ever closer to losing my mind, losing my way...

"Do you think you can do that?" he said firmly. "Do as you're told?"

A frown gave my answer and my thoughts raced, wondering when he would lead me over to the other side of mortality. I tried to read his expression and gauge if he really planned on doing this.

I'm not ready.

Jadeon replaced the showerhead and threw down the sponge. Water cascaded again, spraying over us both and around us. I stole those few short moments to steady my breathing.

"Orpheus warned you about the need for punishment." Jadeon gave a ghost of a smile. "As Dominion, I get to deem which punishment is appropriate."

My back struck the tiled wall and all air left my lungs. "What are you going to do?"

"This." He leaned low, his mouth kissing my right breast, sucking the nipple. His teeth grazed the delicate flesh and his arm wrapped around my waist to pull me closer to him.

My eyelids fluttered shut, responding to his mouth's taunting, and my thighs shifted apart, allowing his hand to advance between them. His fingers rubbed my clitoris in delicate circles, leisurely pleasuring. I wanted to grab locks of his hair, but only moments before he'd denied me this. Arms by my side, I felt powerless, beholden to him to keep me standing.

"Well?" His fingers slowed to a hypnotic pace. "Have you learned your lesson?"

Our eyes met and I drowned in his deep brown gaze, catching those few specks of hazel in his irises. Despite knowing what that meant, I couldn't resist him, couldn't pull away from this intoxicating rhythm.

Yet some part of me still needed to defy him.

He frowned, picking up on my rambling thoughts.

"Then you leave me no choice," he said, sliding his left hand down my back and resting it against my lower spine, pushing me toward his other hand that lay at the crest of my thighs. His fingers bestowed masterful flickering strokes, causing my moans to echo.

How could I fight him off if he turned me during an orgasm?

Dizzy with pleasure, my head lolled to the side, my lips parted. I wanted more of him, needed him inside me. His arched brow revealed he'd caught my need, my unbound desire.

Water cascaded over my chest and shoulders, caressing me from above as his fingers caressed below, sending shivers from his touch. These relentless sensations between my thighs forced me to pump against his hand, yearning for this moment never to cease.

"Ingrid," Jadeon murmured. "Surrender to me." His fingers nudged past that delicate cleft and plunged inside. My channel rippled around his strokes that set into a hypnotic rhythm. His thumb strummed my clitoris in perfect timing with his thrusts.

My arms flung around his neck, my nails buried in his flesh, and my body betrayed me. Or perhaps it was my mind. It was hard to keep up with my scrambled thoughts. I screamed my rebellion, soon to be snatched away by an orgasm. My entire body shook as I exploded with desire and ached for him.

I fell against him, my mewling silenced as my mouth pressed into his wet chest, tasting him. Carried away to the place of forgetting, I was too far gone to think, to care. My entire body shuddered and my breasts trembled. Captured by this endless searing pleasure, I came hard, screaming his name.

When those last ripples of pleasure finally left me, Jadeon hugged me into his chest, his arms wrapped tightly around me. My legs felt weak, useless. Where his fingers had brought bliss now delightfully tingled, sending shivers throughout my body, which was wracked by pleasure.

He held the world at bay.

The water cleansed, washing away any threat as peace embraced us, promising nothing could touch us.

"There." Jadeon kissed my forehead. "Now as far as punishments go that wasn't so bad, was it?"

CHAPTER 11

My entire body tingled in the wake of Jadeon's touch, and despite exhaustion pulling me down toward sleep I wanted to hold onto this moment, hold onto him being here.

Dressed in my pajamas, sitting up with my back pressed against the headboard, I felt lulled from our post shower tryst, the wake of my orgasm relaxing me.

Embarrassed that Jadeon might eavesdrop on my musing, I turned my attention onto more mundane thoughts, focusing on my cereal instead and dabbing a drop of soymilk from my lips.

Jadeon sat in the corner armchair with his long legs stretched out. "I can't recall ever being quite so disturbed," he said, watching me spoon in another mouthful of Special-K. "What must that taste like?"

"It's the only thing I have to eat," I said. "It's got chocolate bits in it."

"I should have ordered food in for you."

I wondered if he knew I'd eaten a Mars Bar for lunch. "It's better than the stuff you eat." I gave a wry smile.

He rolled his eyes. "At least blood is nutritious."

"So is this." I raised the bowl. "Says it right there on the box."

"You believe everything you read?"

"Yes, and sometimes I even believe what people tell me." I placed the bowl on the side table.

"Ingrid, this time apart from you has been hard for me too."

"Then help me understand it."

"You must trust me."

Tugging up the bedsheet, I said, "I'm trying."

I liked this room, *his* room, more for its contemporary taste than anything. Even though Jadeon had never lived here, he'd made sure the place was decorated tastefully. From this tall headboard I rested against, to the antique armoire with a TV tucked inside it, and I loved the sprawling walk-in closet. The black and white prints of lilies on the far wall seemed so different from his usual taste and added an arty flair.

Jadeon gave the softest hint of a smile, as though he too savored our time together.

I wanted to reach out and grab his hand, pull him into bed with me and feel his body next to mine again. Feel his strength, his weight, his love. To have those strong fingers of his return to mastering my body like he'd done within the hour beneath that hot shower. My eyes fluttered shut with the realization he could of course hear every thought.

"Sure you don't want me to get you something more palatable?" On my reaction, he added with a smile, "To eat?"

"I've lost my appetite. Waiting to be turned into a vampire kind of does that to a girl."

"I did warn you it would happen." He arched an eyebrow. "Didn't say when."

"Do you still love me?"

He went to answer and looked away, his frown deepening.

Within came the deepest fracturing of my soul, and it was hard to tell if something nameless had buried itself deep inside of my chest or crawled its way out, ripping my insides apart as it went and leaving behind a hollowed heart.

Reacting to my haze of confusion, he said, "I'm sorry to be the cause of so much pain for you."

"Then love me. Be with me. Hold me."

He tilted his head back and stared at the ceiling. "I'm doing everything I can not to devour you right now. Please don't make it any more difficult." The tips of his fangs disappeared as he closed his mouth, his kissable lips hiding them.

"You still have feelings for me?" I said, reading that tell-tale sign of a vampire's desire.

"I'm very fond of you."

"You're still angry because I turned up at that place?"

"I'm angry with myself for not getting through to you."

"You realize why I came there tonight?"

"We have our own people working on it, Ingrid."

"Care to share what you have?" I pulled myself farther up the headboard. "The odds of finding Beatrice decrease by 50 % if no solid lead is found." I shook my head. "Usually I ignore those kinds of stats and place my full attention on doing what I do best."

"We've doubled our efforts." He paused. "Her home was undisturbed, which indicates the kidnapping didn't occur there. She may have been snatched after the car accident. Beatrice is very well-liked. Trust me, we have everyone working on this."

"Your files, your reports," I said, "I want them."

He sighed deeply. "I thought you weren't working this aspect of Hauville's case?"

Easing up my left sleeve, I showed him my circled brand. The one that both he and Orpheus had given me. "You think this now puts me in danger, don't you?"

He conceded with a nod. "For centuries Orpheus used the symbol to protect his Gothicas, but we're now concerned Hauville might use it to distinguish girls he's developed a taste for."

"More girls have gone missing?"

"Ingrid, we're not doing this."

I glared at him. "He's missing. Do you know that?"

"We'll find him."

"You think his motivation is sexual?"

"Possibly."

"Something is telling me it might not be."

"Place all your attention on those cases in your in-tray." He sat forward and rested his elbows on his knees.

"How do you know I have an in-tray?"

He shrugged. "You have an office."

"Listen—"

"This is not up for discussion."

"Who showed you the photo? Orpheus?"

He sighed. "What we have so far is tenuous."

I caressed my face to ease my frustration. "I'm being kept at arm's length by my department, by you, and Orpheus."

He interwove his fingers. "It's best if you let us deal with this."

"Are you making any headway?" I balled my hands into fists. "Beatrice is Anaïs' lover. She's asked me to help her."

"Stay away from Anaïs. She's more reckless than you and that's saying something."

"What will happen to her?"

"Orpheus is with her now."

"Please tell me he won't hurt her."

"I'm sure she'll be fine."

"I thought you hated Orpheus?" I said. "You're arch enemies."

"Things change." Jadeon leaned back. "Orpheus has behaved with you so far. Please don't give him an excuse to take liberties. I get to read his thoughts too."

I blushed wildly.

"A friendly warning, that's all. He's obsessed over you in the past. You know how unpredictable he is."

"And yet you're best buddies now?"

He paused, brightening suddenly. "It's good to have all that behind us."

"Can we talk about what happened to you and him?" I said, having been closed down by him last time I tried to discuss it. "You have specs of hazel in your irises. And Orpheus has a brown ring around his." Something told me these were the aftereffects of what they'd both been through three months ago.

"I can't..." He flinched.

"Jadeon?"

Tension marred his face. "It's a blur."

"What do you remember?"

"Vampires aren't meant to get headaches. Thinking about it gives me one. Talking about it makes me..." He winced in pain.

"When you're ready," I whispered. "I'm here for you."

"You will never visit the Athenaeum again," he snapped. "I do my part to protect you, exhaustively so. You need to work with me on this. We had this discussion in Trafalgar Square. We agreed it's safer for you keep a low profile. Stay away from the underworld. Stay away from me."

"Those were your words. I don't recall getting a word in."

"Ingrid, this is bigger than both of us."

"What is?"

He blinked several times, his gaze not meeting mine. "My position does not allow for such luxuries as—"

"Love?"

The silence encroached into our space, forcing a rift between us and threatening to ruin everything. All the groundwork I'd made over the last hour was seemingly now lost. Our reunion tonight had been an illusion; a lie rearing its ugliness.

Hating the quiet, I broke it. "You berated me in front of the elders—"

"To placate them," he said. "They were ready to turn you. Orpheus would only have been able to hold them back for so long."

"Why do they want me turned?"

"You saw too much."

I looked incredulous. "It's a library."

Something in his stare made me pause.

Not just a library?

"Anyone breeching my command to stay away from there risks their own death," he said.

"You would never hurt me."

His silence stunned me.

My lips quivered at his sternness. His change of demeanor had gone from friend to antagonist in a heartbeat.

"Get some sleep," he said. "I'll have my driver take you to work tomorrow."

I eased my way down beneath the covers. "I'll take the tube."

"No, you won't." He pushed himself to his feet and came over, sitting beside me on the edge of the bed. He pulled the blanket up and over me.

The sensation of his fingertips caressing my scalp made my eyelids flicker.

"You're not going to turn me while I'm asleep are you?" I said.

"That's actually rather a good idea."

"Not exactly reassuring."

"You're a difficult woman to get through to."

"Promise me you'll not shut me out again."

"You have a remarkable future. Please don't mess it up because of me." He climbed onto the bed beside me and pulled me back toward him, wrapping his arms around me. Despite the blanket being between us I felt his warmth, his strength, and that comforting scent reached me. He was intoxicating.

He pulled me tighter. "Know that I share your pain when it comes to us not being a possibility."

"I thought you were trying to comfort me?"

"Enlighten you." He pulled the blanket higher over my shoulder. "Let's savor these last few hours together."

Surrendering to his hand stroking my damp locks and ignoring my tear soaked pillow, I gave up this impossible fight of wills and drifted asleep.

CHAPTER 12

The cold water felt good.

I captured more of it in my cupped hands and splashed it over my face to awaken me, drenching my chest. My discarded dress, bra, and panties lay on the bathroom floor as a reminder of last night. That faux diamond bracelet rested on the side of the sink where Jadeon had slipped it off my arm. Proof he'd really been here. I fought the urge to stare at the shower and lose myself in the memory of him in there with me and all those sensuous things he'd done. I blushed, my thoughts flittering over the details: his voice, his touch, and everything else about him that I loved so much. The kind of love that hurts.

Jadeon's presence lingered. His face haunted my every thought. He'd left during the night, leaving nothing but an imprint of his body against mine.

Staring into the mirror, I found my face looked fresh enough, easily hiding my lack of sleep, though smudged mascara gave away a night of reckless abandon.

Although grateful to have survived a trip into the very heart of a vampire's lair, Jadeon's annoyance left me feeling bereft and ashamed I'd let him down.

Loathing the hold he still had over me, I silently cursed him.

"Being mortal suits you," I told my mirrored self. "Let's stick with that, shall we? And while you're at it, let's see if we can stay alive." There, I'd appropriately chastised myself.

God I missed him.

What is wrong with you? I snapped at myself.

Last night Lord Jadeon Artimas had sensuously burned me up from the inside out in his usual seductive fashion; *that* was what was wrong with me.

I leaned in closer to my reflection. "Get a grip."

Grabbing my silk robe from the back of the door, I pulled it on.

If I was going to catch the 7 A.M. tube to Scotland Yard, I was going to have to hurry. Being late-phobic meant I'd rather die than fail to be at work on time.

Heading barefoot into the kitchen, I stopped in my tracks.

Studying my arms, I tried to see if anything was different. The color of my flesh was pink and normal looking. No paleness there, and my reflection had certainly appeared the same. There, see, I had a reflection. Daylight flooded in through the blinds. If I'd been turned that would be bad. Very bad.

Caressing my brow and nursing this headache, I realized these spiraling thoughts were closing in and making me incapacitated. I grabbed the bottle of Tylenol from the kitchen counter and clicked my way into it. I took two, swigging tap water to wash them down.

I ripped off the photo of the Eiffel Tower and threw it across the room. It merely landed a few feet away, mocking me. France, the country Jadeon and I had promised each other we'd visit back when things were normal. Well, as normal as they get when you're romantically involved with the undead.

It's for the best, my reason butted-in and it had a point, making a good argument for things not working out. Jadeon did spend his days sleeping and his nights, well, doing God knows what, and I had a job to do that involved following the law and making sure everyone else did too. Incompatible was an understatement. We were oceans apart, not meant to be, a bad fit. So why did my mind lead back to him with every waking thought? I was spellbound, that was it, having fallen prey to his seduction. It didn't help that he was the sexiest man I'd ever met. Okay, vampire.

This was so unlike me. I was the girl who ignored my heart's calling and did what had to be done. This crazy crush was addling my brain.

My hand rested on the fridge door and I mulled over whether

to brave the cheese stick. It was only slightly less dangerous than entering a vampire lair with no real plan, and later falling asleep with one of London's most dangerous vampires beside me. Yet somehow I'd survived that experience unscathed too.

Jadeon, my darling nightwalker, was lost to me forever, and last night he'd reiterated the fact. I sucked back tears, trying to reconcile we were over. That cheese stick sounded good right about now.

I flung open the fridge door—

Gone was that lone carton of soymilk, the tin of tuna, and moldy life-threatening cheese stick. In their place was more food then I'd ever had in there. I reached in and pulled out the small pot of Beluga caviar.

Seriously?

So let me get this straight—

I couldn't contact him, yet Jadeon felt entitled to interfere with my life in any way he saw fit? He had no right to go inside my fridge. No right at all. I threw the caviar back in and slammed the door.

I stormed back into the bathroom.

Within twenty minutes I'd taken a quick shower, donned my blue silk shirt, pencil skirt, two inch heeled pumps, and tied my hair back in some kind of semblance of a chignon.

Heading out, I was more than ready to throw myself into work and get this day going.

Oh no.

There, standing curbside was Henry, the chauffer from last night. He saw me, tipped his hat, and opened the passenger door of the Rolls.

I strolled up to him, offering a polite smile. "Henry, isn't it? I'll be taking my car, but thank you for being here. Sorry to waste your time. Please don't come back. Ever."

"I can drop you off around the corner of Scotland Yard," he said in a strong Cockney accent.

"No thank you. Please excuse me. I'm running late." I turned on my heel and headed toward my Rover. My car's left back tire was flat. I spun round and glared at Henry.

He gave an unconvincing look of surprise. "I can help you change it if you like?"

"I'm going to be late."

"There's fresh coffee and a bagel waiting for you." He peered through the black tinted window. "Wasn't that a bit of luck?"

"Bit convenient." I pointed to the wheel.

"It's a good thing I'm here." Henry gave a knowing nod.

With clenched teeth, I cursed Jadeon. He had no right to push me away one minute and seduce me with bagels and coffee the next. Something told me that puncturing my rear wheel, or getting someone else to, was the least of what he would do to keep control of me. This was his way of tracking my whereabouts, I was sure of it.

"Madam." Henry opened the passenger door. "We don't want you to be late."

Reluctantly, I lowered my head and climbed in.

The aroma of fresh coffee hit me and I breathed it in, hating that I wanted it this much. Leaning back against the leather seat, my fists clenched in my lap. "Aaaahhh."

"Music, ma'am?" Henry offered.

"Sure. Why not."

A backdrop to all this misery might be just what I needed.

Coldplay's *Paradise* blared through the car's speakers. Henry turned up the music, drowning out the sounds of traffic.

I eyed the large cup of Starbucks as though it were the enemy and took a peek inside the brown paper bag, expecting to find evidence and not the toasted salmon and cream-cheese bagel, which in no way was I eating.

Henry peered up at me via the rearview mirror. "Apparently all the tubes are running late, ma'am," he said, pulling the Rolls away from the curb. "Good old British Rail."

I snapped and took a bite of the bagel, resisting the urge to roll my eyes in ecstasy as the texture of rich salmon mixed with the tang of cheese. The cucumber added freshness. Other than the bowl of Special K last night, and not counting the Mars Bar I'd had for lunch, I hadn't eaten a proper meal in over twenty-four hours. The coffee tasted good as well, and I conceded I had a long day ahead. Fueling up on carbs and caffeine was actually a good idea.

I'll allow you this one, Artimas.

Peering into the rearview to better view Henry's eyes, I asked, "How long have you worked for Lord Artimas?"

Henry turned the music down. "That's restricted I'm afraid." He gave an apologetic shrug.

I sat back. "I can always use Scotland Yard's database."

"Well for that you'd need my last name, ma'am."

I took another sip of coffee to hide my annoyance. "I have this number plate memorized."

"I have a message from Lord Artimas." Henry steered the Rolls around another car waiting to park, its indicator flashing. "He knew you'd want to question me and asked that you respect my privacy."

"Do you know who you're actually working for?"

"I do, ma'am, yes."

"Tell me what you know about him."

"Lord Artimas is one of the wealthiest men in Cornwall. A Peer of the Realm. You're a lucky woman."

"We're not dating."

"I just thought—"

"We're friends."

Though from last night's adventure, *friends* wasn't the first word that came to mind. Lovers was more appropriate. Fuck-buddies even. But he hadn't fucked me, had he? He'd held back on his own pleasure, merely concentrating on mine and giving me the most mind-blowing orgasm I'd had in months.

I took another bite of bagel.

Henry's cufflinks bore the insignia of a parachute with wings. Those, and his short haircut, revealed he was ex-army, a retired paratrooper.

I mulled over the idea that Jadeon knew I'd interview Henry at the first opportunity. He'd warned Henry about me. Still, like most men, Henry probably underestimated what I was capable of. The art of an interrogation was to make it seem more conversational, lull the interviewee into thinking we were sharing a nice little chat and get them to a place where they wanted to talk about themselves. All I had to do was push the ego button and sit back and listen.

"Lord Artimas has saved my life on numerous occasions," I said. "I don't know what I'd do without him."

"He's been very good to me too, ma'am."

"Jadeon's very selective about who he hires. You must be special. You're not just his driver are you?"

He stared dead-ahead at the road.

"Thank you for driving me today. I hate being late."

"My daughter's the same way. Very punctual."

"What does she do?"

He twisted him mouth, contemplating going there. "My daughter works for a colleague of Lord Artimas."

"That's how you got this job?"

"Yes, I was in the army before this."

And, bam, there it was. The door opened to his world like I'd pushed play on a movie.

"My dad was in the army," I said. "Served in Afghanistan."

"Where's he now?"

"Retired," I said, not wanting to share he'd committed suicide when I was fourteen; my ability to shove that one away into the recesses of my consciousness was legendary. After taking another sip of coffee, I said, "What does your daughter do?"

"She an executive assistant."

"A goth?"

His eyes flashed with surprise.

I held his stare until he broke it off to concentrate on the road ahead.

"She's one of those well dressed goths," he said. "Although she always dresses in black, she looks classy."

"I imagine if she's working for Orpheus she has to be," I said. "I've had the pleasure of meeting many of his employees and they're all well-educated and high-achievers."

"I didn't tell you she was working for him." Henry looked worried.

I gave the sweetest smile.

"This job comes with a mighty fine pension," Henry said. "I consider myself a lucky man. Wouldn't want to do anything to threaten it."

"I think Lord Artimas is the lucky one," I said, and I meant it too, though I detected he had no idea he worked for a vampire.

"You have the same tattoo as my daughter." He raised his

eyebrows to make his point.

I realized he'd seen my brand last night when I'd travelled back with Orpheus. My bracelet must have slipped after Orpheus had manhandled me out of the Athenaeum.

"That tattooed circle?" he said. "The latest fashion?"

I twisted my mouth to indicate it wasn't up for discussion.

"Ma'am, to be honest I've never heard anyone talk to Orpheus in the way you did last night. He doesn't intimidate you?"

"I'm not a Gothica."

I caught that tell-tale sign of tension as he swallowed hard, and with a brief flush of his cheeks he'd told me his daughter was.

"Henry, if that is indeed your real name, can I expect your complete discretion?" I raised my hand to make my point. "Because you are assured of mine."

"Of course." He beamed the widest smile. "How's your bagel, ma'am?"

"Delicious, thank you. Where's your daughter now?" I tried to make it sound casual.

"The company insists their employees are fluent in at least one other language," he said. "She was sent to Rome to brush up on her Italian. In fact, the company has sent her entire department overseas."

"Sounds fantastic."

"I talked to her last night on the phone. Orpheus has put her up in this really swanky five-star hotel. She's staying in a suite. Great view of St. Peter's Basilica."

"Lucky girl. I'm sure she deserves it." I gave a nod, doing my best to process what he was telling me without showing any reaction. Hauville's threat had resulted in Orpheus sending every last Gothica out of the country. They really did know something I didn't.

Henry held up on his promise to park around the corner from the Yard. After an extended narrative of reassurance from him that discretion was his highest prerogative, I thanked him and got out of the Rolls.

It was hard to contemplate that Henry's little girl was heading for vampiredom, and depending on how long she'd been a Gothica she might soon take the final step into immortality. Henry seemed like such a great father. I wondered what might have been the trigger that pushed her into becoming a servant of Orpheus'.

Though something told me Orpheus was a goth girl's dream come true.

CHAPTER 13

On the way to my office, I stopped off at Nick's cubicle.

His focus was on his computer screen and he looked like he was doing something fancy with complicated coding.

"Hey there," I said, snapping him out of his trance.

Nick spun round. "Hey boss."

"What are you working on?"

"Chief Inspector Brook's computer crashed so I'm trying to salvage his hard drive."

"I hate it when that happens."

"I set him up with an external hard drive a few months ago and apparently he took it home and attached it to his laptop." Nick opened his mouth in a silent scream.

He made me smile. "When you're done saving the boss' arse will you do me the most amazing favor?"

"Sure."

I handed him a post-it note. "Can you find everything you can on this building in Pall Mall?"

He took it from me. "The Athenaeum? What's it for?"

"It's for off the record."

He tilted his head back. "Looking for anything in particular?"

"Names, dates, schematics. Anything you find."

"You want me to hack into their computer system?"

I flashed a look of surprise.

"Because that would be illegal," he said.

"And highly inappropriate."

"Give me an hour."

"You're the best."

With Nick's cyber detective work set in motion, I headed to the staff break room and poured myself a large mug of coffee. After resting it on the table, I slid two pounds into the vending machine and punched the keypad to deliver lunch. A packet of salt and vinegar crisps and a Marathon Bar fell into the lower pocket and I fished them out. The promise of improving my diet after I'd resolved my latest case was a tried and tested lie I'd been telling myself since graduating from the academy. Seriously, I knew this stuff was bad for me but the idea of wasting time eating a sandwich made me cringe.

"I see you're planning on visiting me in the morgue sooner rather than later."

Dr. Riley Russell critically eyed my snacks and I felt like I'd be caught red-handed at something more sinister than buying crappy food. He looked decidedly old-school with those round-rimmed spectacles, yet appeared dashing in scrubs. His white coat barely covered a small stain on his scrub top that I in no way wanted to know about.

"Good morning," I said, slipping my snacks into my handbag to conceal the evidence.

"Seriously, inspector," he said. "I'm worried about you."

"I promise to start eating right tomorrow."

"Why don't I believe you?"

"More disturbing is you calling me, inspector." I frowned.

"You didn't get the memo? The one from the higher-ups reminding us that informality is against Met policy."

"I filed it away in the bin," I admitted.

"Me too."

"Shouldn't they focus their energy on solving crimes?" It sounded pedantic but reasonable.

"Have you seen Constable Noble?"

"Just got here." I gave a smile.

"Do you ever turn that radar off?"

"No. How long?"

"And go against policy?" he denied my probing with panache.

"Please tell me you don't think I'll have an issue with it?" I said.

He looked uncomfortable, shifting from foot to foot and glancing away.

I felt deflated. "Am I really considered that stuffy?"

"Well you are considered a high-flyer. You are the Met's blue eyed girl."

"Hardly. You and Helena had an argument?"

"How do you do that?"

"If it makes you feel any better it's a trait that's as equally annoying to me. I see more than I want to. For crime fighting, it's an asset. For everything else I see too much." I gave a shrug. "What was it over? Your argument?"

"Us driving in together. She's scared she'll get reprimanded. Or worse, transferred to another station."

"Not by me I hope. I'm sure you'll work through it."

"You won't say anything, will you? I mean, mention it to her. She'd be furious."

"About what?" I winked at him.

"She thinks the world of you," he said. "She wants to be you when she grows up." He let out a chuckle.

"Way to make me feel old, Dr. Russell."

"Riley, and choose a salad next time. They have a cafeteria here you know."

"How else am I going to get my antioxidants?" I picked up my mug and waved goodbye.

"That's dark chocolate," he called after me.

Within the hour, I'd settled into my office and started making good headway pouring through my stack of files. In-between sips of coffee, I went over Hauville's phone records, which had stopped the day he went missing. There was nothing out of the ordinary. Hauville's bank records reflected no activity on his accounts. None of his emails had been replied to. Most of them were from friends questioning why he'd gone silent. Some were responses to what they'd seen on the news about him and his alleged case. A futile attempt to reach out to him.

Hauville had left with his wallet, car keys, and phone, and he hadn't left a letter as far as his wife told us. Every hospital in London had been contacted and no John Does fitting his description had turned up. To expedite the identification process, we'd obtained Hauville's dental records. His medical records revealed no health concerns that might account for his sudden disappearance. The report just in from Interpol had nothing on him. Hauville had vanished.

I made my way up to the seventh floor and strolled through the offices of the Met's missing persons department. I soon reached the corner office. Inspector John Werner was hard at work at his desk, his nose buried deep in a file. His paunch revealed he'd long given up the beat and the collection of donut wrappers stacked high in the bin beneath his desk divulged his love of sugar. Though if he was going to drop from a heart attack, I hoped he would at least wait until I'd left the floor. His bushy gray eyebrows rose in greeting.

"Hey there," I said, trying to ignore his nicotine stained fingernails.

"What brings you to this neck of the woods?" he said.

I leaned against his doorjamb. "I was wondering if you had anything on this missing girl's case."

"Come in."

I moved closer to his desk. "The case connected to Hauville."

"Take a seat." He gestured to the chair next to his.

"I'm only popping in. Won't take up too much of your time."

"Nothing on that one. We're close to tying up a sex trade ring working out of the East End. Did you hear about that one? Sick bastards. Promising foreign girls help with getting their British citizenship and then trapping them in a sweat shop. As well as performing other duties."

Bile rose in my throat.

"Yeah, we're all going to need a shit load of therapy after this one," he said.

"So nothing at all from that photo found on Hauville's computer?" My hand caressed my cheek to hide the horror of the images I'd just caught on his computer screen. The girls were also being beaten. Some of them were painfully young.

He followed my stare. "If we find anything I'll let you know."

"I appreciate that."

"Maybe you'll have to put Hauville away on the fraud case alone. At least you have that." His phone rang and he reached for it. "Yes," he snapped, resting his elbow on the desk in a frustrated pose. "Got it. Okay. What time? Look, can I call you back?" He hung up without waiting for an answer and focused back on me. "To be honest, that photo is pretty vague."

"If you find anything, can you send it to me?"

"Sure." He arched a bushy brow. "Chief Inspector Brooks is getting a briefing on this case right now."

"Anything being kept on the down low?"

He glanced past me, checking we wouldn't be overheard. "Look, Hauville has played many a round of golf with the Prime Minister."

"So any info I get will be filtered?"

The phone rang again and he picked it up. "Hello." He rolled his eyes to show his frustration.

I took that as my cue to leave.

At 10 A.M., Sgt. Miller arrived for our early morning meeting and sat opposite, ready to cross-reference what we had.

"Isn't Helena joining us?" I said, fanning out the files on my desk.

"Dental appointment, apparently," Miller said.

The side of his mouth twitched and I read that small hint of a lie. I let it go, wondering if Helena had been affected by her argument with Dr. Russell last night and needed time to decompress. Although I didn't like the idea of her dating someone at work, there was no way I'd consider myself a curmudgeon when it came to love. Especially after my romantic affiliations with a Lord of the Underworld. I cursed myself for going there and pushed all thoughts of Jadeon far from my mind, determined to at least do something right today.

"Helena mentioned something about a root canal," Miller added, bringing my mind back to focus.

No, Miller wasn't lying, though he knew Helena was.

"She didn't mention it to me," I said casually.

"That surprises me." Miller held my gaze this time.

I gave a nod, letting it go, deciding it wiser to stay out of people's private lives, particularly the relationship kind.

"Can you do me a favor?" I said.

"Anything for you, ma'am."

"Can you get me a report on a motor vehicle accident?" I said. "It happened at Oxford Circus on the 8th, around 10 in the evening."

"Sure. Want to tell me what it's related to?"

"I'm looking into something for a friend."

"I'll check in with traffic."

"Perfect."

Miller had worked at Scotland Yard for decades, which meant he'd have the kind of contacts that wouldn't question him. The report would be offered up willingly.

"How did the visit to Hauville's executive assistant go?" I asked.

Miller cleared his throat. "Ms. Lawrence has worked for Lord Hauville for over fifteen years, so her loyalty was a hard nut to crack."

"Any hint of an affair?"

"Didn't get that vibe. She looked around sixty if that helps form an impression. Smart, patient, protective of her boss. The Rottweiler kind."

"Did she offer anything new?"

"All we got out of her was a rave review of her boss. Filled in a few of the gaps about what they've been through lately. Their daughter's passing hit him hard. Hauville fell into a brief depression. Ms. Lawrence did say something interesting though."

"Go on."

Miller sat back. "Well, you know when someone dies the family very often keep their bedroom just the way it is. At least for a few weeks or even months."

"In homage to their loved one's memory?"

"Exactly. Well apparently Ms. Lawrence visited the family home the day after Olivia died. The Hauvilles weren't home and she had a spare key at the time, so she popped into the child's bedroom to place a vase of roses in there. According to her, Olivia's bedroom was empty. Stripped bare of everything. Even the bed."

"Like stripping the memory of her?"

"Weird, huh?"

"It kind of is." I sat forward. "You mentioned Ms. Lawrence

had a key?"

"Dr. Hauville asked for it back."

"Did Dr. Hauville tell her why?"

"No."

"Interesting."

There was a knock at the door and Nick entered. "Ma'am, got a question for you."

"Let's see if I have an answer," I said with a smile.

"Don't you ever knock?" Miller chastised him. "We're in a meeting."

"I knocked," Nick said. "This is kind of urgent."

"What is it?" I glanced at the envelope in his hand.

Nick came closer, his usual pale complexion even paler. "What's the policy when your computer, or correction, the computer you're working on gets stolen?"

"What are you talking about?" Miller said.

Nick swallowed hard. "I went to the loo and was only gone a minute. When I came back to my desk, Chief Inspector Brooks' computer was gone."

"Shit," said Miller.

Nick looked like he was about to throw up. "I'm freaking out a bit."

Miller and I swapped a wary glance.

"Well, the place has cameras everywhere," I said, standing. "Let's go check out the security footage."

Chief Inspector Anthony Brooks appeared in the doorway. This fifty-year-old with a well-used face easily ruled the room, and his tall, slender figure proved he could still go a round of racquetball and win by a mile against the junior officers.

Nick side-stepped out of his way.

"Sgt. Miller," Brooks said, his face taut with tension. "Can you give us a moment?" He glowered at Nick. "You're staying."

Miller was up and out of his chair, moving faster than I'd ever seen him in an impressive reaction to Brooks' demeanor. I threw Nick a glance, hoping he'd get my subtle smile reassuring him. With Miller gone and the door shut, Brooks pointed to the seat opposite mine, gesturing for Nick to sit.

I remained standing. "Mr. Green's just reported your computer missing, sir," I said. "I can assure you we are on it."

"Oh I know where my computer is." Brooks glared at Nick. "It's what the fuck he was doing on it that I want to know."

A slew of possibilities came to mind, yet none of them fit any of Nick's M.O.s, which was clean cut and by-the-book. Unless of course I'd read him wrong.

"I just had the Home Office on the line," Brooks snapped. "Asking why I'm hacking into one of their computer systems."

My stare shot to Nick's and slowly, reluctantly, found its way back over to Brooks. "Sir, are we talking about the Athenaeum in Pall Mall?"

"You know about this?" he said sharply.

"I authorized it," I said, sensing Nick's immediate relief. "Unofficially."

Brooks stared at me in horror. "Shut down whatever you think you're doing." He raised a hand. "I don't want to know." He puffed out his cheeks in annoyance. "Is it related to the Hauville case?"

"No, sir," I said. "But—"

"Jansen," he snapped. "You've riled up some very senior civil servants. I'll see what I can do to put the fire out. No more misappropriation of personnel or Scotland Yard's computers. Understand? Or I'll be using you as a civilian consultant."

"Yes, sir." I cringed, wondering what kind of connections Jadeon and the elders had with the British government.

I mean, what the hell? I'm not sure what I expected but it certainly wasn't this.

"May I ask if the report's come in on the kidnapping case?" I said, hoping to change the subject and regain some of the respect he'd once had for me.

Brooks gave a dismissive sweep of his hand. "Your fraud case is solid, so don't lose any sleep. Once you get a hit on his whereabouts arrest him."

"What about that girl?" Nick asked, and visibly cowered when Brooks glared at him.

Brooks ignored him. "We're thinking the photo was downloaded from a European porn site. Looks German if you ask me. S C & O ran the girl through our face recognition software but nothing came up."

"So that's it?" Nick dared to clarify.

Brooks looked annoyed. "Not come up with anything new have you, Jansen?"

I dropped my shoulders, dejected that I couldn't in any way share *why yes, sir. She's a vampire. And that brand on her left forearm is the mark of a Gothica. Got one myself actually. So when it comes to all things undead, I'm your girl.*

My forearm itched right over my brand.

"Didn't think so," Brooks said. "Stop wasting police time hacking into government computers. My retirement's coming up in less than a year. Don't fuck up my pension." He stormed out and slammed the door behind him.

"Nick, I'm so sorry," I said.

He held up the manila envelope he'd come in with and waved it in the air. "You owe me one."

CHAPTER 14

Outside the front door of Scotland Yard, I breathed in the smog.

At least it wasn't stuffy office air recycled by the over chilled air-con. I peeked inside the envelope that Nick had given to me and marveled that he'd managed to get anything in the short time he'd worked on Brooks' computer. Why he'd used that one to access sensitive information left me reeling. Wasn't there some way to hide his cyber tracks so that the British government hadn't been alerted? Still, other than Brooks' verbal warning it looked like we'd gotten away with it.

A long list of names ran the full length of the page. Nick had accessed associates of the Athenaeum. Thrilled with my new evidence booty, I tucked the envelope back into my handbag and headed out in the direction of St. James' Park tube station, looking forward to studying this list when I got home. A glass of wine and an evening of researching these members lay in my future.

My feet stuck to the pavement—

Parked on Dacre Street was that same Rolls Royce that had brought me to work this morning.

Henry leaned casually against the back door and his face lit up in a smile when he saw me. "Evening, ma'am. How was your day?"

"What are you doing here?" I kept my voice low, not wanting to draw any more attention from the passing pedestrians, some of whom were Scotland Yard employees.

"I'm not here to take you home, ma'am." He peered up at

glass windows of Scotland Yard.

"What are you doing here then?"

Henry tilted his head toward the passenger door, hinting I was to get in.

"I'll walk," I said, trusting my gut, which was telling me to put distance between me and the car.

Henry opened the rear door. "Best not keep him waiting, ma'am."

Swallowing hard, I hesitated, not sure if I was up for another round of verbal sparring with Orpheus.

"We'll be back here tomorrow in the same spot otherwise." Henry gave a sympathetic look.

Resisting the urge to glance back and see if any of my colleagues might be catching this unusual drama unfolding, I lowered my head and climbed in.

There, sitting comfortably on the far leather seat and dressed in a sharp black pinstriped suit, pristine white shirt, with his silk tie undone, sat Jadeon.

Settling into the seat next to him, I felt grateful for the distance between us. All this posh cream leather and perfect trim everywhere was unnerving. If this was merely a quick visit for my nightly chastisement, I didn't feel up for it. Weren't we meant to keep our distance from each other?

Jadeon captured me with that fiery gaze of his. He oozed a brooding sensuality, highlighted by his unyielding confidence. His heady cologne reached over the scent of leather, stirring feelings I had no right to feel. Back in Scotland Yard I was a force to be reckoned with, but in here with the Lord of the Underworld I found myself crumbling.

I jumped when Henry shut the door. The soft lighting did nothing for my unease.

"Henry," Jadeon said calmly.

The privacy glass slid upward, providing a black glass window between us and Henry. The Rolls effortlessly pulled away from the curb. I wondered where we might be headed. Home, if last night's drive was anything to go by.

"If you're here to continue," I titled my head to make my point, "where we left off last night—"

"That's not why I'm here." His tone was deep, smooth,

cultured, and he threw me off balance as he always did with that dominating look. He held out his hand. "Give it to me."

"Excuse me?"

"I won't ask you again."

My mouth felt dry and I licked my lips to moisten them. I squirmed in response to his steely stare. A twitch of his lips revealed his awareness of how he affected me, as though he drew a dark pleasure from it.

His hand returned to rest by his side. "Very well."

As though time had stood still, he now held an envelope in his hand. He hadn't moved at all, or at least I hadn't seen him move. Jadeon casually peeked inside the manila envelope. I dove into my handbag searching for mine, disbelieving it was the same one I'd tucked in there less than a minute ago. Sure enough, the envelope was no longer in there.

"You blinked," he said, folding it in half and tucking it into his jacket pocket.

"That's police property," I said.

He peered beyond the window, taking in the building fading into the distance. "Something tells me this information was accessed illegally," he said. "Shall we return to Scotland Yard and discuss the matter with your superiors?"

"That won't be necessary." I wondered how ridiculous it would look if I dived on top of him and tried to get it back.

From his raised eyebrows, I wasn't the only one musing how impulsive I might be.

"What is it with you and Orpheus kidnapping me and whisking me off without my consent?" I said. "You two have a lot in common." I knew how to push his buttons too.

"Last night," his eyes narrowed, "we both agreed it would be safer for you not to pursue any further inquiry into the Athenaeum—"

"I didn't agree—"

"I've not finished." He sounded eerily calm. "The warning was articulated clearly that should you ever again show any interest in that building there would be serious consequences."

Something shifted inside my chest, a thrill of excitement. My head screamed something to the effect that I was on to something big. "It's a government building?"

"Even after the threat of turning you?" He looked exasperated. "What is it going to take to reach into that thick skull of yours?"

"It's my nature," I blurted. "Just as it's your nature to bury your fangs into a victim's throat."

"You're hungry. It's making you grouchy. You're not eating properly. I'm worried about you."

"I ate that bagel this morning. Thank you for that by the way."

"What did you eat for lunch?"

"Well…"

"I'm taking you to dinner." His hand flew up in defense. "You might want to revise your response." He'd read my thoughts of refusal moments before I'd dared to speak them.

Resisting the urge to sulk, my attention drifted back to that envelope inside his pocket. My envelope. I hoped Nick had made a copy. Pushing that thought out of my mind and hoping Jadeon wouldn't catch it, I sunk into the leather.

"Do you have anything new on Beatrice?" I said. "This is important to me."

"As it is to me." He shook his head. "No new leads."

"I'm going to search Hauville's property in Windsor."

"My men found nothing. They did a thorough sweep of the land. Hauville's not hiding out there."

"You've used my skills on other cases in the past. Which I did in fact solve for you. Why are you refusing to involve me in this one?"

"Ingrid, we have detectives on it. Our detectives."

"What are they? Ex-MI5? Ex-SAS? Retired police?" Are they qualified?"

"Ingrid—"

"Promise you'll come to me if they don't make any headway on this."

"Out of the question." He leaned forward and brushed a stray hair behind my ear. "I refuse to place you in any more danger."

We drove the rest of the way in silence with him staring out of the window and me doing the same and hating not knowing where we were going. Within twenty minutes, though it felt longer, the Rolls pulled up outside Micelles, an Italian bistro off Caxton Street.

Once out the car, Jadeon led me inside. The mere touch of his hand as he took mine sent a shiver through me. His firm grip made my legs weaken. As though sensing the effect he was having on me, he squeezed my hand and I melted in the wake of his heart-stopping smile that contradicted his deadly demeanor.

Maybe I'd get the chance to persuade him to give me my envelope back if I played it right.

The place looked like a little Italy, with frescos on the ceiling, the walls a mixture of brick covered here and there with dark green and blue shades of paint. Numerous family portraits made it feel like we were stepping into a home and not a cozy restaurant. Arches ran the full length of the seating, offset by a long mahogany bar at the end. Leather booths lined the dining room. Jadeon and I followed the maitre d' to one of them.

It all seemed so surreal, me ordering lasagna and salad and Jadeon ordering Rigatoni Del Casa, even though he wouldn't eat it. He went on to order a bottle of Chateau Mouton Rothschild, a 1989 vintage, which sent the already spiraling blonde waitress into a tailspin. The fact Jadeon was gorgeous and now evidently rich was apparently all too much for her. With flushed cheeks and a trembling hand, she took our menus and scurried off into the kitchen.

I gave him a *there, see?* look to indicate I wasn't the only one disarmed by him.

Despite his stunning looks, Jadeon really did blend in. He merely exuded the air of a successful businessman or some other impressive profession. His supernatural quality was kept in check. He'd had two hundred years to perfect mingling with ease; a predator's advantage.

Jadeon folded his arms. "I forgot to order you garlic bread."

I leaned back. "Didn't want to offend you."

"We won't be kissing, Ingrid," he said it with a smile.

"I didn't mean that. You know vampires and garlic. Deadly combo."

"Please, say it louder." He rolled his eyes. "The couple in the back booth didn't catch it. Unlike everyone else in here." He shrugged. "Anyway, that's a myth."

"Like asking permission to enter? I mean a room. I meant a room." I blushed wildly.

He gave a wry smile. "Myth too. Can you imagine the practicality of it?"

Seriously, it made me wonder if he was using his paranormal skills on me and it wasn't simply his mesmerizing aura making me giddy.

Our bottle of wine arrived and Jadeon declined to taste it. "I'm sure it's fine," he told the waitress, breeching wine etiquette.

She poured the full bodied red into two tall stemmed glasses. I waited for her to leave.

"Can I have my envelope back?" I said.

"I'm going with no."

I wanted to pounce on him and grab it.

A frown marred his face. "Let's pretend you didn't just think that."

I slumped in my seat. "I visited St. Michael's."

"I know."

"I was looking for you."

"So I heard."

"Your brother Alex looks well."

Jadeon flashed a smile. "He's doing great. Seb's good company for him. They both seem happy."

"Are they having an affair?"

"Nothing is off limits to you, Ingrid, is it?"

"Just interested."

"Alex is head over heels in love," Jadeon said. "So is Seb." He pointed at me. "No more spontaneous visits to The Mount. Understand?"

"Seb is my friend too."

"As he is mine. I need to protect him. Your visits to Cornwall draw unwanted attention."

Dejected, I folded my arms. "Paradom's still at the castle then?"

Jadeon arched a brow.

"He's not a problem for you?"

Jadeon waved off the idea. "Never."

"So what's it like being...you know who?"

"Excuse me?"

"Being Dominion?" I whispered.

"It would be much easier if I wasn't chasing a detective out of trouble every five minutes."

"So you're keeping busy then?" I said, happy to rile him up.

Jadeon nodded, seeing where I was taking this. "Keeping the peace is my main goal. Maintaining order. We dictate rules to our community and when they fail to abide by them we decide on a suitable punishment. A final death is never taken lightly."

Stunned by his words, I reached for my glass and took a sip. The heavy, rich flavor did a dance on my tongue and I closed my eyes before I could stop myself. This wine was expensive. Probably worth a week's salary.

Final death.

His words echoed in my mind like the darkest nightmare screaming the reality of what he really was.

"I would have ordered you a nicer wine," he said. "It's the best they had."

I took another mouthwatering sip and considered how Jadeon could never drink it. His expression softened a little and it made him look younger, vulnerable even. The waitress reappeared and set our plates of food before us, asking if we needed anything else.

"Garlic bread, please," Jadeon said. "Everything looks great." He eyed his plate of rigatoni as though he really looked forward to tucking into it.

When she left our table, his face returned to that intensity he wore so well. Despite the awkwardness of Jadeon merely nudging his food around his plate with a fork, I tucked in, taking a big mouthful of lasagna and almost burning the roof of my mouth. God, I was hungry.

Jadeon quickly handed me a tall glass of ice-water. Taking a gulp, I gestured my thanks.

"Now I can relax," he said, placing his fork on his plate and reaching for his wine glass. He took a sip, or at least it looked like he did.

With another mouthful of lasagna balanced on my fork and paused midair, I gave him an incredulous stare.

He tilted his head toward the bar.

We'd attracted attention, or more accurately Jadeon had. I took in the crowd of five dolled-up women standing at the bar and all of them had zeroed in on Jadeon. They giggled amongst themselves when they caught him staring back. These mood inducing low level lights didn't help to soften his ridiculously breathtaking face. Those girls were bewitched by him.

Jadeon flashed me a mega-watt smile. "How's your wine?"

"How do you do that?" I said. "Be furious with me one minute and nice to me the next?"

"It's hard to stay angry with you for long." He lowered his gaze. "I'm not the only one garnering attention. The barman hasn't taken his eyes off you since we arrived."

"He's probably gay," I said. "And he's scheming how to get rid of me so he can get to you."

Jadeon rested his fingers against his brow to let me know he was listening to the man's thoughts. "No, he's definitely coveting an all-nighter with you."

Unable to resist, I glanced over at the barman. He ran a tea towel over a tumbler, stealing glances our way. He looked around twenty and wore a tight black shirt and baggy jeans. The barman turned away when he saw me staring.

The idea of dating mortals had become so boring. I'd been spoiled with too much adventure and ruined by the masterful touch of someone who knew the female form all too well.

Squeezing my thighs together, I suppressed these feelings that threatened to make me beg Jadeon to take me home so we could reenact that shower scene from last night. There came a need so deep. My body yearned for him, ached. I suppressed it as best I could and took another sip to distract me.

Braving to look at him again, I said, "This is delicious." Seeing his uneaten food, I continued, "Sorry, I didn't mean—"

"After a century or two, one ceases to think about it." He pushed his plate to the side. "The only concern is insulting the chef."

I smiled, allowing myself to enjoy this time with him. "You know you are conditioning me to misbehave. Every time I mess up in your eyes you reward me with your presence."

"Ah," he said. "I've failed you."

"Hardly."

His stare burned through me. "Every waking moment I'm thinking of you. What it is to be with you. To taste you. Be inside you. Hear you scream as I make you come."

My fork slipped from my fingers and clanged on the table.

"Wanting to make love to you this much is killing me." He stretched his arms out on either side of the booth. "You can see the wisdom in choosing a public place."

"I thought you didn't love me anymore."

"I'll always love you." He brushed his fingers though his black locks. "I'm ashamed."

"Of what?"

"Part of me wants you to mess up so that I have no choice but to turn you. Bring you over to me." He caressed his forehead. "I hate myself for it." His hand swept over the restaurant. "All this and more will be lost to you."

"I'm scared of what we have."

"We have nothing. I've had to let you go in order to save you. My world is full of doom, and death, and secrets, and lies. Your world, the one you make better for being in it, is full of beauty and innocence and promise." He raised his hand. "Please, let me continue."

I nodded, wanting to speak so much that the words of passion for him burned me up from the inside.

"Everything we have shared I cherish," he said. "From the memory of seeing you for the first time in the National Gallery. The most beautiful creature I'd ever set eyes on." He beamed a smile. "Baring in mind I'm talking centuries, so that's saying something."

Everything disappeared and it seemed we were the only ones here.

Jadeon reached for my hand, saying, "When I took you out to dinner that night I first met you, I couldn't take my eyes off you. I ached for you when the evening was over. Then later, you trusted me enough to visit my castle." He caressed my hand with his thumb. "You have no idea how many times you've saved me. Not just from the pitiful state I'd gotten myself into after two-hundred years of immortality, but you loved me despite this." His hand rested on his chest. "You deserve a man who can walk with you in daylight. Share a romantic meal like this with you."

His hand gestured to our food. "More importantly, have a child with you. A lover who'll not threaten your life because of your association with him."

That white picket fence was an illusion, and one that inevitably led to divorce, or worse, domestic drudgery. No, that had never been a possibility for me. Though Jadeon's link to the underworld did come with a dubious ability to abide by the law. It clashed with everything I believed in. Everything I'd worked for my entire life.

Jadeon shrugged as though agreeing with my thoughts. "Do it for me. If you truly love me as you say you do. Promise you'll forget me. Forget the world I'm from. You'll stay away. Stay safe."

"I don't know how," I whispered.

"Then let me do it for you. For us. Let this evening be our last, but with the memory that we were honest and kind. That we want the best for each other."

"Jadeon, please—"

"I realize that you need to know how much I loved you."

"Loved?"

A muscle in his jaw twitched. "There are those who would harm you to torture me."

"But I—"

"The elders are expecting me." He let go of my hand. "I promised them I can handle you. That I can get you to see reason. Even after that stunt you pulled today hacking into their data."

I needed a second glass of wine.

Jadeon motioned to the waitress. "Ingrid, the elders have told me in no uncertain terms that if they don't have your assurance that you'll drop your interest in them…"

The waitress topped up my wine and quickly withdrew. She too picked up on this tension between us.

"You won't let them harm me," I said. "I know you won't."

"Listen to me—"

"That place, the Athenaeum—"

"They'll kill you to protect it, Ingrid."

"It's not just a library, is it?"

His face became still, unreadable. "One more question like

that and I won't be able to stop them."

CHAPTER 15

After crashing from the high of seeing Jadeon again, I lingered outside Micelle's with him, stealing these last few precious seconds of having him near. I held his hands and stared into his eyes, soothing my soul for the last time as I prolonged the inevitable.

When the Rolls pulled away with him inside, a terrible grief consumed me, twisting in my gut and threatening permanence. It felt like a part of me had been ripped away. I choked back tears.

I'd refused Jadeon's invitation to let Henry drive me home despite his insistence, telling him I needed to walk off our conversation. Breathing in the post rain soaked air helped calm me a little. London's smog lifted and an earthy scent rose from the pavement. The city's frenetic energy served as a welcome distraction. Late night shoppers scurried by, plus a few tourists walking with maps and locals making their way home from their 9-5 jobs.

London, such an extraordinary city with its astounding architecture and intriguing history, yet I had never belonged here. Jadeon's love had been the closest feeling to home I'd ever had.

We left things on a positive note as only Jadeon could, with his reassurance all immortal matters would be ruled with an iron fist. I'd promised to let him find Beatrice. With Jadeon's supernatural advantage, I believed it wouldn't be long before she was home and safe again in Anaïs' arms.

I had a visit to make before I could finally lay to rest this part of my life. Not that I had any choice but to put it behind me.

Conceding it was over left a deep chasm where my heart should be. I wondered if this ache would ever go away.

In a daze, I found my way to the tube station and stop by grueling stop made my way to Notthing Hill.

Within the hour, I stood in Anaïs' living room. Nothing about her place hinted at what she really was. More interesting still, Anaïs showed no surprise at all with my visit. She was dressed in black yoga pants and a white T-shirt, her long black hair pulled tight in a ponytail and her makeup flawless.

The decor looked like it had come right out of an interior design magazine. I'm not quite sure what I expected Anaïs' place to look like but this wasn't it. The high ceiling widened an already spacious room. Modern lighting and plush furniture made the place feel welcome, and other than the enormous black marble fireplace there wasn't a hint of goth.

I tried a smile to lessen the uneasiness.

"The Lamborghini's number plate?" she said. "That's how you found me?"

"I ran it through our database. I didn't expect to find your car registered."

"You wouldn't have found me if I didn't want you to."

"Ah."

"Anyway, the car's gone now. Orpheus confiscated it."

"The Lamborghini?"

"He was furious with me for taking you to the Athenaeum."

"I'm sorry."

"Don't be. I took his Viper."

"You stole his car?"

"It's blood red. I much prefer it actually."

"What will he do when he finds out?"

"Why?"

"I'm worried about you."

"I'll be fine."

"Are you having sex with him?" I said.

"No." Anaïs threw her head back in laughter. "Would you be jealous if I was?"

"No." I flushed wildly. "Yoga?" I pointed to her mat.

"Yes, I love it. Do you do it? You have a yoga body. Tall and lean."

"I'm a runner. When I get the time, that is."

The conversation felt surreal, forced even, but it would soon be over. I really had to get home and prepare for tomorrow. A good night's sleep awaited me. That lasagna and fine wine that Jadeon had spoiled me with made me sleepy.

"Orpheus sired me," she said. "We have a special connection."

"You're not frightened of him?"

She lowered her gaze. "I don't drool over him like all the others. That's probably why he's drawn to you. You're in love with Jadeon. It appeals to Orpheus' masochistic side. You're the ultimate challenge. Still, he must respect Jadeon because you'd belong to Orpheus' in a second if he wanted it so."

"Don't I have a say?"

"Of course not." She blinked at me. "You think about Orpheus sometimes, don't you?"

"Not like that."

Her smile oozed with an easy charm, taunting me.

No, there was no truth in what she was intimating. *Was there?*

"I was worried about you," I said quickly. "We never got the chance to speak after you left the Athenaeum."

"I'm sorry for leaving you there."

"Oh, Anaïs, that wasn't your fault."

"I let you down."

"Orpheus can be very persuasive."

She gave a thin smile, but it quickly faded.

I glanced over at her couch. "That's nice."

"Beatrice bought it for me." She gestured to it. "Take a seat and I'll pour you a scotch."

"No, thank you. I'm not staying."

"I have Dalmore 64 Trinitas."

I frowned, stunned that she knew what I liked to drink.

"I have visitors who drink booze," she said. "Mortal friends."

"Do they know you're a vampire?"

"Course not."

"You live here with Beatrice?"

"Yes." She strolled over to the marble mantle piece and

picked up a silver frame. She smiled fondly at it and brought it back to show me.

I took it from her and sat on the couch, studying the photograph. In it, Anaïs wore an elegant short black dress. She'd flung her arm around Beatrice, who didn't look a day over twenty. The girl's smile was captivating. The moment reflected happier times. Remembering that other photo of her captured in chains was hauntingly painful.

"She looks angelic," I said.

Thoughts formed just out of reach but didn't rise to the surface of my consciousness, as though answers lay deep within the recesses of my mind, promising to come together and form facts. My mind revisited the evidence room filled with Hauville's personal belongings: boxes of folders, private letters, and a few stuffed animals. All of it now catalogued. All of it useless.

Anaïs leaned forward and rested her index finger right between my eyes. "In here lies the answers."

"I've been assured everything is being done to find her."

"By Dominion?" Anaïs nodded in response to her question.

"Jadeon has reassured me he has his best men on it. You have to trust him."

"Right."

"What is it?"

Her lips curled into a sinister smile. "I saw the footage filmed through the fox. It's rather interesting. Places you right at the scene, Ingrid. In Hauville's secret room before the warrant was served."

My throat tightened and I held her stare.

"Something like that would ruin a career," she said.

"Anaïs, what are you saying?"

"I'm worried about Beatrice. I'm a wreck. I can't think straight enough to find her."

Yet Anaïs looked flawless, unchanged from the day she'd been turned, with no sign of strain showing any of the turmoil she was going through.

I reached for her hand to comfort her.

Anaïs pulled back. "Orpheus will give you the footage filmed of you in exchange for your cooperation."

"Orpheus has always had my full attention." I sat up

straighter. "He's the one who kept information from me, remember?"

"This case is going nowhere."

"Orpheus never mentioned this."

"Well he is now. Through me."

"Jadeon wants to handle it." I hated losing control of where this was heading.

"You're handling it now," she said, rising from the sofa and heading off toward the glass fronted bar on the other side of the room. She poured a large scotch into a tumbler and brought it back to me.

With a shaking hand, I took it from her with no intention of drinking it. Jadeon hadn't mentioned anything about footage filmed of me. I wondered if Orpheus had kept it from him too.

Anaïs pointed to the frame resting on the couch beside me. "You're going to find Beatrice, or Orpheus will send that footage of you to Scotland Yard."

In a daze, I took a sip. The liquor burned my throat.

"Your mind has all that evidence in there waiting to rise to the surface," she said.

"Blue illuminate?" I said faintly. "You're going to force me to drink it?"

"I'm offering it to you. See it as a solution to your problem."

I pulled back the tumbler and stared at it in horror.

"It's scotch, Ingrid. I don't keep the spell here."

I set the glass down on the side table. "Orpheus would never go against Jadeon's wishes."

"They merely use each other."

It didn't make any sense. Jadeon had insisted he could find Beatrice, and Orpheus had convinced me they were working together. Jadeon had warned me of the danger I'd put myself in if I pursued any kind of contact with the underworld, yet here I was with Anaïs, and right now I wished I'd heeded his warning.

Hesitating, I tried to read the truth in her threat. "This is a bad idea, Anaïs."

"Having your mind open up so you can connect the dots and find Beatrice is the only option left."

"Let me think about it." I rose to go. "I'll call you tomorrow."

"Oh, Ingrid, Ingrid, Ingrid," she used my name in a threatening chant.

I froze, my glare fixed on her.

"Orpheus doesn't negotiate," she said.

"I have to go home."

"Sure, right after we take a trip." She set off across the room and picked up a set of car keys on the table.

"Where are we going?"

"You'll see."

CHAPTER 16

Redruth's Carn Brea Castle had a magnificent view of the ocean.

Atop a hill, this grand landmark rose elegantly out of the ground. The fact that its brickwork had stood the test of time was a testament to the craftsman who had built it back in the medieval era.

We had arrived just after 9 P.M., with Anaïs driving the Viper hard. Had I not been in a stunned silence and lacking sleep, I might have been able to enjoy the passing countryside. I had a soft spot for Cornwall. My happiest memories of spending time with Jadeon occurred here on the west coast of England. It was known by many as God's country for its varied coastline, golden sandy beaches, and sprawling moors.

Anaïs led me inside the castle with a confident stride, which was an indication she knew this place well. She walked with verve, every sure step proving she was on a mission and nothing was going to stop her.

Within minutes, we settled in a sitting room. Cream colored couches faced each other and large arm chairs were positioned here and there for ease of conversation. Large rugs were strewn upon the floors and paintings showcased other Cornish landmarks, hanging low on the thick walls, designed to keep in the heat. All very homey, very welcoming.

Still, I didn't want to be here.

Letting out a deep, steadying breath, I peered out of the arched window from the castle's uppermost floor and watched children playing on the grassy bank below. "This is a school?"

Anaïs joined me and peered out. "Orphanage."

Ten or so teenage boys ran the full length of the green lush lawn, kicking around a ball and avoiding the boulders clustered left of the castle. Beyond, a long fence ran the length of the cliff overlooking the ocean. Unruly waves rolled in the distance. A storm brewed out there too.

"How many of those children try to climb that fence?" I said, half in a daze.

Anaïs shrugged.

"Do any of them ever run away?"

"They wouldn't."

"Are they strict here?"

"They're well looked after. They're loved, which is not always the case in places like this."

I turned to her. "What are we doing here?"

"You'll see." Anaïs kept her focus on the garden. "Try to see it from my point of view."

"I've been warned that if I don't withdraw my interest in the underworld—"

"Find Beatrice. That's all we're asking of you."

"We, being you and Orpheus?"

"I'm doing you a favor. You want to solve this case as much as I do."

The door opened and a thirty-something redhead strolled in. "Anaïs, it's a pleasure seeing you again," the woman said. "You've brought a friend."

The woman's green eyes were mesmerizing, though not iridescent, and were all the more emphasized by her tan. A true Celt if ever I saw one. Despite her petite frame, she held the confident air of a woman in authority. Her snappy blue suit made me wonder if she was the governess. One thing I was sure of, she was mortal.

"Mirabelle, this is Ingrid," Anaïs said.

Mirabelle smiled. "Any friend of Orpheus is a friend of ours."

"Is this Orpheus' place?" I asked.

Mirabelle looked surprised. "He knows you're here, right?"

"Of course," Anaïs said, not missing a beat. "Mirabelle's the headmistress." She turned to her. "Thank you for seeing us on such short notice."

Mirabelle lowered her head in fake scorn. "No need to be so formal."

They chatted away, catching up on time lost since they'd last seen each other.

The idea that Orpheus had anything to do with an orphanage was startling and more than a little disturbing. I made a mental note to ask him just what kind of involvement he had here.

Mirabelle didn't radiate anything sinister. For these children's sake, I hoped my radar was right.

A cool breeze blew in through the window. I loved Cornwall, yet this visit was altogether different. I wondered how far St. Michael's Mount was from here. I hoped Jadeon would burst through the door at any moment and save me from this, whatever this was. A supposed jaunt to imbibe some concoction Anaïs called blue illuminate. My thoughts drifted to how Jadeon would react when he found out that Orpheus was coercing me into something so unpleasant. So unknown. So dangerous.

"The entire faculty ensures the children feel at home," Mirabelle said, turning her attention on me. "Loved."

"Is this a Catholic school?" I said.

Mirabelle twisted her mouth. "Goodness, no, my darling. Wiccan."

"Oh." I tried to hide my surprise.

Mirabelle nudged up closer. "The children are brought up to respect God, nature, and each other. They are taught that they are world citizens. The lines that divide humanity such as religion and politics are studied so they better understand the world they are born into."

"Can they have a religion?" I asked, "I mean other than Wiccan?"

"Of course. That's Jonathan." She pointed to one of the children kicking a ball around.

The neatly dressed teenager stopped in his tracks when he saw Mirabelle at the window. He waved up at her.

She waved back. "His parent's died in a car accident when he was six. Despite there being a will, other members of his family refused to take him. Jonathan's a darling boy. We're delighted to have him here with us at Carn Brea. His parents were devout Catholics, and as such we honor his parents' wishes and he is taught Catholicism."

"Does he go to Mass?" I said.

Mirabelle's eyes twinkled. "Jonathan's an altar boy." She headed over to the two beige couches facing each other. "Let's sit."

I joined her, taking a seat next to Anaïs.

Mirabelle sat on the couch opposite ours and kicked off her shoes, bringing her feet up bedside her. "Tea is on its way up." She smiled her approval. "So how do you two know each other?"

"Ingrid's helping me find Beatrice," Anaïs said.

"You mentioned that in your call." Mirabelle peered over at me. "We can't quite believe this has happened. Beatrice is a sweet, sweet girl." She looked over at Anaïs. "How are you doing? You two are so close."

"I'm holding up." Anaïs returned her focus to me. "Ingrid's promised to find her."

"That's wonderful," Mirabelle said. "The more people we can get on this the better."

I wondered if Anaïs had mentioned to her that I was a policewoman. I decided it was best not to say anything about it until I'd felt Mirabelle out a little more.

"How do you know each other?" I asked, looking from Mirabelle to Anaïs.

"I lived here for a short time," Anaïs said. "Before I became a Gothica."

"We did try to set her on a traditional path," Mirabella said. "Anaïs has always been strong willed."

"Orpheus bought you here?" I asked Anaïs.

"After he found me begging in Convent Garden," she said. "Still, I didn't stay long. It's too quiet here and I wanted to be near Orpheus."

Mirabelle shrugged in confirmation of Anaïs' explanation. "We couldn't persuade her to stay. We were quite proud of her when she became a Gothica. It felt like such a natural pathway for her. Her destiny." Mirabelle looked upon her with affection.

"We're kind of against the clock," Anaïs said.

Mirabelle's eyebrows knitted together. "Ingrid knows what this entails?"

"She does," Anaïs told her.

Nausea welled in my gut along with panic. Having no idea what any of this entailed, I hated Anaïs for saying I did. My glare shot to her.

Mirabelle caught it. "Something wrong?"

"Usual nerves," Anaïs said, seemingly appeasing Mirabelle.

The door opened and a teenage girl dressed in a grey school uniform entered carrying a tray. A teapot and cups balanced upon it. She carefully placed it on the table before us.

"Thank you, Poppy," Mirabelle said, leaning forward to pour tea into a cup. She added milk.

I waited to see if she poured herself one. She did, confirming my suspicion that she was indeed mortal.

I refused the cup she offered, too suspicious of what might be in the tea. "No, thank you."

"Of course not," Mirabelle said. "You're partial to more delicate tastes."

She thinks I'm a vampire?

I sat forward, ready to correct her.

"Mirabelle, thank you helping us tonight," Anaïs said quickly.

"Of course. It's my pleasure." Mirabelle flashed her a smile.

The young girl headed for the door, glancing back to take one more look at Anaïs. How captivating Anaïs must have appeared with her rock star black leather pants and edgy T-shirt, along with her long black mane and heavy eyeliner that oozed rebellion. A seductive combination to an impressionable teenager of Poppy's age.

We waited for her to leave.

"We perform a ceremony," Anaïs said to me, offering a smile of reassurance. "It's tradition."

"I'm sorry?" Though my expression was more *what the fuck?*

Mirabella waved her hand to gesture it was nothing. "Our ancestors worshiped a vampire who protected them. We're talking a couple of centuries back now, of course. Cornish witches have long been associated with vampires. I'm surprised you don't know that being a vampire yourself, Ingrid."

I went to correct her. Surely she could see my irises weren't luminescent? Unless she assumed I was wearing contacts.

"Ingrid's looking forward to this," Anaïs interrupted again, her glare hinting I wasn't meant to correct Mirabelle's misconception.

I offered a forced smile. "Blue illuminate, what's in it?"

"A few herbs," Anaïs said.

"And a drop of ancient blood," Mirabelle said. "Amongst other things. You'll find it a rather luxurious experience."

Slowly, I pushed myself to my feet and strolled over to the window, trying to compose myself. I regretted coming here and putting myself in this predicament. Regretted being beholden to Anaïs and her crazy scheming. Beholden to Orpheus.

"Give us a moment," Anaïs said as she joined me by the window.

Mirabelle rose. "Something wrong?"

"Not at all," Anaïs said. "Please, gather the others. We'll meet you there."

Others?

My stare shot to her and I wondered where the hell we were going now.

Mirabelle hesitated, not missing my reaction, but then on Anaïs' glare she conceded with a nod. "Very well." She left the room.

"Blood?" I snapped.

"Thinking of backing out?"

"Hell, yes."

"Very well," Anaïs said calmly. "I'll call Orpheus." She went to leave.

"Give me a moment." My fingers gripped the window ledge. "Let's discuss this rationally. I can investigate this case better without having my mind altered. You have to believe me."

"We've given you more than enough time to prove that," she said.

Hugging myself, I shook my head, not wanting to hear this. "I need more time."

"More time to mess up Beatrice's life?" she snapped. "You've even turned your back on Jadeon."

"What? No, he's the one—"

"You think you're better than everyone else."

"That's not me." Confusion muddied my thoughts. "What are you saying?"

"How long has this case been on your desk? How can you live with yourself for failing so terribly?"

"It's being dealt with by another department. By Jadeon—"

"You and I both know you're the only one who can find her. You and no one else. Beatrice's blood will be on your hands. Please, Ingrid, you have to step outside your comfort zone and do this."

I grabbed Anaïs' arm. "Mirabelle thinks I'm a vampire."

"It doesn't make any difference whether you are or not. Within the hour your brain will be firing off all cylinders. Your mind will be sharper than it's ever been."

"You're blackmailing me. It doesn't exactly illicit trust."

"Seems to me you don't have any choice."

"Where is it?" I said. "I want to look at it."

"They keep it under lock and key in the chapel. But you won't be drinking it here."

"I...I can't, Anaïs."

She ran her fingers through my hair. "Yes, you can," she cooed. "And, yes, you will."

My feet became unsteady. My limbs weakened from having her so close. She was so dangerously controlling. Anaïs' ironclad grip guided me out of the room.

The rest was a blur.

Anaïs told me she'd booked us a room in the five-star Camelot Castle Hotel. Apparently I'd need somewhere to sleep off this 'Alice in Wonderland' elixir that Anaïs was threatening me with. We drove there in record time with her at the wheel of the Viper, the speed so dangerous I doubted we'd actually get to the hotel in one piece.

My thoughts raced, trying to make sense of this, trying to find the words that would persuade Anaïs to change her mind and give me a second chance to find Beatrice without frying my brain in the process. This was the consequence of missing all the signs of manipulation. Of course I knew people were more likely to mess up when they were out of ideas and pushed up against a wall. I knew this all too well. I'd failed miserably to eat properly over the last few weeks and get the rest my body needed. Fatigue had set in.

Sitting on the edge of the four poster bed, I took in the room. The hotel Anaïs had chosen was luxurious. Lush furnishings surrounded us and antiques gave the illusion of turning back the clock to a Victorian era. Another time, another life. The fireplace had been lit prior to our arrival and flames licked high in the hearth, providing a welcome warmth to my chilled bones.

Was I really going through with this?

No, I wasn't.

Anaïs sat beside me. "Would you like some water?"

"I'm not staying," I said. "Please let me talk with Orpheus. Surely we can come to some kind of an agreement?"

She sighed. "Maybe it's time you faced the fact your life is a lie, Ingrid."

I stared at the door, willing my courage to take over as I ignored her threats and braved the consequences.

"There's something I have to tell you," she said. "You're not going to like it, I'm afraid."

From her expression, I knew I wouldn't.

"Vampires are incapable of feeling love," she said softly.

"I don't believe that."

An uncomfortable silence followed.

My heart didn't believe that either. After all, Jadeon loved me and had told me this on so many occasions. He'd also proven it with every action, and even now validated how much he cared by staying away. Keeping me safe. Sacrificing his happiness and mine. And I was failing him by being here and breaking the promise I'd made.

"Jadeon used you."

"What?"

Anaïs ran her hand up and down my back. "It's not your fault. Don't blame yourself. It's done so smoothly. You never see it coming."

"What are you talking about?" I snapped.

"You really never suspected?" she asked surprised.

"Suspect what, Anaïs?"

She looked incredulous. "Yet you're so damn smart."

"What are you trying to tell me?"

"Did it happen like this for you? You were lured to a

meeting in a public place like a library or an art gallery? A place where your guard was down. Jadeon garnered your full attention and then seduced you off to somewhere even more glamorous. A place that ensured he'd take your breath away."

My gut wrenched. She's was lying. Surely she was? *No, stop talking...please...*

Anaïs nodded knowingly. "You were lured to Jadeon's castle, I imagine?"

I shot her a wary stare.

"Though it could have been his luxury yacht," she said. "Working girl's love yachts. Castles are more practical though."

"Jadeon doesn't have a yacht."

"Of course he does. He's rich and lives in Cornwall, for goodness sake."

"He never mentioned it."

"I find that rather interesting, don't you?" She flashed a look of surprise."All that decadence is so outside your realm of experience. I imagine it's rather intimidating at first. Soon, though, it becomes addictive. Like his money."

"I never cared about his money."

"That's refreshing to hear." She looked solemn. "Orpheus is no different. Well, he makes a point of getting off on watching you suffer." Shaking her head in disbelief, she added, "I mean choosing drab women because they're more likely to be grateful is downright taking advantage."

"Why are you doing this?"

"Surely you don't believe Jadeon is exclusively seeing you?" She looked puzzled.

My mouth went dry.

"When was the last time you had sex with him?"

I broke her stare, not willing to allow my thoughts to lead to the pain waiting for me on the other side of truth. We'd not made love in months. Yes, he'd pleasured me, but we'd not...

Oh God...

"A few months ago you were working on a case," she said. "Girls had been murdered and dumped, one of them at Stonehenge. Alex was accused as the perpetrator. Jadeon offered to take care of you. He did, after all, want to protect his brother. Protect the underworld. Distract you as it were. It was the only way he could save Alex."

"My investigation—"

"Jadeon managed to derail it." She threw her hands up in exasperation. "The culprit was never brought to justice. Am I right?"

"Why would Jadeon stay friends with me now?" I rose to my feet and backed away from her.

"To keep track on what you're doing. What you know."

I slammed my hand to my mouth.

"Has Jadeon ever told you he can't be with you because he needs to protect you?" she said. "That's kind of the party line. Works every time."

I cringed, my throat tightening with tension.

"Yeah, for some reason mortals fall for that," she said. "Orpheus and Jadeon played you perfectly."

"I don't believe it."

She pushed herself to her feet and came closer. "Vampires are incapable of feeling love. Hell, we don't even feel pleasure."

"But Orpheus? His club, Belshazzar's?"

"I know, right? Truth is, the only pleasure we get is to watch someone else's."

There was a knock on the door and Mirabelle entered. "Well, are we ready?" She paused halfway. "Bad time?"

Anaïs wrapped her arm around me and hugged me against her. "Ingrid, what I'm trying to tell you is that it wasn't your fault that you fell for it."

A sob caught in my throat.

Anaïs looked back at Mirabelle. "She's upset over Orpheus. I've told her what a rogue he is." She stroked my back again. "He's playing with you. He can't help himself."

"I have to talk with Jadeon," I said.

Anaïs sucked in a breath. "Jadeon is even crueler than Orpheus. Isn't he, Mirabelle?"

"Jadeon does have a reputation for being ruthless," Mirabelle agreed. "I wouldn't want to cross him. Have you been intimate with him? Did he break your heart?"

More tears fell and I swiped at them in a daze.

"Ingrid, I know you're hurting." Anaïs reached out for the glass bottle Mirabelle was holding and she took it from her.

"This will deaden your pain."

The glass bottle with its filigree silver top was delicate and inviting. Anaïs removed the stopper.

Outside, the cry of seagulls sounded as they flew by the window. Outside, where my old life begged me to find it again.

"You need to be seated." Mirabelle gestured at the bed.

I went to tell her that I wasn't a vampire and felt Anaïs' grip on my arm tighten.

"Sit," Anaïs said.

Lowering myself onto the edge of the bed, I stared at the fluorescent blue liquid swishing in the bottle. Tinges of red spiraled through the blue like colored ribbons. There was no way I was drinking it.

A chanting filled the room.

Mirabelle was joined by two other young, female Wiccans, and just as she'd dressed in a bodice and long full skirt so were they. Their medieval get up only added to what felt like insanity. Asking how I'd gotten here was a mute point now.

"Behold, I give you blue illuminate," Mirabelle said.

If I refused to do this, Orpheus would send those tapes to Scotland Yard and my career would be over. Perhaps, just perhaps, Anaïs knew what she was doing. If I drank this, I might very well find myself enlightened and able to find Beatrice.

"I need more time," I said, begging her with my eyes.

"No," Anaïs said, "No more wasting time."

Anaïs lifted the bottle and rested the tip against my lips. I nudged her hand away.

"Drink it, my dear," Mirabelle coaxed softly. "It'll soothe your heart."

"Deaden the pain," Anaïs silently messaged me.

But would it help me forget Jadeon's betrayal? No, these were lies. This was Anaïs' dreadful manipulation. Her motivation was clear.

"You want proof?" Anaïs said firmly.

I gave a slow, careful nod.

"Why do you think Jadeon branded you as a Gothica? Marked you clearly as belonging to Orpheus?"

"To protect me?" I whispered.

"He gave you to Orpheus," Anaïs said. "This was Jadeon's

way of proving he serves him. Just as we all serve Orpheus."

"No, Jadeon is Dominion," I said. "Jadeon rules the underworld."

"Have you seen them together recently?" she said. "Do they appear like enemies to you?" She shook her head. "Even when the evidence is right in front of you." She gestured to the room. "Where is Jadeon now?"

With eyes lowered to the floor, I tried to think straight. I struggled to gather all the pieces of this distorted puzzle yet nothing added up, nothing made any sense.

"Do this, Ingrid," Anaïs cooed. "Or your career will be over. Your choice."

There was no choice. Without my work, I was nothing. It was all I had ever known. My work defined me.

"Open," Anaïs' said, pressing the bottle to my mouth again.

I had never lost Jadeon because he had never been mine to lose. Anaïs poured the liquid into my mouth. The taste of bitter apples... and something else...peppermint? That familiar sweetness of vampire blood tingled on my tongue and curled down my throat. My legs turned to jelly with the realization of what I'd done.

This dreadful danger.

I collapsed back onto the bed and stared up. The ceiling bore down on me. The walls closed in. There it was. That familiar daring willing me to fly too close to the flame.

Into its very center.

A slow deliberate chanting echoed around us...

I was spellbound.

Time slowed as electricity sparked between all of us. I reached out to caress the fine holographic strands of red dancing before my eyes. These were quickened by the vibrations that swarmed, drowning me, entering me. Something within recognized these hypnotic, melodic sounds and calmness descended. Celtic words were spoken softly, a familiar incantation reaching into my soul, twisting and turning and causing me to tremble.

A whisper found me in the dark. "She'll achieve infinite awareness."

Sparks of desire shot down my spine, directly to that delicate place between my thighs. Blood rushed to my groin and my sex clenched in anticipation.

"She looks so beautiful." A Cornish lilt came out of the quiet.

How can it work so fast?

But I couldn't ask, couldn't speak. My voice was snatched by a yearning so intense I questioned fighting it. I tried to hide my ascending bliss, this building orgasm, the curling of my toes the only clue to these secret sensations.

Blushing wildly, I knew they were watching.

Stillness emphasized their focus remained on me, but I was too far gone to care. I was coming hard, moaning my pleasure, stunned by these erotic spasms causing me to writhe and twist upon the bed as though taken by an invisible lover. My breathing grew shallow, ragged, and my heart readied for wherever this moment took me. Taut fingers gripped the bed sheet as my head turned, whipping my hair from side to side. My hands laved the sheet and then let go to reach out to prevent me from falling—

Freefalling.

A door opened and closed, but first came a rustle of skirts, along with whispers that were impossible to catch. The stillness revealed the women had gone, leaving Anaïs and I alone in the dark.

"Anaïs," a deep male voice broke through the silence. "Did I just see my fucking Viper parked outside?"

I recognized that pissed off tone.

Orpheus.

But I was too weak to raise my head, too far gone to protest. I descended further out of my depth and sunk into the unknown.

Into oblivion.

CHAPTER 17

I turned my gaze away from the needle.

The smell of bleach, or something similar to bleach, filled my nostrils and I willed myself not to throw up. Hanging out in the morgue wasn't one of my better ideas, but then again I wasn't exactly rational right now, even if I pretended I was.

"What am I testing for again?" Dr. Russell asked.

A pinch in the crook of my left arm let me know the needle was in. I felt the pressure of the specimen bottles being switched out to draw more blood into each one. Dr. Russell placed the tubes safely on the silver tray beside him.

"Chemicals," I said. "A drug screen, toxicology, that kind of thing."

"I'm going to test your Vitamin D while I'm at it. You're looking pale." He removed the needle and pressed a cotton wool ball into the crux of my arm. "Want to tell me what's going on?" He replaced the cotton ball with a Band-Aid. "Please tell me we're not talking date rape?"

"No. I don't meet strange men in bars."

He removed his gloves and threw them in the bin. "Glad to hear it."

I just date vampires until my self esteem is decimated beyond recognition.

He labeled the bottles. "Well considering I haven't taken a blood sample from a living person in over a decade that went better than expected."

"Glad you told me that now."

"I'm sure if you were doing drugs you wouldn't volunteer your blood to Scotland Yard's coroner. So that leaves me to wonder. Why the hell am I testing your blood for drugs?"

"Can we discuss this later?"

His shoulders dropped. "Has anyone ever accused you of being insufferable?"

"They may have hinted at it, yes."

He frowned down at my London Times Newspaper. "Is that today's?"

"Yes." I scanned the articles, trying to see what headline he'd caught.

"The crossword's done."

"Did it on the way in."

"How long did it take you?"

"I don't know." And then it hit me. It usually took me an hour to complete, yet I'd finished the crossword puzzle in less than twenty minutes this morning after purchasing a copy from a vender outside the tube. I'd searched for a distraction from this gut wrenching pain brought on from last night's revelation.

It hadn't worked.

My mind wandered back farther.

I'd awoken with the mother of all headaches, feeling hungover. The cause of it found its way back to me in all its glorious dysfunction. My thoughts dragged me along until I recalled last night and the consequences of falling for Anaïs' blackmail. She'd driven me to Cornwall in a stolen vehicle, put me through an erotic witches' ceremony, and forced me to drink an unknown substance known as blue illuminate.

Reckless. No change there, then.

Nothing unusual to report. This was my customary modus operandi of chasing danger and mingling with its cohorts, otherwise known as irrationality and regret. I caressed my forehead to ease the tension.

"You got number 21 across," Dr. Russell said.

"Acadian. Early French settler."

"Impressive."

I twisted my mouth, having to agree this was a little unusual, but I'd put it down to fatigue, infused with way too much coffee. Not to mention having my heart split in two by the revelation of how foolish I'd been over the last few months. Everything I knew had been a lie. I'd been apparently used and abused and had offered myself up willingly to the process. I only had myself to blame and the shock of it all was so startling it threatened to incapacitate me. Last night, I'd fallen into unconsciousness in a hotel room with Orpheus' voice fading into the background. The next thing I remembered was waking up at home and finding a vase of red roses on my bedside table with a note card scribed with the letter *J*.

After shoving them in the bin, I vowed never again to fall for the charms of the undead. See, addressing them as what they really were was actually a good start to getting over the worst mistake of my life.

Swallowing back tears, trying to dislodge this lump in my throat, I marveled at my ability to remain stony-faced.

"You okay?" Dr. Russell said.

"Fine, thank you. How are things between you and Helena?"

He looked relieved. "Much better. We drove in together."

"I have a feeling your bridge sessions are good for the agility of her mind."

Dr. Russell blinked. "We really are playing bridge, Ingrid."

"I know." I tapped his arm playfully. "So, when will these be back?"

"It usually takes a week, but I'll see what I can do."

"I appreciate that, and if we could keep this on the down low."

He pointed to the tubes. "You're labeled as Jane Crossword Doe."

"Clever."

"I have my moments."

Within the hour, I was back in my office and downing my third mug of coffee of the morning, self-examining every action to see if there was indeed any change in my ability to process details faster. Other than the crossword, nothing out of the ordinary stood out. The speed with which I read was the same, and as I rifled through my files in my in-tray nothing popped out as a new revelation.

I found myself in some halfway land wedged between relief and disappointment.

Perhaps Anaïs had merely been manipulating me all along, hoping she'd convince me to help find Beatrice? I understood her desperation. Still, she'd put me through the ringer both physically and emotionally, and if anything Anaïs had threatened my ability to function at my optimum.

I took two more Tylenol and chased them down with a gulp of coffee.

I grabbed all the files out of my in-tray and set them before me. It was time to close these once and for all. Enthusiasm surged though my veins with the possibility of finally getting on top of my workload. With these taken care of I'd be able to dedicate time to finding Beatrice. Though it would still have to be off the record.

An envelope slipped out from the stack and slid across my desk, spiraling to the floor. Inside was a gold embossed invitation to the annual police charity ball. I'd completely forgotten about this event being held tomorrow night at the Waldorf Ritz in Covent Garden. The last thing I needed was a social event where I'd need to pretend everything in my life was business as usual, and all I had to look forward to was an evening of enduring small talk. Surely I was bright enough to figure a way out of it?

Mulling over that idea and refusing to let this week derail any further, I went in search of Sgt. Miller and Constable Noble to inform them of today's goal, which was wrapping these cases up.

Within the hour I'd debriefed them on the day's plan and they were both up to speed. Helena didn't bring up her dental appointment, and though I doubted that's where she had been I felt a girl had the right to privacy. Our job was so stressful at times that taking a mental day off was allowed in my book. Though for me there could be no such luxury. I had to put off going home and curling into a ball on my bed until the weekend.

Yes, two days of licking my wounds while watching back to back episodes of Doctor Who and enough chocolate to lull me into a sugar coma was in my future. Who was I kidding? A torrent of grief welled beneath the surface, threatening to flood out at any minute. There was nothing that would soothe this knot of pain wedged in the center of my heart. *Nothing.*

My ability to make polite conversation with Helena and Miller hid the fact that anything was wrong. With Helena at the wheel of our police rover and Miller sitting in the back seat, we made our way through London traffic.

"Anything on that car accident?" I asked Miller.

He leaned forward. "There were two cars involved. A Ford Escort and a BMW. The driver in the Ford was over the limit. He was arrested and charged on scene. This is the bit I imagine you're interested in. The driver of the BMW disappeared. Whoever was driving that vehicle would have been seriously injured. They wouldn't have gotten far."

"Do you think someone dragged the driver from the car?" I asked.

"Witnesses on the scene didn't see anyone."

"Who was the BMW registered to?"

"It wasn't registered."

"Was it stolen?" Helena said.

"No," Miller said. "Purchased in Dagenham and never registered." He sat back. "Get this, the car was apparently bought with cash."

"Is this a new case for us?" Helena said.

"I'm looking into it as a favor," I told her. "Any reports from local hospitals?"

"All MVA patients admitted to London hospitals that night had registered vehicles," Miller said. "I'll send traffic's report over to you."

"You always have the most difficult cases," Helena said.

I smiled her way. "*We* have the most difficult cases."

She beamed a smile.

Our first stop was at Regency High School on Mayberry Street to check on this building that had sustained a spate of vandalism. The security system had caught the activity of thirteen-year-old Bryce Arnold spraying red paint on the science lab walls and sabotaging the computer equipment. The lawyers defending Bryce were delaying him being expelled despite the obvious danger to the other children. His parents donated heavily to the school so the case was being delayed by the headmaster, or so it seemed.

Much to Miller's chagrin, I forced all three of us to spend

the morning in a spare classroom enduring a month's worth of security recordings and tracking Bryce's every move throughout the school.

Hours later, Miller and Helena both agreed it had been worth it when we found last Monday's footage of Bryce in the home economics lab, alone, trying to set light to a wastepaper bin. Bryce had been interrupted by other students entering the class and they'd evidently caught him in the act, but had been too afraid to report him. Our vandalism case was upgraded to arson, which was all that was needed to get Bryce thrown out of school and add a juvenile conviction that would stick.

After grabbing a quick lunch at a Greek cafe, Miller, Helena, and I drove over to Rumple Street to check in on Sally Summers, our domestic abuse victim.

We found Mrs. Summers rolling pastry at her kitchen table, flour splotched over her face. Her tired eyes and worn out smile revealed she took little pleasure from her domestic duties. Makeup applied earlier had made a good go at concealing her black eye. Her husband's abuse wasn't letting up.

Sgt. Miller and Helena stood at the back of the kitchen and let me do all the talking. My speech flooded out like a Shakespearean sonnet. A plead for Sally to see what she was enduring and offering her a way out of this miserable life.

"He's under your skin," I told her. "He threatens you and then pulls the 'feel sorry for me card.' I'm afraid it's the classic M.O. of an abuser. He probably tells you he'll not survive without you."

Sally rolled the pastry, half-listening.

I grabbed the rolling pin. "I know you're scared. I'm scared too. I'm terrified that tomorrow, or next week, I'll be the one zipping up your body bag and watching the medics wheel your lifeless corpse off to the morgue. Your husband's getting more violent. He is going to kill you. It's a matter of when, not if."

She glared up at me, aghast.

As did Helena and Sgt. Miller, who'd never seen me so agitated.

"I know how it works," I said. "They seduce you with their charm. Tell you what you want to hear. Make you feel special, needed. As though without you their world will fall apart."

Tears rolled down Sally's cheeks.

"They woo you," I continued calmly. "Take you to places you never dreamed you'd see. They take your breath away. There's this sense you'll never find anyone quite like them again. Your self-esteem is decimated. You're grateful for the scraps of affection they give you no matter how few they are. But this is not living. It's a slow death, and you and I both know we deserve better."

Silence.

"You deserve better," I corrected.

"I do," she muttered and wiped white powder and pastry off her hands with a stained cloth.

"We'll get you out of here and place you somewhere safe," I told her.

"Thank you." She looked as stunned as Helena and Miller.

I squeezed her arm and handed her over to my colleagues to wrap up the arrangements for her extraction.

Waiting for them in the car, feigning to be busy on my BlackBerry, I tried to cease my hands from shaking. My outburst might have just saved her life and it had also revealed a lot about mine. Both Miller and Helena knew well enough not to discuss what they'd witnessed. I hoped they put it down to my versatility and hadn't picked up any hint of personal experience. I kept my life private and it was going to stay that way.

Miller asked to visit a local cafe to pick up some tea before making our way over to our next destination.

Sipping the dark brew while gazing out of the window, my thoughts kept circling back to Jadeon. Scrutinizing each and every moment we'd ever spent together, my mind searched for missed signs of his artful deceit but found none. Thus proving the genius of his cruelty, just as Anaïs' had so deftly explained. I'd never seen it for what it really was. *For what he really was.*

We arrived in Highgate within the hour. The on-going dispute between two neighbors had been seemingly settled. Happy the Chihuahua was no longer digging up next door's flower beds apparently, which was a good thing. Unfortunately the reason was he'd been missing for two days now, and despite the owner, Mrs. Simms, placing flyers all over the neighborhood they'd been no sight of him.

Standing on the front step of Mr. Lazlo's house, the neighbor who had initially filed the complaint against Happy, I listened intently to his denial of all knowledge of the dog's whereabouts while reading every nuance of what he didn't say from his animated body language.

"Oh bloody hell," I said, reaching into the boot of the rover and fishing around for a shovel.

Despite Helena's look of horror, which matched the dog owner's as she watched from her front porch, I made a beeline for Mr. Lazlo's garden via the side-alley. Though Lazlo had only given a brief nod of permission, it was all I needed to enter his property.

I should have been searching for Beatrice, but no, I was on the hunt for a lost dog. Everything was wrong with this picture.

Everything.

Several calming breaths later, I continued on down the garden. After a rudimentary search of the flowerbeds in the far left-hand corner, I spotted the disturbed shrubs and began to dig. With a gloved hand, I wiped away more layers of dirt from the remains of the decomposing Chihuahua.

Terror stricken, Mrs. Simms peered over from her side of the fence.

Miller turned toward her. "I'm afraid it looks like Happy's dead,"

How poignant that statement was when applied to my own life, I mused.

I offered her my condolences as Miller set about arresting Mr. Lazlo. Happy's owner wailed us out of the garden.

We were back at Scotland Yard by 5 P.M.

I now had the task of completing the reports before I could finally drop these files into the records department. No longer would they haunt my in-tray. After thanking Miller and Helena for their help with today's crime fighting activities, I sent them both home.

Miller expressed his admiration for my ability to get things wrapped up so quickly, and even went on to question my caffeine intake. I wondered if blue illuminate was finally kicking in. More alarming still, I'd forgotten to ask about any possible side effects.

Well it's too late now, I scolded myself.

After doing a quick Google search on the stuff and predictably coming up with nothing, I reminded myself the blood results would end up revealing what I'd put in my body. Stretching my arms out wide and twisting my back, I tried to ease the tension out of my weary limbs. If I was going to get out of here by a reasonable hour, more coffee was needed.

I grabbed a large mug of vanilla blend from the staff break room and returned to my desk. Clicking open the program, I set about documenting the day's activities in standard reports. My fingers swept over the keyboard faster than they ever had and I couldn't help wonder if I really had imbibed something magical.

Halfway through the second report, I shot to my feet.

Jadeon leaned casually against the doorjamb as though nothing was wrong with him visiting Scotland Yard. He looked beautiful, his face serene and framed in a dark flock of hair, his iridescent brown irises locked on me with that familiar intensity. One of the many reasons I'd fallen for him. I found myself melting in his presence, surrendering, *failing*.

"What are you doing here?"My heart pounded with the danger he'd put himself in.

He'd put me in.

Then it came back to me in all its painful glory. Everything he'd ever done to me. All those lies. A wave of gut wrenching betrayal made my legs go unsteady.

"How are you?" he said, looking devastatingly sincere.

A shrill shattered the quiet.

I reached for the phone. "Jansen."

From the reception desk, Constable Rutledge informed me that a gentleman was on his way up to see me. Despite the call being late, I thanked him.

And returned my focus. "What do you want?"

Jadeon raised a manila envelope.

"What is it?" I said.

"Orpheus wants you to have all the recordings." Jadeon shut the door. "Footage filmed through the fox. It's all here. I've watched it myself. You're not in any of them despite what Anaïs told you. She also lied about Orpheus threatening to send them here. That was never his intention. Anaïs also lied about us."

"Get out."

Desolation swept over his face. "Surely you don't believe—
"

"She explained everything."

Jadeon drew back, his expression aghast.

"I thought you and I weren't meant to be speaking?" I fisted my hands on my hips. "For fear of alighting the elder's wrath?"

"Your peace of mind is worth it."

"Do they know I'm still mortal?"

"I can be very persuasive."

"Manipulative."

"Actually, I'm not."

"I have evidence to the contrary."

He stood taller. "You have hearsay, which is not the same thing."

"Do you have a yacht?"

He hesitated. "Why?"

"Just asking."

"Technically, it belongs to Alex."

"Why never mention it?"

"It's not like I can take you out on it to sunbathe." He shrugged. "I bought it for Alex for his two hundredth birthday. Seemed like a reasonable gift considering the milestone. Do you want to go out on it?"

"No."

Confusion marred his face.

My glance at the wall clock warned his time was up.

He reached into his jacket pocket and removed a flash drive. "A record of Hauville's movements leading up to his disappearance."

"Anything stand out?" I said.

"I'm afraid not, but you might catch something we didn't."

"Why didn't anyone approach him? Ask him what he'd done with Beatrice?"

"We were about to when he went missing."

"That's it?"

He placed the flash drive into my palm and invisible sparks were set off merely with his touch, sending shivers into my fingers. I snapped my hand back, throwing him a glare not to try any kind of seduction.

Worry clouded his eyes. "You didn't drink blue illuminate."

My legs wobbled at the humiliation. "What?"

"Your blood test will validate—"

"How do you know about that?"

With a tilt of his head, he gave me that look. "You were minutes away from drinking it when Orpheus swapped out the bottle. He replaced blue illuminate with schnapps from the hotel bar, added Ambien, and a spot of his blood to give you an orgasm to convince everyone in the room, including you, that you had in fact just imbibed it."

I cringed; flushing brightly.

"Orpheus didn't tell Mirabelle he'd done it so that Anaïs wouldn't suspect."

"But—"

He arched a brow. "You're smart, Ingrid. You don't need some concoction to make you smarter. Besides, blue illuminate is reserved for vampires. The stuff would fry a mortal's brain."

"Why not let Anaïs know he'd switched them out?" I said.

"She's fragile. You've seen her. She's not herself. Orpheus is doing his best to help her through this difficult time."

"So Orpheus allowed those witches to put me through that for nothing?"

"He's trying to appease Anaïs." He gestured his sincerity, or attempted to. "He's trying to handle her the best way he can."

"What about me?"

"Well, your relationship with Orpheus is complicated."

I rolled my left sleeve up to reveal my circled brand. "Why did you give me this?"

"To protect you."

"You marked me as his."

"You'd stepped into a vampire's lair. They were going to either kill you or turn you, Ingrid. That saved you."

"Did you give me to Orpheus?" I said. "Is that what this is really about?"

His expression hardened, his jaw tensing. "Do you want to belong to him?'

Jadeon should have left the door open. There was no air in here.

"Ingrid?"

"I need you to leave."

"We need to talk this through."

"Out."

"At least give me the chance to—"

"Now."

He stepped forward and rested the envelope on my desk. "Don't let the memory of me become a stain on your life."

I reached for the phone. "Security will escort you."

"Listen to me—"

"We can upgrade it to SWAT if you'd prefer."

"I care deeply for you."

"You're a monster." My hand stayed on the phone. "And I'm drawing on as much reason as I can in order to deal with you."

He sucked in the deepest breath. "I will always love you."

"Then you'll be wasting your time. Like you've wasted mine."

Jadeon looked lost, and for a moment I believed he might be, and that his heart ached right alongside mine. But this was the mistake I'd made on so many occasions when I'd allowed his deception to devour my life and steal my love that he wasn't worthy of. That he could never reciprocate. His gaze swept over my office as though the words he needed lay just out of reach.

As quietly as he'd appeared he was gone.

I stared at the place where he'd been standing, the loneliness threatening to choke me, and slumped into my chair before burying my face in my hands.

CHAPTER 18

The Waldorf Hilton's grand salon had apparently been influenced by the style of Louis XVI. Or so Inspector Brooks' wife, Nadine, informed me. We sat beside each other at the senior officers' table. The charity ball was in full swing.

And I didn't want to be here.

Fine food, wine, and good company should have all added up to a pleasant evening, but I felt too riddled with guilt for taking time off. Though it was hard to feel down for long. Nadine really was the life and soul of the party. She was a forty-something stay-at-home mom. Plump and extraordinarily pretty, with long blonde hair fluffed to perfection and kind blue eyes. She had a laugh that made you smile. During the course of the evening, she'd shared with me her story, telling me she'd given up teaching to devote her life to her children and support her husband's career. It wasn't hard to tell that Nadine was a tremendous influence on Inspector Antony Brooks, and from their gestures of affection toward each other they were still very much in love. Nadine and I had read many of the same books and much of our conversation centered on literature, art, music, and our mutual love of chocolate.

The other four guests at our table knew each other well from the way they shared jokes and had an easy comfort. I recognized several of the senior officers who I'd briefly met a while back at Scotland Yard. Their wives chatted away with the familiarity of good friends.

Taking in the splendor of the high ceiling embossed with

gold, which continued down the pristine pillars surrounding us, I marveled at the grandeur. Well polished hardwood floors added to the lavishness. I really was doing my best to enjoy myself. Or at least pretend to.

I'd reluctantly dragged myself away from the recordings filmed in Hauville's office that Jadeon had given me last night. Having only made it halfway through, I still wasn't convinced I hadn't been caught in any of them. It was the only piece of evidence I had on the darker side of Hauville's case. Considering how I'd come across this footage, it would remain for my eyes only.

Distracted, I let out a long sigh.

All this luxury should have been a welcome escape from all the crazy activity I'd immersed myself in over the last few days. After all, what else would I be doing tonight? Curled up on the sofa while picking at a Chicken Tikka Masala, with my laptop open and waiting to appear on surveillance footage as the leading lady. Damning evidence that would lose me my job and put me in prison. I hoped Jadeon was right and I wasn't in any of them. My stomach was tied up in knots with the guilt of not pursuing Beatrice's disappearance. Being misled from it at every turn wrenched at my nerves and decimated my trust.

Instead of creating some genius excuse about why I couldn't make it this evening, I'd searched my closet for a suitable outfit and pulled out this long, red evening gown with a plunging back that I was currently wearing. I'd matched it with these strappy four-inch heels to complement my dress. The faux diamond bracelet on my left arm that Anaïs had given me went perfectly, though more importantly it hid my circled brand.

Some part of me wanted to prove I could move on. Though my heart hadn't gotten the memo. My thoughts kept drifting back to Jadeon. Sipping my chardonnay, I tried to convince myself I'd not made a mistake. And why was I the one feeling guilty?

I reminded myself this event sponsored one of Scotland Yard's most beloved charities, that of Salvador Moran's Children's Foundation. I'd felt compelled to donate a little myself, though by the look of the other guests all dolled up in the finest regalia money wasn't an issue for them. The men all donned black tie and the women's dresses were some of the finest I'd ever seen.

No, not the finest.

That honor went to the gathering of vampires I'd witnessed mingling within the foyer of the Athenaeum. The aristocratic nightwalkers who I'd chatted away with casually, seemingly without a care in the world. I had glimpsed such extraordinary beauty, a compelling peek into the underworld, and seen just how glamorous it could be. There had been so many striking women there that Anaïs' accusation of Jadeon taking other lovers made perfect sense. How had I ever considered I was the only one? What was I compared to these breathtaking immortals who oozed perfection and raw sexuality. My naivety knew no bounds.

Way to lift your self-esteem Ingrid, I silently berated myself.

"This event gets more posh each year," Nadine said, pulling my attention back into the room.

"This is my first time here," I said.

"You've only been at Scotland Yard a couple of months, is that right?"

"Yes, I transferred up from Salisbury."

"How do you find London?"

"I'm getting used to it. Do you enjoy living here?"

"I was born here so it's all I've ever known." She leaned in closer. "Let me know the next time you get an evening off and I'll show you the London I love."

"I'd like that."

"At least the band isn't too loud."

With a nod I agreed, grateful we could talk without having to shout over the music.

Nadine scooted closer. "From what my husband tells me you're a high-flyer, Ingrid."

I looked away.

"Don't be bashful. We need more officers like you." She narrowed her eyebrows. "I'm having such a problem watching the news these days. So much seems to be going wrong."

"The world's always been like this," I said. "Only the media makes sure we hear about it."

"That's true, I suppose." Nadine topped up her husband's wine. "I know, dear, we really should let the waiter pour, but they haven't swung by our table since the last full moon." She winked at him.

Inspector Brooks melted. I couldn't remember seeing him look so, well, normal.

It was the kind of relationship I coveted. One where you've been together so long you finish each other's sentences, fulfill each other's needs, and where you get to curl up in bed together at the end of a long day.

Distracted by my romantic musing, I took a mouthwatering bite of steamed black cod with fennel, the tomato and mushrooms enhancing the flavor. A sip of chardonnay made the taste even more delectable.

"Wonderful food, isn't it , inspector?" Nadine said, shaking me out of my foodie-trance.

"If I'm aloud to call you Nadine, please call me Ingrid."

"Such a pretty name. Why did your mother name you that?"

"After Ingrid Bergman."

"Well, you're certainly as beautiful as her. Your mother named you perfectly."

"Aren't you lovely to me," I said. "It's much more flattering to get a compliment from a woman."

"That's true. You don't know how refreshing it is for me to get out. I chopped up my husband's waffles the other day just like I do for my children. We have two sons. Dillon, who's one, and Thomas, who just turned three. I didn't even realize I'd done it." She looked over at her husband with affection. "Anthony ate it. Didn't say a word."

We shared a laugh and it drew attention our way.

Nadine went on to share the same story with the other guests at our table, delighting everyone with her self-effacing humor, which made her all the more adorable. I'd always enjoyed meeting the families of my co-workers. So much information could be garnered from merely watching their interaction with their loved ones. It was good to see Chief Inspector Brooks was liked just as much at home as he was at work.

"Could I have a quick word with your husband?" I asked.

"Of course. Let's switch places." She took my chair.

I took hers and waited for Brooks to finish the conversation he was having with Lieutenant Hailey.

"Sir," I began when I got Brooks' attention. "Anything new

from S C & O about Hauville's computer?"

"Jansen," he said, "don't you ever take the night off?"

Nadine's elbow poked my rib. She was staring across the table and her expression was one of awe.

Orpheus stood a few feet away and he was suavely dressed in black-tie, his mega-watt smile directed at me.

"Inspector Jansen," he said with a smile. "It's good to see you again."

Startled by the danger my table guests were under, not to mention the entire room, I tried to find the words to keep him calm and prevent the impending carnage.

No words came.

"Ingrid, are you going to introduce us?" Nadine asked with a glint of amusement, admiring the dashing specimen of a man before us.

Brooks shot up, pushing his chair back, and rounded the table toward Orpheus. I shot up out of my chair too, ready to assist.

"Lord Velde, it's good to see you, sir." Brooks proffered his hand to Orpheus and shook it. "How are you?"

They patted each other's backs in a gesture of manly greeting. These two had met before, so it seemed, and from their demeanor they appeared to like each other.

What the hell?

"Chief Inspector," Orpheus said. "I see you've bought your lovely wife." His smile hit its mark and Nadine's eyes widened in wonder, her face flushing.

"Would you do me the honor?" Orpheus offered his hand to me. "Dance."

Nadine poked me again, blinking her excitement.

"Sorry, can't." I sat back down. "My shoe. Strap issue." I gave him an *oh well* look and feigned interest in my napkin, folding it several times like I'd taken up origami. For goodness sake. I aimed for my best stony-face, hoping to give nothing away. If there was one thing I knew how to do well it was this. How many times had I needed to feign nothing fazed me, like when I sat through a suspect's confession.

Orpheus strolled around to my side and knelt at my feet. His left hand discreetly slid up my calf and beneath my dress as his right hand feigned fixing the shoe strap with the same ease that I'd faked it was broken. My foot tingled as his fingers ran along the strap, caressing, sending shivers up my spine.

Displaying the same elegance with which he'd knelt, Orpheus rose with a predator's grace and held out his hand again. "There, that should do it." He gave a wry smile.

"Ingrid, we won't let you say no," Nadine said.

From Brooks' glare, he wasn't letting me off the hook either. I threw my head back in what I hoped was a convincing laugh and accepted Orpheus' hand. He squeezed mine tight and led the way through the pathway of tables toward the dance floor.

"How are you?" he said.

"I'm not doing this," I whispered.

"Yes," he said. "You are."

We stepped up onto the raised area.

My thoughts scattered, an action drill forming in my mind of how I was going to handle the moment when Orpheus started attacking each and every person in the room.

"Bit defensive," he said.

"Just doing my job to protect everyone."

"Talking of deadly, you look stunning."

Making a passing sweep of the many faces, I imagined a strategy.

"Ingrid, I'm insulted."

I glared at him.

"I'm merely removing you from your third glass of chardonnay," he said. "The last thing anyone needs is a tipsy Ingrid grabbing the mic and singing karaoke. Trust me, they'll be begging for a quick death." He wrapped his left arm around my waist and pulled me into him. "You've been a little unpredictable lately. I'm looking out for you."

"Unpredictable?"

"Yes, I'm taking into account driving to Cornwall in a stolen vehicle."

"But I—"

"My Viper, to be specific. If that wasn't bad enough for Scotland Yard's finest and brightest, you went on to top it by imbibing in an unknown substance."

His body felt all hard muscle and uncompromising, and I

was powerless to resist. Three other couples danced around us, helping to shield us from prying eyes.

Orpheus' chest pressed firmly against mine. His expensive cologne sparked all my senses, as though trying to convince me this was a good idea. His left hand rested on my lower spine where the dip of the dress ended, touching naked flesh and sending shivers of electricity between my thighs. In this slow dance, his left cheek was close to mine. His masterful hold swayed us slowly to a rendition of Etta James' *At Last*.

I am out of my mind to let this happen.

I was dancing with Orpheus at a high-profile event, wavering between the need to arrest him and the desire to get away. Never had a more surreal moment found me. These two worlds I'd managed to keep separate clashed in the worst kind of way. This nightmare played out in slow motion. His grip tightened, reminding me of his strength, and his temperament that, if provoked, could become depraved.

"What are you doing here?" I said.

"This is my party, Ingrid. I run the Salvador Moran Foundation."

My jaw dropped, shocked that Scotland Yard was unwittingly sponsoring a compromised charity.

"My work to protect orphans goes back centuries," he said. "It's my finest obsession. Other than you, of course."

"I look forward to taking more of an interest in your extracurricular activity."

He yanked me against him. "Be a good girl."

"Sure, if you drop the theatrics."

"Word of advice, remember who you're talking to." His lips brushed over my cheek.

My legs weakened and he sensed it, his fingers splaying over my lower back until I'd found my balance again. The chardonnay hit me. I regretted putting myself in harm's way by compromising my agility. Orpheus was the last person I'd imagined seeing tonight and I wasn't exactly dressed for combat.

"You look beautiful," he said, as though trying to soothe my rambling thoughts.

"Strange how a tux camouflages."

"If this is your attempt to arouse me it's working."

"Let me go."

"I like it when you fight me."

I flushed. *It's the wine,* I reassured myself. I'd failed to censor my booze intake.

"I imagine you wish you were dancing in Jadeon's arms," he said softly.

I pushed thoughts of Jadeon away and rested my head on Orpheus's shoulder. It was better this way. I didn't want him reading my expression, and if a dance was all he wanted he could have it. Not that I had any choice.

"You will never be off the hook, Orpheus," I whispered, "for what you did to those girls."

"Boring doesn't suit you, Ingrid."

"Listen to me," I snapped. "I'm only placating you in order to protect the public. God knows how they'd react if they knew about…"

"Vampires?"

"Shush."

"If I really disgust you that much why are you so aroused right now?"

My breath caught in my throat. *"Because you're using that preternatural sexual manipulation to turn me on,"* I silently berated him

"Actually I'm not," he whispered close to my ear. "I don't need to."

A jolt of pleasure slithered up my spine. "I'm warning you."

"Ever considered that's just your natural attraction to me making you so wet?"

I went to pull away.

He yanked me back.

A dull throb settled between my legs and I realized it was useless to fight him. This was Orpheus, and from all I knew about him resistance wasn't an option. I had no choice but to relax and let him lead the dance, lead me.

"That's more like it," he cooed.

The song changed to something more angst ridden, though I wasn't really listening to that female vocalist singing about lost loves and painful pasts. I was too caught up in this moment and struggling with this urge, this inner voice coaxing me to succumb.

His hold tightened. "From what I hear your last meeting with Jadeon didn't go so well."

"Anaïs has been very informative."

"She's desperate, Ingrid. She'd tell you anything to get you to help her."

I lifted my head to look at him. "I don't like being manipulated."

"You weren't by Jadeon. Ever. Although I do admit to being guilty of it as far as you're concerned, but then again you're a challenge I can't resist. The chase is too alluring." He stepped back, turning on his heel with my hand in his, and led me across the dance floor toward a table.

With a nod from him, the three couples sitting there rose and took to the dance floor, allowing Orpheus and I privacy. He pulled out a chair and waited for me to sit.

He took the one beside it. "Shall I order you some coffee?"

"No, thank you," I said.

Orpheus stared down at my bracelet. "How very decadent."

I traced the stones along the gold band. "Anaïs gave it to me."

"That's quite a bit of bling." He broke into a smile.

My gaze shot to it.

"You're looking at a million pounds worth of diamonds. At least."

I lowered my arm, having had no idea the thing was real. *Oh God*, I'd blatantly flashed the thing in front of a table full of Scotland Yard's finest. I hoped it wasn't frickin stolen.

"Anaïs really does love you." He shrugged a shoulder. "She has a funny way of showing it, I know. See it from her point of view. She's angry with me for not resolving this issue fast enough."

"You have to find Beatrice. I first heard about this a week ago and so far no one has any leads." I shook my head. "How long exactly has she been missing? Three weeks?"

"We're pouring all our resources into it, I can assure you."

"So I'm told." I shook my head. "It's not enough. You need me."

"Out of the question."

"You're losing precious time. Keeping me out of this is a mistake."

"Putting you in danger is the mistake."

"You and Jadeon are both so stubborn."

"You have no idea how much your words hurt him." Orpheus reached over for the decanter and poured a tall glass of water. Ice clinked into the tumbler.

"That wasn't my intention." I took the glass from him, my mouth dry and thirsting.

"You called him a monster."

Oh, fuck. I did.

Caressing my brow, I tried to ease this throb in my forehead.

"Do you remember the evening you first met him?" He rested an elbow on the table and twisted to face me. "Let me refresh your memory. I sent you the postcard of Raphael's portrait of Saint Catherine of Alexandria, with the invitation written on the back to attend the gallery at a specific time. I knew it would stir your intrigue and you'd visit the National Gallery. After tracking Jadeon's every move for two centuries, I knew he'd be admiring the same portrait. The one on your postcard at that very same time you were meant to be there. He's a creature of habit. Well, was."

"You set us up."

"I thought you'd end up arresting him and that would be the end of that." He raised a hand. "I don't need to bore you with how it backfired and you're now his lover and not mine. Your obsession with Jadeon is more than evident. I will tell you this though, *you* seduced Jadeon."

I shot a look at the tables around us, hoping no one was eavesdropping.

"Jadeon walked away from you in the gallery, remember?" Orpheus gave a nod to confirm. "You pursued him into the next room. You were like a hummingbird flittering before him. You wouldn't go away. Ingrid, it was you who asked Jadeon out to dinner that night. Evidently, you were very persuasive."

Conceding there may have been some truth in this, my shoulders slumped in defeat.

"Imagine that," he said. "Totally out of character. You certainly had me impressed."

"Jadeon introduced me to the curator—"

"Mr. Teddington."

The very first night I'd laid eyes on Jadeon had changed my life forever. Had I been told he'd been sculptured out of rare marble by a master craftsman I'd have believed it. Majestic in the way he moved; an unmatched grace in both his physicality and heart. Whatever I thought I knew about vampires this wasn't it. He was a supernatural God in all his perfection.

That night in the gallery I'd been smitten at first sight. Jadeon walking away and me never seeing him again had stirred an uncommon panic, alighting a dark yearning, a fear this chance would never be repeated. I'd never dared to question it. The meeting had felt so spontaneous, fortuitous even. And now Orpheus was admitting to arranging our rendezvous and fracturing the innocence of that night. It all made sense now.

"Coming back to you?" Orpheus said dryly.

"But Anaïs told me—"

"A bit of truth interwoven with a lie." He shrugged. "Mostly lies."

"You were never going to send that footage of me to Scotland Yard?"

"There is no footage of you."

"Why are you here?"

"For Jadeon."

"Since when have you ever cared about him?" My words felt scratchy in my throat as I remembered Anaïs telling me they were indeed close. Close enough to continue this manipulation? Drag out this cat and mouse game that was destroying my life?

"Having sired Jadeon, I feel his every emotion," Orpheus said. "It was fun for a while. Well two-hundred years to be exact, considering that was how long I tortured him. But I'm over it now, and with that in mind I know I have no right to say this but, hell, you deserve the truth."

"Which is?"

"Jadeon loves you. He always has and always will. I know what the elders have demanded of him. It's an impossible request considering the magnetic pull between you both. Jadeon's been working to find a way through their demands so you can be together."

"He has?"

"Very much so."

I held my breath. "Are vampires capable of love?"

He looked affronted. "We feel love deeper than any mortal."

The tang of lemon water tasted bitter, like the bitterness of this ruse.

"Two-hundred years ago, a young lord was turned into a nightwalker, as was his younger brother." He was talking about Jadeon and Alex, his tone low, bleak. "My hate for Jadeon went so deep that I took from him what he loved the most." Orpheus lowered his gaze, the intensity burning as his words unfolded. "I kidnapped Jadeon's childhood sweetheart, Catherine De Mercy. Jadeon pursued her by tracking me. He followed us to every corner around the world, searching us out. As his sire I held the advantage, always knowing where he was at any given moment, and could evade him easily."

It was impossible to hide my horror.

"Jadeon never gave up, Ingrid. Despite Catherine choosing the church over him long before I took her. Jadeon sacrificed every waking hour to save her. For two centuries. Now if that's not love, I don't know what is."

"Why are you telling me this?" But I knew, and the pain I'd caused Jadeon found its way back to me.

"The reason you're still mortal is because of Jadeon."

The blur lifted; memories that had lingered out of reach for so long now cleared perfectly like a fog dissipating from the darkest dawn.

"Catherine still chose the church over him," Orpheus said. "And even after everything he'd been through Jadeon gave her his blessing."

"Where is she now?"

"I have no idea. She and I don't exactly see eye to eye."

"Do you feel remorse?"

He breathed in a long cleansing breath and his expression changed to unreadable.

"I'm considering the source," I said. "How can I trust you?"

Orpheus' focus locked on something across the room and he pushed to his feet. "That's why he's here."

Across the sea of candlelit tables, standing in the

entranceway, was another well-dressed guest. An exotic vision of loveliness that was Professor Lucas Azir. He too wore a tux, his dark eyes sweeping the room, searching for someone, searching for *us*.

My focus snapped back to Orpheus. "How has Jadeon forgiven you?"

"We are brothers. Not of blood and flesh, but of an order that goes beyond your understanding."

I tried to comprehend his words.

He looked resigned, as though about to share something with me.

I held my breath.

"Ingrid, I was out of control. I was wreaking havoc. Jadeon stopped me in my tracks and all that happened between him and I changed me. Irrevocably. For someone over four-hundred-years-old and stuck in my ways this is a small miracle."

"Are you trying to tell me I don't have to be frightened of you anymore?"

"You reminded me of Sunaria. That was why I obsessed over you."

"So now you have her again I'm safe?"

"It all depends how you define safe."

"You like playing with me, don't you?"

Orpheus' hand squeezed my shoulder. "Jadeon better make you *his* fast."

"Why do you say that?"

"If he doesn't claim you soon, I will." Orpheus threw a wave to Lucas. "Goodnight, Ingrid."

Caught in the wake of Orpheus' presence, the imprint of his body against mine lingering from our dance, my face flushed from the residual burn of those fierce hazel eyes. His saunter was that of a man of prestige, a man of wealth, an easy confidence garnering looks of admiration. Goose bumps rose on my forearms and I felt the full effect of being this close to an interminable force of nature.

He and Lucas were too far away for me to catch what they were saying. After sharing a few words and a shake of hands, Orpheus strolled toward the exit, nodding here and there at the other guests, his authority evident.

Lucas made his way over to me and I rose to greet him.

"This is all very nice." Lucas gave a smile. "May I?" He gestured to the chair next to mine. The very same one Orpheus had been sitting in moments before.

Despite the joy of seeing Lucas, I still felt wary. Trust was a long way off.

"Wine?" Lucas looked around for a waiter.

"No, thank you." I glanced back at the pathway Orpheus had taken.

"I'm glad you can see firsthand the good work O is doing." Lucas motioned to the room. "All of the funds go directly to his charity."

"O?"

"Term of endearment," he said. "I forgot myself."

"I'll take a rain check on advocating for his sainthood, if you don't mind."

"Well, I wouldn't go that far."

"Considering there's a ban on vampires interacting with me, I'm one lucky lady." I raised my brows in mock indignation.

Lucas went to answer and something caught his eye.

Nadine stood before our table. "Ingrid, I hope I'm not interrupting."

Lucas rose to his feet to greet her.

"Of course not," I said, standing too.

"We're off," she said. "Apparently something has come up that Antony has to attend to back at Scotland Yard." Her gaze found Lucas. "Ingrid, where are you keeping all these dashing men hidden?"

Lucas took Nadine's hand and kissed it.

She blushed. "And here I was thinking it was impossible to meet any decent gentleman in London."

"Thank you for making this evening so lovely," I said.

"I feel the same way." She caught her husband's smile. "Must dash. I'll get Antony to give you my email if that's okay?"

"I'd love that."

"Are you on Facebook?"

I shook my head. "Last thing I need is one more way for criminals to keep track of me."

"Hadn't thought of that," Nadine said. "Take care." She

threw Lucas and I a wave goodbye and rejoined her husband.

Scrutinizing Chief Inspector Brooks' expression, I wondered what might be so important to pull him away from this event. Maybe this was his way of making a polite extraction.

My attention fell back onto Lucas. "Orpheus asked you here?"

"We've all been worried about you," he said. "Even Orpheus."

"Well I'm fine." I rubbed my forehead, mortified with how the last few days had gone and the fact that everyone seemed to know about it.

"Orpheus drags me to these things because he loves to see me squirm," Lucas said. "He knows I'd much prefer to be digging up bones. Oh dear, what does that say about me?"

"You're adorable."

"This Hauville situation has us all shaken up."

"Apparently Jaden and Orpheus are investigating it," I said. "Reading minds is an advantage."

"Undoubtedly. It's good to see you." Lucas held my hands in his. "Don't want to embarrass you in front of your friends," he let go and took in the room, "colleagues."

"Never."

"Good. It's just that when I heard you'd felt betrayed by us my heart broke. Quite literally. You've been nothing but a friend to us."

"Really?" I sat back. "Then why do I feel I've become a burden?"

"Would you like to take a walk?"

With a nod I conceded that a walk would be a nice distraction. After retrieving my purse from my table and saying goodbye to the remaining guests, I headed out arm in arm with Lucas.

Lucas edged me along faster. "Time is of the essence, so please forgive me for my lack of small talk."

"What's going on?"

"Understand this," he whispered. "With Dominion taking his seat of power there came many changes in our constitution. All for the better. But change is never easy and there is always resistance."

"What are you saying?"

"You're life is threatened by those who would see the fall of Dominion."

A cold sweat came over me.

"We've all tried to keep you a secret. Protect you. Should your relationship with Dominion become known it would have disastrous consequences."

"That's why Jadeon pretended he didn't know me when I visited the Athenaeum?"

Lucas pulled me toward the elevator. "Don't go back there." He summoned the lift with the push of a button.

"Well, you needn't worry," I said. "Jadeon and I are over." I brushed a stray hair out of my face. "Orpheus explained everything, but after what I said to Jadeon he must hate me."

The elevator opened and Lucas shuffled me in with him.

Assuming we were using the lift for privacy, I relaxed a little and leaned against the glass wall. "Are you staying here?"

"I do sometimes. But not tonight."

The lift ascended.

"Don't ever mention the Athenaeum again," Lucas said. "Ever."

"What are they keeping in there?"

Fear marred his face. "If they even knew you had an inkling—"

"But that's just it. I don't. I only saw a library."

He placed a plastic keycard into my palm. "God knows how much I love you. I'd hate to see anything bad happen to you."

"What's this?"

The lift came to a stop and the doors slid open.

"Your last chance to speak with the only person who can help you." He nudged me out onto the floor and stepped back in. He punched the button for his descent. "Suite 877."

The doors closed, the lift taking him away from me.

Standing alone on the eighth floor, I stared at the Waldorf's keycard.

CHAPTER 19

The indicator flashed green when I swiped the keycard to access room 877.

In the far corner, a golden lampshade threw a soft illumination. The vastness of a penthouse with vintage-styled wallpaper stretched out before me. Persian rugs were scattered here and there and the usual touches of luxury, like the plush sectional sofa with matching armchairs. A dining room table was surrounded by six high-backed chairs. Windows ran along the far wall, all of them rising from the floor to the ceiling, their dramatic green drapes drawn back to reveal London's shadowy nightscape.

I recognized that distinctive gait. That height, those broad shoulders, and an intensity that even with Jadeon's back to me sent me reeling. From where he had been staring out of the central window, he turned slowly.

Lowering his gaze, he held mine.

Here was my second chance. An opportunity to explain and mend the damage. Take back those things I'd accused him of. Jadeon's stare followed mine down the corridor and into the bedroom, the end of a four-poster bed showing. A luxurious burgundy bedspread hung low.

"Orpheus?" Jadeon said, cringing.

"I didn't know you'd be here," I said.

Head down, Jadeon strolled past me and went for the door.

"Wait."

He gripped the door handle. "I had no part in this."

"I'm sorry—"

"Ingrid, you have every right to be angry with me." He gave a nod. "I should never have invited you to St. Michaels."

"Jadeon, please—"

The door closed and I was alone again. The quiet leeched in from the stillness, reaching into my bones.

Running through the suite, my stomach lurching, threatening to spill its meal, I thrust my hand over my mouth, desperately scouring for the bathroom and cursing each wrong room.

I dry heaved into the toilet, retching until my stomach could take no more, then I collapsed beside it, my strength fading. Jadeon's haunting look of pain was too much to bear. The white marble floor, the white towels folded into perfection, and that enormous sunken bath were so far removed from my world of the ordinary. I struggled to push back feelings of inadequacy. I didn't belong here.

Curled up on the bathroom floor, my tears wet the tile beneath my face. I lay in a heap staring at nothing. I cursed at my inability to find the words that might have persuaded him to stay.

Love; at times it seemed this was the only thread of commonality that Jadeon and I had. So many times I had questioned why I was unable to let him go, why was it impossible to forget him. His beauty had been an obvious draw, but his kindness, his humor, his intelligence had all be traits I admired. The profoundness of having lived through two centuries, having all those experiences, and his continued willingness to share what he had learned with those in his life. His generosity toward his friends and family, his unending desire to make their lives a little easier, endeared him to me. He was a true leader, a man of the people, and I still believed I could be a part of his new life.

His embrace, his kiss, his enduring affection, how would I learn to live without him? This ache twisting in my heart would never lift.

A knock at the door startled me.

Rising from the floor and wiping away tears, I hoped Jadeon had changed his mind and had come back to me. Hands clenched into fists, I willed myself not to mess this chance up again. I had to let him see what he meant to me. I refused to live in a world where he played no part in it.

Opening the door and peeking left and right, I saw no one. My heart sunk and that awful ache came back to me. Closing the door, I gave myself a few moments to gather my thoughts, assuming I'd imagined the knock. I needed to hear it.

The room fell dark.

Backing up, I tried to discern what I was looking at on the ceiling. I strained to keep up with movement zigzagging toward me. My heart thundering and my hands shook as I fumbled my way.

I almost tripped on my own feet.

He landed with a thud and flew at me, forming a chokehold with his hands around my throat. This monk-like figure squeezed all air from me. His soulless black eyes stared back with an expressionless face. His breath was stale. My gasps were the only sound, my windpipe disallowing any air. I dug my thumbs into the creature's eye sockets.

He flung me across the floor and I tumbled backward, losing my balance, crashing onto the coffee table. Pain shot through my skull. Dazed, on my hands and knees, I crawled away, my limbs weak and useless. Blood trickled down my forehead and reached my eyes.

Dragging me toward the window, he slammed me against it with such force it cracked the glass. Another smash. My scream was silenced as he shoved again. He was relentless, and my forehead hit the pane over and over as my hands pressed into its coldness. Tell-tale spider webs fractured the glass, leading to the deadliest fall.

Another shove.

Another sound of someone crashing into the room. Those hands lifted off me, then blackness flooded my senses and stole my consciousness.

I awoke in Jadeon's arms.

"You're safe now," he said, hugging me against his chest.

Looking around us, my throat constricted in terror.

"He's gone," Jadeon said.

I caressed my forehead to feel for that cut yet felt nothing.

"Healed," he said, alluding to bestowing a drop of blood on my wound.

With his help I climbed to my feet, taking in the surrounding mess of scattered glass, a green velvet curtain off its rail, and that coffee table pushed out of place. The thought of the hotel staff finding all this sent a wave of angst.

"We'll take care of it," he said.

I reached around Jadeon's waist for support, feeling bruised and shaken. "Who attacked me?"

"Later."

Despite needing answers, he was right. I felt too weak to tackle that at the moment. "What if he comes back?"

"We've posted guards."

Yet something in his demeanor hinted that might not be enough.

He led me into the bathroom. My reflection kept nothing from me. My hair was disheveled, matching my expression. My mascara was smudged beneath tired and frightened eyes. I shuddered at how close I'd come to going through that window. My dress was twisted, creased, and stained in blood.

Jadeon didn't have a reflection.

He caught my look of surprise and waved it off, showing he was used to it.

I turned my back on the mirror. "Cold water gets blood stains out," I blurted. "Hot water cooks it into the material."

Jadeon gave a crooked smile. "I'll bear that in mind." He wet the face cloth under the faucet and dabbed it across my forehead.

"Not that you do your own washing."

"No."

I nudged away his hand. "You should have warned me."

He lifted me up and sat me on the bathroom counter. "And have you looking over your shoulder every five minutes?" He held me firmly by my shoulders, his stare insistent he was right.

"At least I'd have been prepared," I said. "How long has he been trying to kill me?"

He looked away.

"Jadeon."

"Since you turned up at the Athenaeum."

My throat tightened. "You've kept him away from me?"

"Until today, yes."

"But aren't you Dominion?" I said. "Aren't you meant to have some kind of authority?"

"He's from the old guard." Jadeon looked solemn. "I'm dealing with this as diplomatically as I can with the elders. It's a delicate process. We're bringing a thousand year old tradition into the 21st century and there's bound to be a jerk reaction."

"I didn't see anything at that place," I said. "Just a library. That's it."

"I know."

The memory of that vampire's pale face flashed before me again and I cringed. "Who is he?"

"A guardian."

"Of what?"

"It doesn't concern you."

"It does now. Well, are you going to tell me what I nearly died for?"

"You must believe me when I tell you you're safer not knowing."

"They think I know what's hidden in that place. Isn't that the same thing?"

"No, it's not."

My lips trembled when I envisioned that sheer drop. "Does Orpheus know I'm in danger?"

"Of course."

I wondered if Orpheus might have better protected me. His ruthlessness was legendary, his ability to do whatever it took without compromising. No doubt he would never have let that monk leave the room alive.

Jadeon reached for my arm and slid up the bracelet. His fingertips caressed my circled brand. "I hate you having this."

"I thought it was meant to protect me."

"Your bracelet covered it." His jaw flexed with tension. "Not that it would have made any difference. Your attempted murder is connected to me."

I repositioned the bracelet over my brand. "I can't keep this. Orpheus told me these are real diamonds." My gaze shot to his. "Anaïs gave it to me."

His expression hardened. "I'm taking you home."

"You can't order me around."

"Say it."

"Say what?"

"Ask me."

I hesitated and then relented; anxiety rose in my voice. "I'm not your only lover, am I?"

He stared past me, his expression taut as though studying his lack of reflection. I resented the seconds that went by pretending to be hours.

"Am I just one of many?" I said.

"You know me better than that."

I slid off the marbled counter. "I don't know what to believe anymore."

"Ingrid, I want a lifetime of sunsets and sunrises for you."

"Don't you see if I can't have you than all of that is meaningless?" I let out a sob. "Am I anything to you?"

Jadeon eased me back against the wall and held me there. "While you are in this world there can be no one else for me." He rested a fingertip to my lips. "There has been no one else." His forehead rested against mine and his grip tightened around my waist. "I've tried not to love you, believe me. It's more trouble than it's worth."

"No one else?"

"Just you, my darling. Only you."

His hardness grew against my belly and I felt that low thrum below intensifying, wanting him inside me. "Make love to me." I dug my fingernails into his forearms. "I can't bare this emptiness any longer."

His hand reached beneath my dress, sliding up and along my thigh, and he tore my thong free; the snap stung my flesh. That welcome flash of pain proved he really was here.

My breath caught as his blazing stare burned through me with a dark craving. This was where I wanted to be, here, with him and I cherished every moment, every second, of being close to him. Jadeon was the most beautiful man I've ever met, and beneath these soft lights he looked so unyielding and yet so fragile, reminding me why I'd fallen so heavily for him.

"Promise me something," I said.

He lowered his gaze.

"Say it." I grabbed his arms. "I need to hear you say the

words."

"I will find a way for us to be together." His breathing was hard, his face full of lust, an unbridled need surging through him. He gripped my shoulders and spun me around to face the wall. My fingers splayed against the cold tile, but I lifted my hands only for him to raise my gown up and over my head before throwing it to the ground. He nestled into the nape of my neck, bestowing relentless kisses down my left shoulder then the right, kissing down my back as he reached for my bra strap to unclip it then ease it down my arms and off. Turning to face him again, my hands ruffled through his lush dark locks.

He lowered his head, his mouth drawing upon a nipple, sucking, dragging his teeth along it. His tongue lavished affection on one while his fingers tweaked the other.

"I love you," he whispered in-between teasing. "You're in my every waking thought."

"I can't live without you." My fingernails dug into his firm chest. "I refuse to live without you. Whatever the danger."

His fangs were at my throat, grazing my flesh. "No more recklessness." His mouth found mine, our battling tongues fighting each other for domination. "That isn't a request."

"There you go again ordering me around."

He held my chin up with a fingertip. "You're bound to me. If you're truly ready to become my mate you will do as I say."

With his left hand, he gripped both of my wrists and pinned my hands high above my head and imprisoned them there. With his right hand he reached low between my thighs, nudging past that cleft and massaging my clit with a firm finger, preventing my words and leaving them unspoken. His full attention was upon delivering mind-blowing circling strokes to the center of my universe, making that secret place need him, yearn for his touch never to cease.

Weakly, I whispered, "Trying to find another way to control me?"

He was unrelenting in strumming my clit, flicking ever faster. "I do control you." Keeping this steady rhythm, he pressed his chest against mine and kissed me, stealing my breath away with an unmatched fierceness, his tongue lashing mine, punishing.

I was close to coming.

The thought flashed through my mind that this was all he would give me, this pleasuring and nothing more. I moaned my fear.

"Oh, Ingrid," he said sternly, close to my ear, "you can be assured I'm going to be fucking you tonight. Hard."

The frisson in my chest shot to my groin and my pussy clenched in expectation.

"But not in here," he said, guiding me into the bedroom with my hand in his.

Dazed and struggling to keep up with his determined pace, I trotted behind him, my thighs trembling with the sensations that still tingled from his touch.

Hardly noticing the luxury bedroom, I vaguely took in the king size bed with its burgundy bedspread fluffed and welcoming. Thick drapes pulled across floor to ceiling windows. A dark wooden dresser stood against one wall. A chaise longue sat in the corner and several armchairs. Elegant and simple and understated.

Naked and vulnerable, I sat on the edge of the bed watching Jadeon make quick work of undressing, until he stood before me glorious in his nakedness. His erection hard and ready and primal in its length. This perfect creature of the night promised the darkest of pleasures. My heart felt so fragile, threatening to shatter if I ever lost him.

"Stop thinking," he demanded.

And he neared me, pushing me back up onto the bed until he lay upon me, his hands holding mine above my head again, pressing them into the mattress. How I had coped with us being apart I didn't know. Couldn't understand how I had managed to go on without knowing this man was in my life. His firm sculptured chest pressed against mine, his virile scent alighting my every desire.

I wrapped my legs around his waist, swooning as his hardness caressed along my cleft, stroking against that wetness as though gauging my readiness.

"God, you are beautiful," he said.

With one thrust he entered me, filling me, stretching me wide, sending shockwaves of pleasure through me. Crying out with desire, my hands wrapped around his shoulders to hold him tighter. I gasped in time with his thrusts.

He stilled and raised himself onto his elbows. "I need to know you're safe. Give me this one thing."

Rocking my hips, I demanded he resume. "Only when you give me what I want."

Jadeon grabbed a fist full of my locks and eased my head back, exposing my throat. He coveted my blood. I knew it.

"Ask," he said.

"I want you."

He thrust with a relentless pace, punishing me with pleasure. "You will always belong to me." His mouth pressed against my throat, licking, threatening a bite. His tongue teased my flesh.

"I belong to you."

"And you will do as I say." His fangs grazed my skin.

"Yes." Shuddering in ecstasy, I buried my face in the crook of his neck, no longer able to fight it, fight him, succumbing to his demand of me as his mouth found mine again and he bruised my lips, opening them wider to master me.

"Look at me when you come," he said huskily.

Our limbs entwined, my hair whipping to either side of my head as he cupped my rear for better control, driving into me deeply, his body pounding against mine. The sound of our sex slapping each others mingled with our moans of desire.

"Your eyes on mine," he demanded. "When you come."

Shockwaves of pleasure burst from me. My internal muscles drew more of him into me and snatched my breath away. His cock molded perfectly inside of me, withdrawing and slamming back into me with frenzied passion.

He stilled above, the warmth of all he had to give sending more spasms of pleasure, making my orgasm go on and on and on. A thousand little earthquakes fractured within and without, causing me to shake violently and come hard.

Coming together, I kept my eyes upon his and disappeared into his immortal gaze.

Undone...

Unbidden, I was completely his.

CHAPTER 20

Stirring from the deepest sleep, I reached out across the bed for Jadeon.

I'd not slept this well in what felt like months. We had drifted off in each other's arms and dreamt our way to separate sides. I craved to be close again, feel his warmth and snuggle into his chest. His masculine scent lingered on my pillow, stirring memories and sending a thrill of contentment up my spine.

My hand slid over an empty sheet.

The bedside clock flashed a fluorescent 3.00 A.M.

The starkness of last night came flooding back, the memory of being attacked and what followed. A night of passionate lovemaking with Jadeon. Why could nothing in my life ever be simple? Despite Jadeon healing the cuts, there were bruises around my body and I ached from where I'd hit that window. I ran a fingertip over the sorest spot on my forehead and flinched, hoping it didn't look as bad as it felt. I pulled the sheet off with me and wrapped it around by body, assuming my dress was still in the bathroom.

Peering at my reflection in the wall mirror, I saw a faint contusion on my upper right forehead. Makeup and a lock of hair would conceal it. My clothes would hide the other bruises on my arms and legs. After falling into Jadeon's arms, I'd soon forgotten about these telltale reminders of my fight for life. There was no doubt that if Jadeon hadn't returned to the room I'd be dead.

Hearing voices, I cautiously made my way out of the bedroom.

Orpheus leaned back against the wall and Jadeon huddled close to him. Their exchange sounded brisk. They were arguing.

Jadeon spun round to look at me. "I didn't want to wake you."

"What's going on?" I said.

"He's leaving," Jadeon said.

I pulled the sheet tight around me.

Jadeon came closer and kissed my forehead. "Go back to bed, my darling. This won't take long."

My body tensed, my mistrust rising. "What won't?"

Orpheus neared me. "I'm sorry for this interruption. I am really."

"Why is he here?" I recognized my bag on the couch.

"A change of clothes from your flat," Orpheus said.

"Which she won't need," Jadeon said tersely.

"You went to my place?" I said.

Recalling all we'd shared last night, all those words of affection and those same feelings of surrendering, of vulnerability, now turned on me in all its karmic glory.

Jadeon reached for my shoulders. "Nothing has changed between us."

"One of my Gothicas was found dead a few hours ago in Holland Park," Orpheus said.

"I thought all of your Gothicas left the country?" I said.

"So did I." Orpheus frowned.

Of course I'd gotten that piece of information from Henry, Jadeon's driver, and from their silence I imagined both of them were gleaning that piece of info from my thoughts right now.

"It's an unfortunate incident," Jadeon said.

"Fuck that," Orpheus said. "This is Hauville's doing."

"Is her body in Scotland Yard's morgue?" Then I realized. "That's why Brooks left early last night."

"Her name is Eden." Orpheus looked devastated. "I thought she was safe."

"Why didn't you say anything?" I asked Jadeon.

"He didn't know," Orpheus said.

"I have to get to work," I said.

185

"No." Jadeon looked vexed. "It's too dangerous."

"Are you saying I can't go in?"

"Yes, that's exactly what I'm saying."

"You can't ask that of me."

"Last night," Jadeon said, "we agreed you'd do everything I asked of you."

I went for my bag and rummaged through the selection of clothes that Orpheus had picked out for me. Considering he'd probably been in a hurry he'd not done too badly. I could turn up in any of these and not look out of place.

Jadeon nudged up against me. "Ingrid, listen to me—"

"We need her on this," Orpheus said.

Jadeon grabbed my arm. "I'm taking you to St. Michael's where you will stay until this is over."

Looking at Jadeon's distraught face, I understood, really I did. What we'd shared last night had brought us closer than we'd ever been and I feared doing anything that might threaten all we'd become. Still, Orpheus was right. This case had dragged on too long and I'd been held at arm's length from the facts.

Jadeon shook his head, as though denying to himself I'd already made up my mind.

"You know this makes sense," I told him.

He glared at Orpheus. "If anything happens to her."

"Get dressed," Orpheus said. "I'll drive you in."

"You keep us informed, understand?" Jadeon snapped.

"It goes both ways," I said.

I hurried to the bathroom and changed into the black slacks, white shirt, and pumps that Orpheus had bought over. I'd have time to touch up my makeup in the car. The idea that Orpheus had explored my flat to extract these few personal items left me uneasy. Yet again he'd proven his sense of entitlement. It caught me off guard that I'd also never seen him this shaken. Eden's death had rattled him.

On the way out of the room, I gestured to the smashed window. "How are we going to explain this to the hotel staff?"

"You needn't worry." Jadeon ushered me out. "Orpheus owns this hotel."

"You own the Waldorf?" It came out high-pitched, embarrassingly so.

"Along with half of London," Jadeon said flatly.

"Let's not bore her with all that," Orpheus said. "Anyway, you own most of Cornwall, Artimas."

In a daze from that revelation, they escorted me down to the hotel exit.

During the journey through London, Orpheus drove the Viper hard, and with little traffic we made our way across the city without hindrance.

When Hauville went missing, so did their only lead. Scotland Yard's case and theirs matched up, equaling pretty much nothing to go on. Hauville had managed to evade these two, which really did point to the fact he'd either left the country or was indeed dead. Right up until Eden's death.

The closeness of last night's precious hours that Jadeon and I had shared had to be forgotten now. We had to focus all our energy on this murder.

After another berating from Jadeon, I was finally allowed to exit the car.

At 4:00 A.M. Scotland Yard was still a bustling place, with phones ringing off the hook, civilian staff scurrying around, and uniformed men and woman going about their usual routine as they worked through their night shift.

Making my way toward Brooks' office, I ran through possible excuses I would use when he asked how I'd learned of this girl's death. I wasn't supposed to know about it yet.

I paused in the doorway when I saw Dr. Russell sitting in a corner chair. "May I come in?"

Brooks narrowed his gaze. "Jansen, what the hell are you doing here?"

"You know this place, sir. Nothing is kept secret for long," I said, entering. "Great party last night." I looked over at Riley. "You were missed."

"I was on call," Riley said.

"You heard about our Jane Doe then?" Brooks said, swapping a wary glance with Riley. "Our good doctor here is about to perform the postmortem." Brooks pointed to an empty chair.

I sat where he pointed, my eyes moving from Brooks to Riley and back again. "What do we have so far?"

"Jansen, I don't remember assigning you to this?" Brooks said.

"I'd love to help in any way I can," I offered.

"A dog walker found the body a few hours ago in Holland Park," Riley said. "She's around twenty-ish. We just brought her body back. No ID. She's never been fingerprinted."

For them I learned she was still a Jane Doe, yet I now knew her as Eden. I should have gotten a last name out of Orpheus. I made a mental note to do that.

"She has that same small circle on her left inner forearm." Riley watched me carefully as though waiting for my reaction. "The same symbol from the girl in the photo. Ingrid, how did you know from the photo it was a brand and not a tattoo?"

I sat back. "Huh."

He waited for my answer.

"Read it somewhere, maybe."

His intense gaze stayed on mine. "I've estimated her time of death at around 9:00 P.M last night."

"Any idea how she might have died?" I raised my hand. "I know it's still early."

"Bled out via an IV," Riley said. "From my preliminary."

"Someone dumped her in Holland Park after she died?" I asked.

"Looks like it," Riley said.

"MIT are all over it," Brooks said.

"Sir, I want in on this one," I said. "My in-tray is clear."

Brooks squinted my way.

"May I see her?" I stood up.

"Don't get in MIT's way," Brooks said.

I headed after Riley.

"Ingrid," Brooks called after me.

"Sir?"

"This Jane Doe was wearing all black. A corset, you know, the whole get up. She's probably a prostitute."

I shook my head. "Sir—"

"IV marks," Brooks added to make his point.

"Sir, someone bled her out."

"Maybe she was too high to realize?"

I leaned on the doorjamb. "Her circled brand links her to

Hauville's case."

"My wife likes you Ingrid," Brooks said. "I like you, but don't take any liberties on this one. Understand?"

I stared back at him with a dawning realization I was looking at me in twenty years. A senior officer with Scotland Yard, hardened and incapable of empathy. I stepped back into his office. "Sir, am I being held off this because I never caught the culprit from the Stonehenge case?"

He shrugged. "You're a brilliant detective. No one blames you."

"But that's the reason why I've only been allowed to work on Hauville's counterfeit activity?"

"Not sure if you've noticed this or not, Ingrid, but Scotland Yard has a specialized department for everything." Brooks' sarcasm allowed him to wriggle out of that one. With a wave of his hand, I was dismissed.

I followed Riley through the pathway of cubicles.

We rode the lift in silence.

The morgue was freezing, and I wondered how Riley coped with being stuck in here for any length of time. The smell of ammonia mixed with something else was nasty. No one would ever want their loved one in this awful place.

There, on the furthermost examination table, lay a green sheet draped over the outline of a body. A sinister image I'd never gotten used to it. We neared the autopsy table and Riley nudged the lighting fixture. He eased the sheet back off her face.

Eden looked asleep. Too pale for life and too sweet for death. Her stillness was eerie. I half expected her to open her eyes and talk to us. Eden had chosen to be a Gothica with the hope of one day being delivered into a life of eternity, yet here she lay dead. Her chance lost. I wished she'd made it to vampiredom, fulfilled her dream. I had of course considered this pathway for myself. Being sired by Jadeon. Becoming his equal. Until last night I'd questioned if this was the only way we could be together. A choice that never really went away. I would rather that then this. Death seemed so cruel when an alternative hovered within reach.

With gloved hands, I eased back the drape from her left forearm and ran a fingertip over her circled brand. No wonder

Orpheus had appeared so distraught. The reality of what I was looking at left a stale taste in my mouth.

She was one of Orpheus' girls. Once under his protection, she'd been murdered and her body unceremoniously dumped in a park. Despite Jadeon trying to protect me he was wrong on this one. I needed to be here.

"I need to see more," I said.

Riley didn't move.

My gaze rose to meet his.

"Your blood results came back," he said.

Oh, I'd forgotten all about those.

Riley strolled over to the sink and slipped off his gloves. He threw them into a bin. "There were traces of alcohol and Ambien. And something else too."

Oh no, not this. Not now when a girl lay dead and her body was a host for evidence. There were clues we needed to gather and study without wasting any more time.

"Let's discuss this later?" I gestured to the drape.

"The lab found high levels of dopamine in your blood."

"A mix up?"

"If you're doing drugs, why let me test your blood?"

"I've never done drugs."

"Cut the bullshit. You had high levels of norepinephrine, serotonin, and dopamine in your bloodstream. Whatever you took would have had you flying." He folded his arms. "Time to talk, Ingrid, or I'm going right back to Brooks' office with this."

CHAPTER 21

The Met's cafeteria was nestled in the far eastern corner of Scotland Yard.

At this early hour it was deserted, though by 7 A.M. this restaurant would be thriving. Senior officers would rub shoulders with junior ranks, staff would pick up their morning coffee, and discreet meetings would be held in private booths as personnel took short breaks from their stuffy cubicles.

This morning however, only a few people ate breakfast in here. They were far enough away from our table not to overhear what Riley wanted to discuss, continuing on from our conversation in the morgue.

Riley had insisted on buying breakfast and was currently at the till paying for a tray of food. He made small talk with the young, brunette cashier. Her stare followed him as he made his way back to me. The cashier was apparently enamored with him.

Riley placed the tray laden with two plates of scrambled eggs and toast in the center of the table. He slid one of the coffees over to me, followed by one of the plates.

"You have an admirer," I said, hoping to break the tension from our current stand-off.

He flashed the girl another smile. "Jane's very sweet."

"Jane?" I glanced over. "She's smitten."

He looked surprised. "I'm only being friendly."

The smell of eggs wafted and my stomach grumbled in protest. I reached for the plastic fork and scooped a portion of golden fluffiness. "You didn't need to do this, but thank you."

He removed his plate and slid the tray aside. "Anything you find in a vending machine is the devil's food."

"Aren't eggs high in cholesterol?"

"Eat up."

First Jadeon, and now Riley was feeding me. I didn't know whether to be embarrassed or flattered that people cared so much. Riley's focus remained on me with a startling intensity and made me hate the fact he had something over me.

"I'm here for you, Ingrid," he said. "You know that."

I lathered my toast with butter. "It always amazes me how doctors can eat no matter what they see."

"We learn to separate." Riley opened a sachet of sugar and poured white crystals into his coffee. "How's your sleep?"

"Fine." I knew he wanted to know why I had Ambien in my bloodstream. "It was a one off," I lied.

"Your doctor prescribed it?"

"I've been working through something."

"Relationship?"

I hid my cringe. I was sharing way too much. Details that might lead to more questions.

Dating a vampire has its challenges. The kind that could never be shared with anyone.

"I heard about the party at the Waldorf," he said. "From all accounts your beau's wealthy and quite dashing." Riley pointed with his fork. "How come we've never met him?"

"Oh, no." I waved my fork to empathize my point. "That was Orpheus." I corrected. "Lord Velde," I shook my head, "Jadeon wasn't at the party."

"Jadeon's your boyfriend?"

"Yes." And it made me feel good to say it.

"He a Lord too?" he mocked. "This Jadeon?"

"Um, yes."

Surprise flashed over his face.

Taking a sip of coffee, my thoughts drifted to last night, skipping over my run-in with danger and fast forwarding to my night of unbridled passion with Jadeon. I wanted to turn back the clock and be in his arms.

"Ingrid, you're blushing."

"Coffee's hot."

"It's serious then? Are we talking marriage?"

"I try to keep work and my private life separate."

"What does he do?"

"He's...an art dealer."

Well was. Now he spends all his time lording over the underworld.

I offered a polite smile, resisting the urge to caress my brow from the tiredness hanging over me. My lack of sleep was taking a toll.

"Your boyfriend's super rich then?" Riley said.

"I suppose."

This felt like an interrogation, and I hadn't had this kind of invasion into my private life since the academy.

He pushed his half eaten plate away. "You won't be the first person to do it. Athletes use performance enhancing drugs all the time. Goodness knows the pressure on you is monumental. The cases never stop coming. But long term illicit drugs will kill you."

"I've never done drugs."

Riley narrowed his gaze.

"I swear."

"The lab identified one of the compounds as a possible street drug. It's potent. The molecular formula of what you took was similar to $C_{17}H_{21}NO_4$."

"That's impressive."

Riley looked intense. "A cocaine-like substance."

What the hell had Orpheus slipped me? Was it merely his blood? Yes, his frickin blood with all its supernatural potency must have manifested as a drug when examined under the critical eye of a scientist.

"Ingrid?"

"I was slipped something," I said. "I was working undercover and..." I hated lying and sensed Riley was too smart to believe it.

"And you failed to report it?"

"That's why I came to you. I knew you'd be discreet."

He sat back. "Start talking. The truth this time."

"Riley, please."

"Do I sound like I'm compromising? Your welfare is my

concern. It's my job to make sure you don't end up with a toe tag." He leaned forward. "Am I getting through?"

"It's complicated."

"Your elitist friends have gotten you into drugs."

"No."

"Cocaine is the drug of choice for the rich. It's powerfully addictive."

I glanced around to make sure no one could overhear. Riley was turning what I'd just told him back on me.

"I've never once taken cocaine," I said firmly. "Never."

He reached out for my face and brushed my fringe aside. "How did you get that?"

My hand shot to my forehead and I remembered the bruise, that tell-tale contusion left by the monk ramming my head against a window. The one I'd failed to cover with enough makeup.

"Helena told me about your visit to see Sally Summers," he said. "The woman you rescued from that abusive relationship."

Great. Helena had shared with Riley my vague admittance to a broken heart.

"Would you like to talk about it?" he said.

"Believe it or not I tripped against a window."

"I don't believe it."

"Riley—"

"I'm taking this issue to the Yard's psychiatrist. You can talk it out with her."

"Why are you doing this?"

"I care about you."

"You have no idea."

"Science has provided an idea in the way of blood analysis." He pushed himself to his feet.

"Okay," I said, my gut twisting with the realization I was stuck and cursing myself for the snap decision to have him test my blood.

Riley sat back down.

"I need to examine that girl," I said.

"First prove you're capable of functioning without crap in your system and maybe, just maybe, I'll reconsider."

"You think I'll contaminate the evidence?"

"I can't risk it," he said. "Now spill."

I rested my chin on my hands, my head spinning with where to go from here. I had no choice but to visit the morgue after Riley had gone home. Only he never seemed to leave the place.

He motioned for me to speak. "I'm listening."

The windows needed cleaning. They were smudged from rain, and beyond them lay the terrace with its well-tended greenery. A welcome escape for those who needed it. The fleeting illusion of serenity.

This gaping chasm of truth, if shared, could wreck my career and have me institutionalized.

With a deep sigh, I began. "There's a secret that goes back thousands of years."

Riley's narrowed his stare.

I was beginning all wrong, so I searched for the words that might buy me some time to fully explain and not have him dragging me off to get fitted for a straight jacket.

"Take your time," Riley said.

I swallowed hard, bracing myself for his impending onslaught of questions, the accusations born out of doubt that would soon follow. "Riley..."

I'm about to turn your world upside down.

He rested his elbows on the table and steepled his fingers.

From the doorway, Sgt. Miller stomped toward us, and the fact that he too was here at this time sent shivers up my spine.

"What's this?" I snapped at Riley.

He looked back at the doorway.

Miller reached our table, out of breath. "Sir, please tell me Helena's staying over at your place?"

"That's kind of personal." He threw me an accusatory glare.

"I didn't say anything," I said defensively, pushing to my feet.

"Helena's mother's going frantic," Miller said. "Helena didn't turn up for her sister's sixteenth birthday party yesterday. She's not answering her phone."

"That's not possible." Riley rose quickly. "We bought her sister's gift together." He shot me a look. "Helena would never have missed it."

Miller's glare darted back to me. "Shit."

195

"What's going on?" I said.

Miller went pale. "As of last night, Constable Helena Noble became a missing person."

CHAPTER 22

I still didn't believe Helena was missing.

Miller and I had driven right over to her home in East London. She still lived with her mother and younger sister. We spent the first hour trying to track Helena's last movements from what they knew. With her hours being so erratic there wasn't a lot to go on. They hadn't seen Helena in over twenty-four hours.

Alone in her bedroom, I scanned her things *again.* I was angry with her for what she was putting her mother and sister through. Valuable police time was being wasted. Denial was easier to chase after then face what was too painful to bear.

Miller was still downstairs comforting Helena's mother and sister and going over all our questions to make sure we'd missed nothing.

I wanted to spot the one clue that everyone else had overlooked. Though Helena's mother had insisted nothing was out of place and everything was as her daughter had left it yesterday morning before heading out for work. Apparently Helena had left Scotland Yard early. Where she'd gone from there was still unknown. The missing person's squad was trolling through security footage to confirm the time she'd left the station.

Glancing at the plastic bag containing her toothbrush, needed for identifying her body if found, I felt a wave of panic. We'd gathered recent photos, taken the names of Helena's friends, acquaintances, and relatives, and we'd made a note of all the places she liked to visit, including coffee shops, parks, as well as her gym.

I mentally ticked off each item on my checklist, running through the possible scenarios. Helena had probably drank too much booze and fallen asleep somewhere and wasn't answering her phone. At her age, this wasn't unusual. A night in the pub with friends that had gone crazily awry and she had several days of nursing a hangover to follow. She'd no doubt suffer for weeks a terrible guilt for missing her sister's birthday. Not to mention having to face the wrath from our higher-ups.

Please, God, let that be the case.

The process of calling every hospital in London had begun. Maybe the pressure of the job had pushed Helena to stay in a hotel for a night or two, in need of solitude. Burn out usually happened in the more seasoned officers, but we had cases of stress showing up in junior officers too, occasionally. Though I'd not seen any sign of strain in either Helena or her work. If anything she thrived during our most tense situations. What was I missing?

"We have everything," Miller said from the doorway.

"How's her mum?" I asked.

"As expected."

"Dad? Where's he?"

"They're divorced."

"Has her mum someone who can be with her?"

"Helena's aunt is driving up from Southampton."

I made one last visual sweep of the room and again nothing stood out. We said our goodbyes, and as with all lost persons cases we promised Helena's mother we'd do everything within our power to find her. It was their eyes that haunted you. That look of terror, their pleading with you not to fail them, fail her.

Miller and I drove back to Scotland Yard together. Other than sharing words of support and a promise we'd find her, we said very little.

By the time we'd returned, everyone was on high alert. Extra officers were brought in and had gathered in the main conference room for the pre-scheduled debriefing. I remained at the back of the room standing beside Miller, both of us receiving critical stares. The truth in their accusations made me sick to my stomach. I deserved it. I'd not been as attentive as I should have been to the constable under my command. Disallowing myself to wallow in self-hate, I focused on what we had so far.

Chief Inspector Abe Flock addressed the room and outlined our plan of action. Flock was a hard-faced, rotund man who scared the shit out of the junior officers, and with good reason. If he caught you messing up, he hung you out to dry as an example. My moment of being publically humiliated by Flock was a matter of when, not if.

Afterward he approached Miller and I, and took us aside to talk privately. We told him everything we knew and answered all his questions as methodically as we could. He shared with us that a press release was set for this afternoon. Flock offered his condolences to us but I could see the blame in his eyes, the need for answers which we just didn't have.

"It doesn't make any sense," Miller told him. "If this is connected to the Hauville case, why target a policewoman?"

"We're not certain that's the connection," Inspector Flock said. "And if Helena has been abducted, the person may not even know she's a policewoman."

"Helena came with me when I interviewed Mrs. Hauville," I said.

Flock shrugged it off. "Does Helena have a boyfriend?"

"Well..." Miller glanced my way.

"Someone here?" Flock realized from Miller's hesitancy. "Well?"

"She's good friends with Dr. Russell," Miller said.

"Our coroner?" Flock looked surprised. "Well, are they fucking?"

I held back on the urge to roll my eyes. "Not as far as I know, sir."

"Then how are they romantically involved?" he said.

"The blossoming of a new love?" Miller cringed. "Off the record."

"It's on the bloody record now," Flock said. "Go interview Russell."

After agreeing with Miller that it was best for me to speak with Riley alone, I returned to the morgue. If I was going to be of any use to Helena I'd have to kick my skills into high gear and put all personal needs aside.

I prayed that Helena's disappearance had nothing to do with Eden's death. I really was going to have to persuade Riley to let me look more closely at the girl's body.

He sat on a wooden barstool, hunched over the lens of a microscope. His ability to keep working considering the circumstances was awe inspiring.

He raised his head. "You found her?"

"Not yet, Riley," I said. "I'm so sorry. Miller and I just got back from her mums."

"How's she doing?"

"She's holding up."

He stood. "Do you have anything? Any leads?"

"Nothing yet. Everyone is on this. We'll find her." I looked around at all the sterility, the starkness of all these clean lines and chrome. "Isn't there someone else who can cover for you?"

"Work is the only way I can stay sane."

"I understand."

"Fill me in." He blew out a sigh. "Every step of the way."

"I have you on speed-dial."

"How are you doing?"

"Other than feeling shitty?"

"Ingrid, this is hardly your fault."

"I'm her boss."

He picked up a tray of instruments. "Still."

I gestured for him to put it down.

His shoulders slumped. "You want to know where I was last night?"

"I'm sorry, Riley. It's protocol. You know that."

"You're not checking on how I'm doing. You're interviewing me."

"Riley—"

"No, that's okay. Of course. Rule me out so you can find her. What do you need?" He cleared his throat. "Last night, of course. I met my brother for dinner at Fred's Cafe in Covent Garden. He's a teacher. I have the receipt somewhere. No, wait. He paid. It was his turn. We take it in turns. I came back here around 0800, right after they found our Jane Doe." Riley raised his gloved hands. "I'll get you his number."

The silence that followed did its bit to strain the tension.

Both of us knew our conversation in the cafeteria was far from over.

"I've filed a complaint," Riley said.

The tightness in my throat nearly choked me.

"See that." He gestured with his head.

There, a few feet away on an examination table, lay a body covered in a green sheet.

"We're slipping," Riley said. "I know that all resources are on finding Helena, but breaching protocol like this is unacceptable. I was only gone ten minutes, and when I returned that was waiting for me. The corpse is male. He wasn't signed in. No toe tag. No record. Just another dead body in my morgue. With no record, I have no idea where he was found. If he came from a hospital. How he was found. Who found him. If there were any witnesses." He shrugged. "You get the idea. Someone was sloppy. I need answers. Now. Someone's getting fired and it's sure as hell isn't going to be me."

"I'll look into it," I said. "Who is the tech tonight?"

"Stewart Palmer. He has no idea where the body came from either."

Bile rose in my throat.

"Find Helena," Riley said. "Then launch an investigation here."

"Got it."

"Oh, Helena left her coat here yesterday morning," Riley said."Not sure if that helps. I imagine she has another one."

"Where?"

"My office."

"Anything out of the ordinary with her?" I said. "Any emotional change?"

"She did seem a little more...secretive."

"In what way?"

"Distracted." He motioned his frustration.

"Specifics would really help."

"The only thing I can think of was she obsessed over the Hauville case. That girl's photo."

"Did she mention she'd found anything?"

"No, but she kept her own copy of that photograph. It really rattled her that the case wasn't being taken seriously."

"We all feel that."

He looked uncomfortable. "Just so you know, we haven't had sex yet."

I threw my hands up in a gesture to show I trusted him.

"You should have asked me that," he said.

"Thank you for your frankness." I gestured to his office.

"Help yourself." He gave a weak smile. "Ingrid, if you have to, search my house. Whatever you have to do to find her. You have my full cooperation."

"I know."

"Oh, and our conversation in the cafeteria this morning," he said.

I hesitated, hating this looming beneath the surface.

"You were going to share something with me before we were interrupted?" he said.

"Let's revisit that another time."

"Let's retest your blood. Tomorrow sound good?"

I hated the idea. "I can do that."

"It's on the back of my chair." He used his chin to point. "Helena's coat."

Riley had managed to make his office cheery. Bright prints hung on the walls and the space was comfortable. His desk was neatly arranged, as was his filing system. All this order was a welcome change from what lay out there.

I recognized Helena's parka hung over the back of a chair. Searching each pocket, I found nothing, other than a tissue. Inside her inner pocket I removed a crumbled piece of paper and unraveled it. The receipt was from Blackly's Tattoo Parlor in SoHo, and it was dated five days ago. The same day Helena had taken off to attend a supposed dental appointment.

Riley hadn't mentioned this, and a tattoo was certainly a conversational piece.

I pulled out my BlackBerry and dialed the number at the top of the receipt. The call didn't go through. We were too far down in the basement to get any reception. Sitting on the edge of Riley's desk, I picked up his office phone and redialed.

"Blackly's," answered a male with a Cockney accent.

"Hey there," I said. "Who's this?"

"Mac. How can I help you?"

"My friend got the coolest tattoo there, and well, we're like bestest friends and we do everything the same."

I could almost hear him cringe on the other end, his impatience welling. Right where I needed him.

"Yeah," I said. "Anyway, I want to get the exact same tattoo."

"I can do that," he said. "Who's your friend?"

"Helena Noble."

He went quiet for the longest time. "Oh yeah. Blonde? Pretty?"

"That's her."

"You want a small, black circle on your left inner forearm?"

A wave of panic. "Yes," I managed, my hands shaking.

"How about Saturday? Noon?"

I slammed the phone down as a cold sweat beaded my brow. Had Helena set herself up as bait? What kind of danger had she put herself in? Where the hell was she?

In a daze, I made my way out of Riley's office.

"You're not taking it then?" he said.

"Huh?"

"Her coat?"

"Riley." I tried to find the words. "Was Helena guarded over her left arm?"

"How do you mean?" His expression became fraught and he stomped toward me.

"What?"

The male corpse that had been lying on the examination table a few moments ago was gone. The green drape discarded on the floor.

"Fuck," hissed Riley under his breath.

I followed his gaze.

A shadowy figure stood stock still in the corner. I knew that face, that monk-like garb, those haunting black eyes.

"Riley," I whispered. "Get in your office. Lock the door."

"Sir, I'm a doctor. Help is on its way." He gestured to his office. "Ingrid, call an ambulance. He must have been in a coma."

I stepped in front of Riley. "Hide. Now!"

The hood slipped off, revealing a flock of white hair. The

vampire flew at us, knocking me backwards onto the floor. Trays of instruments crashed around us, green drape went flying, and Riley's yelling rose above the din.

He let out a death curdling scream...

The creatures fangs buried in Riley's neck, furiously sucking the life from him, tearing at his flesh. A monstrous vision of horror. I ran toward them, bringing my fist hard against the creature's face and punching him hard.

Wide-eyed and dazed, Riley staggered forward and slumped to his knees. The vampire was on me now, his teeth bared, fangs finding my neck. I squeezed my eyes shut, flinching away from his bite. The coldness of his tongue along my neck searched out my pulse. My scream caught in my throat.

He let me go and I tumbled back to the floor.

On hands and knees, I crawled toward Riley, my hands fumbling at his neck, trying to stem his blood loss. Terror raged through my veins.

I scanned the room for that creature, my gaze sweeping the ceiling, the darkest corners.

Riley's face contorted in agony. He was bleeding out. I leaped to my feet and grabbed gauze from the countertop and returned to him, ripping the sterile packet open and pulling out squares of fabric before pressing them against the gouge. Bright red blood soaked through the fabric and more poured onto my hands, dripping onto the floor.

"I'll call an ambulance," I said, failing to hide my panic. Hands shaking, wet fingers slipping, I reached for my BlackBerry. It was useless. If I let go of the gauze, Riley would bleed out faster. My gaze flitted to his office. I had to get to his landline.

A door opened.

Jadeon and Orpheus were beside me.

"Call an ambulance," I yelled. "Hurry. There's a phone in there."

Orpheus took over where my hands pressed, enabling me to straighten Riley's limbs and lay him flat on the floor. Jadeon knelt at Riley's side. Riley was fading quickly, his paleness transmuting into a dusky hue.

Orpheus lifted Riley's chin. "Listen to me. I'm going to ask you a question and you must answer."

Riley prized his eyes open, his pupils dilating.

"Save him!" I yelled.

"Quiet, Ingrid," Jadeon said. "Let him talk."

Riley tried to swallow, tried to catch his breath. He wheezed for life, trying to make sense of this attack that had come out of nowhere.

"We're going to give you a choice," Jadeon said. "To live. To become immortal."

"You're confusing him," I said. "Just do it."

Jadeon held his arm up for Riley to see and with a knife taken from God knew where he sliced through his own wrist. "See?" Jadeon showed Riley how quickly his wound healed. "We're vampires. We can transform you into what we are. Right now. What we can't guarantee is that your soul will live on."

"Say yes, Riley," I said. "Say yes to him."

A lone tear fell down Riley's cheek as he watched Jadeon's wound heal, his face marred with confusion.

"Do it," I screamed.

Yet Jadeon remained calm, cruelly so, as though death held no fear for him even when it had its claws in someone I cared about.

"Orpheus," I begged. "I'll do anything you ask. Just turn him."

"His swallowing reflex is going," Orpheus said, throwing a look at Jadeon.

"Wait." Jadeon grabbed Orpheus' shoulder.

"There's no time," I sobbed.

"Ingrid," Riley gasped. "Don't let them...please..."

"No, you don't mean that," I said. "Riley, you're bleeding. By the time the ambulance gets here—"

"I need to hear a 'yes' from you, Riley," said Jadeon.

"No," mouthed Riley. "I can't breathe."

"The blood loss is effecting his decision," I said.

"Ingrid, I'm sorry," Orpheus whispered and sat up on his heels.

"Hold him," Jadeon told me. "Make it easier on him."

Tears soaked my face, his blood soaking my hands. "You do it. Do it now." I grabbed Riley into a hug and rocked him.

Vaguely, I sensed Orpheus and Jadeon standing behind me calmly watching. Refusing to do what had to be done.

"Whatever you want from me," I called back to them. "I'll give you anything. I'll be anything you want me to be."

With Riley in my arms, I kissed his forehead, trying to comfort him, feeling him tremble then grow still, feeling him slip away. "No. No. No. No. No. Please." I buried my face in the crook of his neck, the agony of losing him too much to bear. Wretchedness washed over me, brought on by the gut wrenching truth that this was my fault.

Riley had tried to save me. He'd taken the time to council me. Yet when he needed me the most I failed him. *Was failing him.*

Hands trembling, emptiness enveloped me as I laid him back down. Jadeon knelt beside me and rested a hand on my shoulder. I shoved his hand away.

"Riley didn't want to be one of us," he said. "He just didn't."

"You misread him." My eyes blurred with tears. "You scared him."

Orpheus picked up a green drape and wiped blood off his hands. *Riley's blood.* "We have to move fast," he said. "We'll destroy the evidence."

"What are you talking about?" I stared at my bloodstained hands. "We need the evidence."

"He has a vampire's bite," Jadeon said. "And your fingerprints are on everything."

Dizziness threatened to drag me to my knees. "What about Helena?"

"We'll find her," Jadeon said.

"Do you think she's in danger?" My body trembled violently. My thoughts scattered.

"We're here for you," Jadeon said. "Whatever you need."

I clamped my hand over my mouth, the shock of it all finding me like a raging nightmare.

"We will find the one who did this," Orpheus said.

"That's not enough," I said. "It's not enough."

"Take a breath." Jadeon grabbed my shoulders. "We need you focused for what is to follow."

"Follow?" I muttered.

"We're going to fake your death, Ingrid," Orpheus said.

"What? No!"

"No one is safe around you," Jadeon said. "Not while there are those still out there who want you dead."

"This is my life. You're talking about my life."I looked at Riley's blood on my hands. I'd caused his death by bringing the attention of the elders to me. I looked at Jadeon for answers. I looked at him to make sense of all this. To turn back the clock. To make it go away.

"I have to call my boss," I sobbed, heading for the phone.

Jadeon stepped in front of me and blocked my way. "It's over." He brushed a loose strand of hair behind my ear. "My darling, I'm so sorry."

The wall clock ticked, each hand sliding forward irrevocably. Time would not wait for anyone, least of all me. The scent of ammonia, the scent of blood, made me queasy. Scarlet smudges were all over my hands, my chest, my face. I was covered in it.

"Please," I backed away.

"This is not a discussion," Orpheus said.

Shaking my head, I searched for the words to make them see reason. "I refuse."

Jadeon's iron-clad grip held my arm. "I'm afraid, Ingrid, the decision's not yours to make."

CHAPTER 23

Breaking into Anaïs' flat had been easy.

Using my pick, I'd entered without difficulty. Nothing but quiet greeted me as I trained my flashlight and scanned the pitch-black living room. The window blinds' effort to shield the room from light was futile at best. The sunlight's threat was unrelenting. Anaïs would only enjoy this space at night. Everything was the same as the last time I'd visited.

Back when my life had been mine.

Back before it was over.

The morgue had gone up in flames, destroying all evidence of Riley's murder, and along with it the young female corpse who was meant to be me. My life had been ripped from me. Apparently my dental records had been switched out and all the other talents that Orpheus had mastered over time had been put into action, ensuring they had successfully wiped my life. My funeral was pending.

There was no going back.

They had taken me back to my flat. In a daze, I'd packed what I could with the warning hanging over me that this was it. I'd never be permitted to return. Orpheus and Jadeon had hovered over me to keep me focused. The chance of my neighbors catching a glimpse of the girl who was meant to be dead from a tragic accident at work wouldn't fair well.

Later that morning, with Jadeon and Orpheus distracted, I'd fled, using daylight as my advantage. I knew it wouldn't take long before they'd find me. For now, though, the sun was the only factor keeping them away. My ability to avoid their mortal servants from tracking me was all thanks to the skills I had learned at the academy. I was now the hunted.

Curled up in a ball on Anaïs' living room floor, hugging my knees into my chest, I cried for Riley, cried for Helena, cried for my life wrenched from me.

I deserved it. All of it.

Through these fog-infused thoughts, I realized, other than Lucas, Anaïs was the only other vampire whose address I had. And I didn't need Lucas' reasoning right now. What I needed was someone who'd understand my desperation, my spiraling, my willingness to do whatever it took to find Helena. Find Beatrice. Do my part to makeup for the mess I had made.

Only now did I understand Anaïs' turmoil. How easily it had been to compartmentalize her situation, sort through the evidence and show empathy for Anaïs and the loss of her lover. How many times in my life had I dealt with the grief of others, merely sharing my condolences and not allowing myself to meet victims in their place of pain.

The rawness of all this agony soaked into my bones.

Crawling to my feet, I couldn't waste another second. Looking around at the several doors leading off to the right and left, I was curious which one led to her bedroom. Sleeping so exposed would be too risky for a vampire. How strange that those we once damn as our enemies come round to be the first ones we turn to in our time of need.

I was going to find those girls.

What Helena and Beatrice might be enduring haunted my every thought and it was hard to think straight. I hated myself for letting them down. The guilt from having encouraged Helena to seek more information on Hauville's case wrenched at my soul.

These self-indulgent thoughts were out of control and threatening to ruin my focus. My attention fell upon the dining room table, moved over to the open magazine, and found Anaïs' car keys.

I left her apartment as swiftly as I'd entered and rode the elevator to the subterranean parking structure.

Car fumes reached my nostrils and unsettled my stomach as I made my way along, taking in the collection of luxury vehicles reflecting the wealth of those living above. A flick of the key fob caused a car to flash its lights. Parked between a Mercedes Benz and a BMW sat a sleek black Viper.

Once inside, I breathed in the new leather smell and clutched the steering wheel, feeling the power yet to be experienced. Had this been any other day I might have found this exhilarating. The key turned smoothly in the ignition. Nothing happened. No purr of the engine. No hum of the car starting. Trying to figure out if I needed to deactivate another alarm, I noted the red button to the right of the wheel and with one push the engine purred awake. The wheel was aligned to the left. An odd design quirk that I was going to have to get used to and fast. With a rev of the engine and a slip of the gear stick, I was out of the parking structure and heading south.

The drive through London was uneventful, and I made a concerted effort not to get a ticket and have my supposedly dead self captured on a traffic cam. Once out of the city, I pushed the Viper to the limit.

And made my way to Cornwall.

Carn Brea's orphanage security alarm was easy to deactivate. I'd have to let Mirabelle know about the weakness in their system. But not today.

Minutes later, I entered the lowest chamber and headed along the dark hallway lined on either side with multidenominational symbols. The door at the end was marked with a pentagram. If what Anaïs had told me during my first visit here was true, this would soon be over and I'd have what I'd come for.

A low growl came from behind me.

Slowly, I turned to face an Alsatian snarling at me. His head was bowed, his teeth bared.

Oh fuck.

I sped toward the door at the end of the hallway, my legs weakening, my heart in my throat. I prayed the door wasn't locked. The sound of paws scraping along the stone floor revealed just how close he was to reaching me. I yanked open the door and slid through and slammed it shut. Blood pounded in my ears. My hands shook uncontrollably.

Moving quickly, ignoring the barking outside, I bolted down

the center aisle with its twenty or so pews on either side and reached the front altar.

I searched for the bottle containing blue illuminate.

At the front of the chapel hung a burgundy velvet drape that ran from the ceiling to the floor. Drawing it back, I found another door. After picking the lock, I entered an even smaller chamber.

There, resting upon another altar, sat that ornate bottle. Bright blue liquid reflected the sunlight flooding in from a skylight, the delicate hue so inviting. Fluid ribbons of red spiraling through the blueness. With the silver stopper out, I sniffed the rosy perfume, a delicate fragrance sweet and welcoming. The essence of a rose garden had been captured and something else too; the scent of a forest at dawn.

The scent of one life ending and another beginning.

Easing a finger inside the neck and wetting the tip, bringing the fluorescent drop to my lips, my taste buds tingled. Carrying the bottle into the corner, I sat on the cold stone floor and leaned back against the wall.

With all I knew about what this stuff could do to me, this was insanity. The deadliest kind.

Don't do it my reasonable self whispered to me in the dimness.

I wanted those girls safe. I wanted this to be over. I wanted this spell to work.

I lifted the bottle to my lips...

CHAPTER 24

I could fly.

Which was pretty damn fantastic, and I questioned why I'd never had a go at it before. Balancing precariously on the top of the balcony of the sweeping staircase, peering down at that familiar chandelier hanging above St. Michael's Mount foyer, I felt dizzy with ecstasy.

And leaped off.

The ground came up way too fast.

A strong arm yanked me up violently, forcing all air from my lungs, jerking me backwards and upwards and shooting pain into my ribcage. The drag of gravity caused my head to spin. I struggled against the loss of control, fighting the hands gripping me. The floor blurred. I was carried up a staircase and along a corridor, onwards through a doorway, and then finally thrust upon a four-poster bed. A door slammed, followed by the click of a key turning in a lock.

Stillness.

Blackness.

A blinding fluorescent light forced me to squeeze my eyes shut, then the light switch clicked off again. My head ached so bad it felt like someone had hit me with an axe. Make that two axes. My stomach twisted with nausea; there was a horrid taste in mouth.

The last thing I remembered was Carn Brea…the chapel…*Oh no…*

His handsome face came into view, that familiar frown

marring his beauty.

"Jadeon?" I rasped.

"Hey." He was right beside me sitting on the bed.

"Horrible dream," I said, my voice scratchy.

"You're safe now."

"Huh?" I tried to remember how I'd gotten here. This was Jadeon's bedroom and I had no memory of coming here. "Are you okay?"

"I'm fine," he said. "I'm glad to see you're still talking to me."

A memory sparked in my brain like a lightning bolt. The rest came in a flood: a ruined life, everything I'd ever known now gone, people, places, and my job now inaccessible. Sleep had held the truth at arm's length, but with waking there came the full force of all that had happened.

"It's my fault," I said. "All of it."

"Nobody else sees it that way."

I was too weak to push myself up. "Had I not gone to the Athenaeum, Riley would still be alive."

"Your connection with me put you at risk, Ingrid. That's why I tried to keep you away from me. To protect you." He shrugged. "I'm ultimately responsible."

"You warned me." My throat felt like sandpaper and I swallowed several times to ease it. "You're trying to make me feel better and I don't deserve it."

Riley had fought for his life in that cold, dark morgue. He'd suffered the cruelest death. Not able to face that right now, my eyes scanned Jadeon's bedroom. Despite his wealth he'd surrounded himself with simple furnishings. Though the four poster bed was a luxurious touch, everything else in here was modest. Like the writing desk upon which rested the helm of a model boat, seemingly rescued from some catastrophe, the mast crumpled in on itself. It had sentimental value, no doubt. There was a side table with a pitcher of water on it and a single glass beside it. The leather armchair in the corner wasn't here last time I'd visited and had been brought in recently.

I peeked beneath the covers, grateful to see I had on a T-shirt and underwear. "Where are my clothes?"

Jadeon pointed to the chair where my overnight bag sat.

Inside it was all I had left in the world. Those few belongings I'd grabbed before leaving my home for the last time.

"Don't worry about that," he said. "I'll see to it you have an entire new wardrobe. Everything you want and need will be yours."

"Thank you." Having always been so independent, it felt strange to rely on anyone for the most basic of needs.

"You left without telling me where you were going." Jadeon sounded hurt. "I've been going frantic."

"I needed to do something. I knew you'd stop me."

He rubbed his hands over his face in frustration. A gesture to control what he was on the verge of saying. He was holding back on what he really felt but his taut expression gave away his annoyance.

I deserved his anger. "Riley," I said. "He shouldn't have died."

"I'm sorry," he said. "Truly I am."

"Why didn't you save him?"

"He would never have been happy, Ingrid. We were repugnant to him."

"He would have come round."

"Only to kill himself later. It was quick." He nodded, as though trying to convince himself. "You were there for him."

"It's because of me he died. Oh Jadeon, you should have turned him—"

"Sometimes the right decision doesn't feel right at the time."

"Helena." I pushed myself farther up the headboard. "I have to find her."

"You need to rest."

I grabbed his hand. "Blue illuminate. I drank the stuff. Did it fry my brain? I feel... weak but other than that..."

"Try to get some sleep."

"How long have I been out?"

"Two days."

"What? No, I have to find Helena. And Beatrice. Find whoever murdered Eden."

"You're suffering from aftereffects." He squeezed my hand. "Ingrid, you didn't drink blue illuminate."

I was stunned, hating the idea of a repeat from last time.

"Orpheus switched it out again?"

"No."

My head fell back onto the pillow. "Was I poisoned?" *Poisoned myself by drinking the stuff. What had I been thinking?*

"Mirabelle found you lying on the floor of the chapel," he said. "She found you unconscious. Apparently their guard dog alerted them to an intruder."

"Bloody great Alsatian." I shuddered. "Did she bring me here?"

"She called Orpheus. He brought you here and then called me. I don't want to alarm you, but Mirabelle had never seen that bottle before." He took a few breaths. "For God's sake, Ingrid, what the hell were you thinking?"

"I needed to solve this case. Put all the pieces together. Most of which I don't have. Apparently blue illuminate is meant to fire up all your brain cells so—"

"Only it wasn't blue illuminate. Which is only reserved for vampires, by the fucking way. Which I told you and you didn't listen. You never listen."

"Those girls need me."

"And you think that frying your brain is going to help them?" He clenched his fists.

"You told me it wasn't blue illuminate."

"Which would have killed you."

"Anaïs said—"

"You're out of your mind do you know that?"

I nudged his arm. "Hey, where'd my sympathetic Jadeon go?"

"I could have lost you. Then what? What point would my life have then?" He grabbed my arm, his face turning to fear. "Ingrid?"

The trembling swept over me, a burning flowing though my veins, my shuddering shook the mattress beneath me. "I feel strange..."

"Ingrid, stay with me..."

The room drifted from view.

The blackness crept into my mind and dragged me under.

I awoke to whispers, the voices familiar. Orpheus sat beside me on the edge of the bed, his brow furrowed and his intense stare critical. Alex lay curled up beside me, his blonde curls ruffled.

"She's awake." Anaïs' said. Her arms were folded across her chest hugging herself; she looked riddled with guilt.

Orpheus gestured he wanted her to step back. He reached for the glass of water on the side table and brought it to my lips. "How's my hummingbird?"

"Not your hummingbird." I pushed it away.

"Not yet." He arched a brow. "Drink."

I took a sip and accepted the glass from him. "Jadeon?"

"He's trying to find out what you drank," he said. "He'll be back soon."

My limbs felt weak, my legs still shaky and useless. Embarrassment reigned like a cloud over my head that would never leave.

"You'll feel better soon," Orpheus said.

I narrowed my gaze, not trusting his kindness. "How long have I been out?"

"A day."

Through bleary eyes, I found Anaïs' face again and she gave a nod to confirm what Orpheus had told me.

"I stole your car," I said to her. "Sorry."

"You can have it," she said. "I want you to have it."

I let out a chuckle and it sounded crazed. "Something tells me it's Orpheus' car I nicked."

"We can add carjacking to your long list of criminal behavior," Orpheus said. "Amongst other things."

"Please tell me I haven't embarrassed myself too much?"

"No such luck." Orpheus gave a wry smile.

Alex stirred and opened his eyes, blinking away.

"Ingrid, I'm sorry for everything," Anaïs said. "Please don't hate me."

"Anaïs," I said. "We've all done what we thought was best."

"I hate myself, seriously."

"Anaïs, please don't do this to yourself," I said. "I've done far worse."

"She knows she's messed up, Ingrid." Orpheus glared her way. "You have a right to be angry with Anaïs."

"It's okay," I told her. "I haven't given up on finding

Beatrice. Once I'm able to stand..." It really did feel as though I could reach into Anaïs' thoughts, and the sensation of trying to access what she was thinking gave me a strange fluttering in my mind, a cerebral caress of sorts. Anaïs really was hurting over this.

"Did you mean everything you said to me last night?" Alex asked me.

I frowned, searching the far reaches of my consciousness to lead me to an answer.

"You don't remember?" He looked hurt.

Wondering what my unconscious self had been up to, I said, "Remind me."

Orpheus grinned. "Let's just say you're best buddies now."

I held Alex's stare, reassured he no longer seemed to hate me. Still, it was disconcerting to think how we'd gotten to this apparent truce.

What the hell had I been up to?

Alex didn't seem in the least bit disconcerted. He slid off the bed and stretched, beaming a smile at me as his eyes lit up with affection. Orpheus lifted the jug off the side table and topped up my glass. I rubbed my eyes, missing Jadeon terribly, feeling so vulnerable, so lost.

"You needn't worry." Orpheus set the jug down. "You're safe here."

"I don't feel any different."

"That surprises me," he said. "Considering."

"What do you mean?" I said.

"Go find her some aspirin," Orpheus said.

Anaïs and Alex left the room, closing the door behind them. It was too late to ask them to leave it open. They had inadvertently trapped me in here with him.

"I need to get up," I said.

"I'm afraid you're not out of the woods yet," Orpheus said.

"What do you mean?"

"Good news first or bad news?"

"Can there be any more bad news?"

"What you drank evidently contained a spell."

I shook my head. "Don't believe in spells."

"Really? I find that interesting considering you believe in

vampires."

"That's because I've seen proof."

"Whatever you drank changed your eye color."

"What?" I studied his face. "No it didn't."

He gave an incredulous stare.

I swallowed hard. "How?"

"We don't know."

"Jadeon never mentioned it."

"He didn't want to alarm you probably."

"What color are they then?" I squinted at him, annoyed.

He reached for the hand mirror resting on the side table.

Peering at my reflection, I blinked in horror at my irises. They'd gone from deep brown to a shocking fluorescent blue. The mirror dropped from my grasp and it landed on the sheet.

Impossible.

My heart hammered against my chest wall, trying to escape my body. My hands shook as I tried to steady the mirror. "What the hell?" Drowning in panic, my entire body trembled. "Am I a... vampire?"

"No."

"You're sure?"

"Did you just ask me that?" He glared. "You have a reflection. Does that help?"

My eyes stung with tears. "But spells aren't real."

"Bright blue irises not proof enough for you?"

I cursed the hours I'd lost and my head crashed back against the headboard. It struck me that my sight could have been lost. What other dangers had I put myself in that I didn't know about? "Where's the bottle now?" I said. "Maybe we can send it to a private lab to get the contents tested."

"I believe Mirabelle still has it. I'll ask her."

"Do you think this is permanent?"

"Have no idea."

"Not exactly comforting," I said. "Is this what happened to Anaïs?"

"It wasn't the same crap she drank."

"How do you know?"

"You're alive."

"Oh, it really would have killed me then."

His eyebrows arched in that oh so sexy way of his. " We believe whoever put the blue illuminate substitute in that room knew you were coming."

"Who?" I slid down the bed and pulled the blanket up. "That monk?"

"No."

"Right, because I'd be dead. Then who?"

"Jadeon believes it may have been Fabian."

I let out a moan. "To punish me?"

"That's not his way."

"Why does Jadeon believe it's Fabian?"

"This is a powerful spell." Orpheus' words came to me, though he had not spoken them. *"An incantation performed by a true master of alchemy."* Orpheus shrugged. "A hunch." His lips thinned. *"Won't show her the room, not yet."*

"Room?" I said

"Did you just..."

I pushed myself up the bed. "Read your thoughts? Yes." Though somehow, I didn't believe it.

"Yet you're still mortal," he thought.

"That's something at least," I said, and on his confusion added, "Still being mortal."

He flinched. *"Oh hell no."*

"I'm not exactly happy about it myself," I said, feeling too dazed to truly believe it. I flicked my fingers for the mirror again.

Orpheus passed the mirror back. *"Bloody hell."*

"I thought you'd seen everything," I said, studying my face, my bright blue eyes.

"So did I." He shook his head in disbelief.

I swallowed hard. "What have I been up to these last few days? Something tells me I've been sleep walking"

"Sleeping. Mainly. *And trying to fucking fly."*

"Oh God, no."

"Guard your mind."

"Please, don't guard your mind." I gave a triumphant smile. "It's the only thing I have going for me right now. Orpheus, could it be possible that you and I are now equals?"

"Absolutely," he said. *"That'll be the day."*

"Oh bloody hell, I really am reading your mind." A

complete and utter breakdown loomed ever closer at the realization of what I'd done.

What had I done?

"Let's get Alex in here," I said, "and see if I can read his mind too."

"Let's not." He thinned his lips. *"She'll freak when she sees the room."* Orpheus' thoughts carried again. *"Shit."*

"What room?"

He looked away.

I pulled off the blanket. "I want to see."

"You're not strong enough to walk."

"This is not a request," I snapped. "Are you going to help me or will I have to ask someone else. Is Seb here?"

"Ingrid—"

"Either you take me or I'll crawl there by myself. You have me curious now." I staggered to my feet. A wave of dizziness hit me hard.

He caught me and wrapped an arm around me, hugging me into his side. "You're painfully stubborn, you know that?"

We headed out and down the hallway. It felt strange to have Orpheus so close, but his embrace was something I needed. Not so long ago I'd fled from his touch, never foreseeing I'd ever demand anything from him. This was going to take some getting used to.

"I can hear you," he said with a wry smile.

"Ha! I can hear you too now."

He rolled his eyes. "Let's hope it's temporary."

"I'm not exactly thrilled myself."

Within minutes, we'd made it to the door that led to Jadeon's art room.

"This is a bad idea," Orpheus thought.

My throat tightened with what I was about to face.

I felt him before I saw him. His presence causing goose bumps to form along my forearms. My chest tingled in anticipation.

Jadeon materialized before us, and even though I'd sensed him I staggered back at his appearance out of nothing. Orpheus grabbed my waist to prevent my fall.

Jadeon prized me from him. "She shouldn't be up."

"You know how stubborn she is," Orpheus said. *"Jadeon, she can hear our thoughts."*

"What are you talking about?" Jadeon looked harried.

I snuggled into his chest. "Did you find out anything?"

"I've sent word that I need to talk with Snowstrom." Jadeon threw Orpheus a questioning stare. *"What do you mean she can read our minds?"*

I sighed. "The illusive Fabian Snowstrom."

"Even if he isn't responsible he should still be able to help," Jadeon said and swapped another wary stare with Orpheus. *"What's going on?"*

My hand rested on the doorknob.

Jadeon eased my hand off. "Back to bed now."

I steadied myself and gripped the handle. "Now you really have me intrigued."

Orpheus came closer. "How about some tea? Seb will make you some."

I shot him a look. "You're being awfully nice. I'm not used to it." A wave of terror slithered up my spine. "Have I hurt someone?" I broke away from Jadeon's grip and pushed open the door.

There were no dead bodies in here, thank goodness. No evidence I had done any damage to anyone or even the room. This was Jadeon's den. The place he liked to wile away the hours and paint. Over a week ago I'd watched Paradom paint in here. There, upon the canvas, was his latest painting and it was stunning. He'd perfectly crafted Jadeon's face with soft pastels, capturing those hazel specks in his fiery eyes, that serene expression of his with delicate strokes. Paradom had almost finished the piece. My attention moved over to what had once been a plain white wall. Paradom had gone mad scribbling ancient symbols all over it, and from the look of things he'd moved on to the far wall and worked out complex mathematical calculations. Paradom had calculated the speed of light with an equation.

How did I know that? How could I interpret so easily what these symbols meant?

Jadeon came closer and again wrapped his arms around me, hugging me close. I leaned against him, finding comfort in his hold while admiring the numerous alchemic symbols and understanding both the sense and the meaning of each one and how they corresponded to each other, while marveling at their brilliance. "Huh."

"*She doesn't remember,*" Jadeon's words carried.

I peered up at him to better read his expression and caught his trailing thoughts. Startled by them, I pulled away. "No." I searched his face for the truth and shot Orpheus a look to confirm what they were insinuating. "That's not possible."

Orpheus gave a slow nod.

Jadeon reached for me. "Take a deep breath, Ingrid."

My throat tightened and that awful blackness threatened to eat me whole again, stealing up on me and wanting to devour my consciousness.

My sanity.

"I drew those?" I stuttered, pointing at the wall. "And painted that?" I motioned to the painting. "Your portrait?"

Jadeon's eyes filled with wonder. "Yes."

I fought the drag, the pull of blackness hankering after me, nipping at my heels, and I crumpled in Jadeon's arms.

CHAPTER 25

What I had been up to these last few days flooded back in a dream-like haze.

I really had tried to launch myself off the balcony in an attempt to fly. Reassuringly it appeared that phase was over. So much so that I'd been allowed some privacy. Alex, who hadn't left my side for days, was now giving me some space.

Those symbols I'd drawn upon the walls had been me trying to figure out what the hell that spell was I'd inadvertently imbibed in Carn Brea's chapel. The spell itself had given me the knowledge to attempt to work out the formula.

Mind blowing.

Jadeon had gathered all the books on ancient incantations from the castle library and given them to me. I'd returned to the comfort of his bedroom and spread out the old texts around me, hoping to decipher these flashes of inspiration. Anaïs had warned that blue illuminate had the potential to make you smarter, but whatever I had drunk had bestowed a supernatural awareness. Though it came and went with no obvious sign of permanence. Not yet, anyway.

When these cognizant flashes occurred, these metaphysical visions of inspiration, it really did feel like my mind was slipping, mainly because subjects on which I had never studied flittered into my awareness. Just this morning my mind had drifted to the castle's history and I'd marveled that the first priory here was founded in 1135. Yet I'd never read that or been told this by Jadeon. Details of that time came to me as vividly as a recollection. Thankfully, these phases didn't last long. The lightheadedness they brought sent me spiraling afterward.

Right now I was feeling normal again. As normal as one feels in a castle with vampires roaming its corridors.

Like the one standing at the end of my bed, his eyes full of concern.

Paradom held out the colorful bouquet of bright pinks and stunning reds and the scent of fresh cut roses filled the room.

I pushed myself farther up the headboard. "Paradom, they're beautiful."

Having been feeling sorry for myself, his appearance was a healthy reminder that someone else had suffered a far worse fate.

"Seb making tea," he muttered. "Tea tastes like iron."

Sebastian made the best tea. His endless tea and biscuit runs were looked forward to, carrying it up those sweeping stairs and along those chilly corridors. He always turned up with a teapot covered with a tea cozy, and though I found this all very amusing the tea was appreciatively piping hot when it arrived. Just how I liked it. Seb's visits were just as warming.

"Sorry you hurt bad," Paradom said.

I managed a nod. A tilt of my head, not wanting to go there, especially with Paradom whose thoughts were apt to wander.

Only last week I'd been in this castle trying to extract Jadeon's location from him. The words Paradom had spoken had been the darkest portent. *"This bridge you cross crumbles beneath your feet."*

Fear slithered up my spine, just as it had when he'd spoken them.

Paradom had warned me. *"There's no way back."*

"How did you know?" I said. "How did you predict this?"

He buried his nose in the flowers and breathed them in. "Beginnings can be scary."

"Let me smell them." I gestured for him to step closer.

"Mustn't stay long."

"Why ever not?"

Sebastian appeared in the doorway. "Because you need your rest." He carried a tray full of breakfast items: a hardboiled egg in an eggcup, sliced buttered whole-wheat toast, and I almost heard angels singing when I spotted the tea cozy covered teapot with a lone cup beside it.

"I'm being well and truly spoiled," I said.

Sebastian laid the tray on my lap. "How are you feeling?"

"Well my headache's gone," I said. "As is my life. Got anything for that?"

"Actually I may have." He looked over at Paradom. "Please put those in a vase and fetch my laptop." Sebastian called after him. "Paradom…"

Paradom paused by the door.

"You picked the best flowers," Sebastian told him. "Good job."

Paradom beamed, revealing the sharpest teeth. He trotted off out the door.

"You let him go outside?" I whispered.

"He's not our prisoner, Ingrid. Anyway, he won't go far. Alex or I stay with him." He shrugged. "The benefit of living on an island."

"Seb, are my eyes really that freaky?"

"That obvious, huh?"

"You're having trouble looking me in the eye."

"Sorry," he said. "They're kind of bright."

"I hope they don't stay like this. I'll be forced to wear colored contacts for the rest of my life."

"Come on now," Sebastian said. "We have a job to do. Beatrice and Helena need finding."

"At least someone is listening to me."

"I'm sorry about your doctor friend." Seb shook his head solemnly. "Jadeon told me."

"Riley was a great doctor and a good man."

"Ingrid, I'm sorry to have to tell you this."

"Say it."

"Your funeral was yesterday."

I moaned. "Did anyone turn up?"

"There was quite a gathering. Turns out you were rather popular." He gave a comforting smile.

I choked back tears. "I suppose that really does mean there's no going back." A lump caught in my throat. "I've lost everything."

"I'm sorry, truly I am. But now that the guardians believe

you're dead they'll stop hunting you." He lifted the tea cozy and poured a golden trickle of tea into the teacup.

"You're not having one?" I said.

"Just had one."

"I imagined how my life might go," I said. "Not once did I ever imagine anything close to this."

"If you'd have told me that one day I'd be living in a castle with a bunch of vampires and a pretty police inspector—"

"Ex-police inspector."

Sebastian lifted the small pot of milk and poured it into the cup.

"I can do it," I said.

"Let me." He used the silver spoon to stir.

"What am I meant to do?" I said. "I'm so lost."

"Well consider this as your home. We're a grand collection of misfits and we're all very happy here."

"Not quite sure how to take that."

"We're one big happy family. Jadeon's installed an 86 inch TV in what used to be the anteroom. We even have wifi. Orpheus is talking about putting in a pool. You know how much he loves to swim."

"How does Jadeon feel about that?"

"You know how amiable he is."

"Not as amenable as I would like," I said, realizing Seb may not know about what really happened in that morgue.

"Paradom will be happy to share Jadeon's art room with you," he said.

Terror found its way back to me. "I don't paint, Seb. At least not before last night when I apparently took it up. Though I have no memory of it. Did you see the portrait of Jadeon I painted?"

"I did take a peek."

"What did you make of it?"

"You've never painted before?"

"The last time I painted was in school. And then I had no talent for it. What the hell, I'm like a Rembrandt or something."

"Let's be thankful it's not Jackson Pollock."

I let out a nervous laugh. "And those calculations."

"All connected to this stuff you drank, apparently."

"Half of me doesn't want it to last, but there's this ego

driven side that's getting off on knowing stuff I never knew before." I studied my hands. "I'm seriously convinced I can play the piano."

"Maybe you and Alex can play a duet?"

"Seb, I've never had a lesson in my life."

"Oh, that's...disconcerting."

I rested my head back, barely holding my panic at bay. "I'm methodical. I study every detail and calculate my deductions based on elemental facts. This is way out of my league."

"Jadeon's working on it. You have to trust him."

"I'm not sure where he and I stand anymore."

"Give it time. All of this is a big shock. Don't rush yourself."

"I'll allow myself the privilege of taking it easy after we find Helena and Beatrice." I lifted the spoon and cracked the top of the egg. "I'm going to need that laptop, Seb."

"Let me know if there's anything I can do."

"There is." I scrunched up my nose. "Keep the tea coming."

"That I can do."

After eating that delicious egg and all of the toast, I finished off the tea and turned on Sebastian's laptop. I slid in the memory card I'd rescued from my flat that captured all the footage shot through the fox from the Bainard Building. Barely aware of the hours slipping away, I methodically studied each frame. Not that it mattered now, but so far there wasn't any footage of me, just as Jadeon had reassured me.

Outside, birdsong trilled though the air.

Loneliness was kept at bay by the sounds of life reaching me from somewhere in the castle. Like the occasional door banging or other sounds echoing up. Even Alex's laughter could be heard, his voice carrying, and he sounded so happy. I'd only witnessed his moody side so it was comforting to know he accepted me being here. I was sure the revving of a motorbike whizzing past my window was Alex riding around the castle with his new toy. From the sound of the engine, it was a powerful bike too. Knowing Alex, he was probably recklessly riding that thing. Though if he did fall off he'd of course be fine. I heard Sebastian telling Paradom to come down from the chandelier. *Again.*

We really were a collection of misfits, and it really was

comforting to know I was welcome.

"Are you up for a visit?" Anaïs lingered in the doorway.

I patted the bed beside me. "Yes please, I'm nose deep in boring Hauville footage."

Anaïs kicked off her shoes and climbed beside me on the bed, leaning back against the headboard. "I promise to make everything up to you."

"I probably would have done the same in your position," I said.

"No, you wouldn't. I was a total bitch."

"You kind of were."

"How can you not hate me?"

"Because deep down I believed vampires feel love," I said. "You caught me off guard, that's all. Look, Anaïs, you came to me for help and I failed you. I've messed up everything and I promise to put things right too. How about that?"

She wrapped her arm around mine. "We do feel love deeply." Her eyelashes lowered. "I can't get over how kind you are to me even after everything. I took you to the Athenaeum. I alerted the elders you existed."

"Oh Anaïs, I've been digging around the underworld for months. I imagine they knew about me long before I set foot in their place."

She rested her head against my shoulder.

"Let me ask you something," I said. "If you know there's a camera in a room and it's your camera wouldn't you glance at it when you walked in?"

"Makes sense." She shot me a look. "You don't think Hauville knew about the camera?"

"Which means it wasn't his."

"Someone was filming him?" She thought it through. "Perhaps he was being blackmailed?"

"Maybe."

"You're right. That is strange."

Jadeon leaned against the doorjamb.

Anaïs was off the bed in a flash, grabbing her discarded shoes and bare footing it out the room.

"You scared her off." I pushed the laptop aside.

He shrugged a shoulder.

"I've forgiven her," I said.

"So I see." He gestured. "May I come in?"

"This is your room."

"I've taken one of the guest bedrooms."

"No, I should be doing that."

He raised his hand to still me. "I like the idea of you sleeping in my bed."

"Thank you for letting me stay here."

"Ingrid, we want you to think of this as your home."

I reached into his mind yet heard nothing.

"Your symptoms are fading?" he asked.

He was right. Whatever ability I once had to access a vampire's thoughts was now gone. I'd been through hell and back and was left with nothing but fatigue. I felt appeasement mixed with the realization it had all been for nothing. Drinking that concoction had nearly killed me, and I cursed myself for believing that anything good could have come from it.

Jadeon shut the door. "I'm seeing Fabian tomorrow night."

"Can I come with you?"

Jadeon hesitated. "We're meeting at the Athenaeum."

"Can't you meet him somewhere else?"

"And risk him changing his mind?"

"Well at least we'll have some answers."

"Yes." He looked away, his expression thoughtful. What was that? Guilt?

"Jadeon, I take full responsibility for my actions."

"As do I."

"I have to find Helena. Her missing is my fault. I asked her to make some discreet inquires into another department in Scotland Yard and put her in harm's way."

"Discreet inquires and getting a tattoo is not the same thing. She went rogue."

"I hate myself for not catching the fact she was scheming." I threw my hands up in frustration. "I've let everyone down."

"Don't do this to yourself."

Caressing my forehead, I tried to ease the tension.

He pointed to the laptop. "Found something?"

"Not sure. I need to go back to the Bainard Building."

"You're not well enough."

My incredulous stare gave my answer.

"This is not up for discussion," he said. "Please don't defy me."

The silence lingered a little too long and I tried to understand the reason for it, trying and failing to read Jadeon's thoughts. That chasm between us that I'd not so long ago crossed, that closeness we'd found, was seemingly out of reach again.

His gaze locked on mine. "Have I lost you?"

"I don't know," I said, wondering how long before grief no longer had its hooks in me.

His face was full of sorrow, or perhaps it was the fact his control over me waned.

"It was never control I wanted," he said. "It was your love."

"You always had it."

"I'm sorry that you have to go through this."

"You warned me. I didn't listen."

"You have to let this guilt go or it will devour you."

I conceded a vampire would know a thing or two about how to endure life. My lips trembled. "How am I ever going to forgive myself?"

"When your life takes a head dive you have two ways to deal with it," he said. "Freefall into the spin or face it with dignity."

"I have nothing now."

"Ingrid, you have me."

"I don't deserve you."

"Love is waiting for you in the center of all that darkness."

"What if I can't get to it?"

"It will find you. I'll find you." He removed his shoes and pulled off his shirt, leaving his trousers on. "If you're choosing to freefall at least let me fall with you." He climbed onto the bed, wriggling beneath the covers and spooning behind me, hugging me into him. "I want you to fall asleep in my arms. I want you to know what it is to feel safe again." His body pressed against mine.

I'd forgotten how wonderful it felt to be held, how comforting it was to have his arms wrapped around me, his fingers interwoven with mine. For now, I gave myself permission to let this self-loathing go, ease up on this guilt that had bored into my heart. This new normal of pain that threatened never to leave.

He squeezed me back into him, soothing my heart.

With everything I'd lost, everything that had slipped away from me, there was one constant, one person who kept me from drowning. And he was here with me. His love reached into the depths of my soul.

Jadeon whispered, "I will always love you."

CHAPTER 26

I took a second bite out of this slice of buttered toast and closed my eyes in satisfaction while soothing my hunger.

Still feeling a little weak, I carried my plate and mug of tea over to the center kitchen aisle and sat. I'd managed to fumble through my bag full of fresh clothes and pulled on my jeans and a white T-shirt. Being dressed again had me feeling half-normal. Though my eye color had become fixed with this vibrant blue and showed no sign of resolving, I had at least ceased to experience black-outs, moments of genius, and the urge to paint masterpieces. Everyone around me had appeared to find that reassuring too. I'd observed all these experiences like a stunned witness, fascinated by the profoundness of human consciousness to stretch beyond its usual boundaries. I wondered if I was the first person ever to go through this. I really hoped Fabian Snowstrom had answers. This was not exactly something you went to your local doctor with.

I was surrounded by characters whose lives were defined by the supernatural, and therefore talking to them about all this was received with a healthy curiosity and not fear and disbelief. I felt like a paranormal parlor game gone wrong.

Now though, it seemed the spell was fading and I was back to my usual knack of having to read expressions along with body language and was no longer able to read the thoughts streaming out of people's minds. How, I wondered, could anyone endure the ability to hear every thought of those around them? Though Jadeon had reassured me it was something he'd adapted to and that over time he'd even mastered the ability to close down his thoughts to the intrusion of others.

In-between sips of tea and bites of toast, I took in the kitchen. I mused what those who had once lived here hundreds of years ago would make of all these modern appliances. I tried to imagine what this room looked like back when there was only a hearth and a central wooden table. They'd only recently renovated St. Michael's and for centuries its appearance had been no different to how it looked back when Jadeon and Alex were boys. Of course the Mount still looked every bit like an ancient castle, but now it had bathrooms, phones, and even televisions installed. All the creature comforts.

More fascinating still was the thought that Jadeon and Alex had been born here over two hundred years ago and still walked the hallways. Sebastian was right to feel excited about being able to spend time with them. Being around those with such a significant perspective felt like a privilege. I never took it for granted.

With daylight came the delivered promise I'd have the run of the place. Even Sebastian had become a night owl, adjusting his schedule to that of Alex's and Paradom's, and was apparently never up this early.

This morning I'd awoken to find Jadeon gone from the bed we'd shared. He'd left while I was asleep. I missed him so much.

Sparrows had stirred me from my slumber, as had the sun shining through my window, waking me from what felt like the deepest sleep I'd had in a long time, and gratefully nightmare free.

***

Jadeon made me smile when he'd told me last night he wanted an evening together. Just us two curled up on the sofa watching a movie together. I had an idyllic evening ahead of me and couldn't wait for the sunset to come fast enough. These moments with him gave me something to hold on to. I wanted to go in search of him and snuggle back into bed beside him, but hunger had gotten the best of me.

You'd have thought I'd found the Holy Grail from the way I'd reacted to the sliced bread I discovered in the pantry. Finding butter in the fridge had made me giddy with happiness. To be honest, after all I'd been through I was grateful to still be alive.

The stainless steel fridge did its best to blend in with the ancient brickwork. I took another peek inside. It was well stocked. There was a box of chocolate truffles in there and a note card on top. I reached in and read it again.

"For you, my darling Ingrid." – Jadeon

He knew I'd find them. It made me smile, reminding me of when he'd stocked my fridge at home. My smile faded as thoughts of having lost everything screeched through my brain.

There came a gentle wave of Jadeon's presence, as though I'd stepped into some kind of time lapse and felt his emotions as he placed all this food in here. I had a sense he took the greatest pleasure in doing this for me.

Washing up my plate and teacup in the sink, I soaked in the atmosphere of the kitchen. I could almost sense Sebastian moving around in here, feel Alex sitting at the table watching him prepare Paradom's usual meal of cat food. There was a warm, safe feeling in here, bringing with it the sense of mutual respect. Peacefulness. After placing the plate and teacup on the countertop rack to dry, I turned around and leaned back against the sink, roused by what I was picking up.

It was as though the room had a residue, the emotions of those who had been in here earlier lingering as an imprint. The mood, the memory of Sebastian and Alex's interaction, had been somehow captured and had remained long after they'd left.

Realizing what my mind was suggesting, I froze.

This wasn't a musing. I was picking up on the energy within the room. How was this even possible?

My head spun with the implications. If I was correct about what I'd detected, I may very well be able to grasp every interaction from here on in, even if I was never present when those conversations took place. Moving quickly, and just a little excited at the prospect, I made my way out and through the foyer and was again stumped by the emotional waves that swept around me in circles.

Just last night Paradom had hung from the chandelier again and Sebastian had talked him down, only something had caused Sebastian to express his panic. He'd raised his voice at Paradom, his sharp words bringing him down from the chandelier fast. A wave of the incident hit me and I realized that Paradom had sulked afterwards, clearly shaken from Sebastian's uncharacteristic outburst.

My gaze swept the ceiling, trying to work out what had caused Sebastian to snap at Paradom. The remains of his fear oscillated around me. Where the chandelier's prong embedded into the ceiling there were huge cracks along the plaster. All that hanging Paradom had done over months had left fractures weakening the structure and making it unsafe. That chandelier probably cost a small fortune. A sigh escaped my lips as I realized these trailing emotions had led me to this clue. This ultimate answer of what had really happened here last night.

Okay, let's not get too excited.

This might be temporary.

Needing to gather my thoughts and process all this, I found the quiet of the sitting room. Settling onto the soft leather couch, I kicked off my shoes and brought my legs up beneath me. The chocolate chenille blanket felt warm and soft against my skin, the material comforting as I pulled it up to cover me. Smoke from the firewood had soaked into the blanket's fibers and I breathed in its hominess.

The vibration of peace should have radiated from this room, along with a welling of happiness shimmering. Yet it didn't match my current mood.

You're tired. You're run down. You're imagining it.

The cozy décor made it easy to relax. It was nice to envision Alex at the piano. His fingers stroking the keys effortlessly as he moved with the music, telling a story with each note he struck. I chuckled at the thought he'd had a century or two to practice his remarkable talent and that was why he was so good. Alex found playing cathartic. He enjoyed getting lost, carried away to a happier times.

Melancholy… *That's what I'm picking up.*

Oh no.

Jadeon had been in here earlier too. In fact, I sensed he'd sat where I was now, his heart heavy and full of concern over what I was going through. There was something else too and I reached for it, tried to fathom what seemed just out of grasp. If I merely listened...

No, that wasn't how to find it.

Settling back, I waited for the emotion to circle round again, as though time had the residual feelings on a loop and all I had to do was wait for them to come back around.

Oh wow, I felt a rush of wooziness at the impact of Jadeon's love for me, saw him sitting forward and resting his head in his hands. The emotion tore him up in a visceral response to what he truly felt. His deep love was a profound and potent longing for me.

Oh my darling, I feel the same way. I hoped he would pick up on my silent message of love for him from wherever he was in the castle.

Reaching out, I tried to catch the wave as it passed by again. I was mesmerized by this moment.

Despite this new revelation, my thoughts felt more focused than ever. I'd survived the strangest experience, yet I had the sense I'd been left with this ability to read the memory of a room. The truth of a moment caught in time.

I shot to my feet, the realization of its implications vivid. Fearing this extraordinary gift might fade, I ran from the room.

I had to get to London.

CHAPTER 27

"I'm bringing the girls home." I ended the note with this.

And left it for Jadeon and the others, making sure to add I was eternally grateful for all they had done for me. I was feeling better. I could do this.

I left it on the kitchen table, reassured that Sebastian would find it when he came down for breakfast. Also leaving a note for Alex, I promised I'd return his motorbike in one piece. I knew he'd understand my need to borrow it.

It didn't take me long to find his Ducati parked out front. Borrowing Alex's helmet, I rocked the bike off its stand and climbed on. After a quick turn of the key, the engine roared to life. I grasped the handle bars, noting the clutch on the left and the throttle on the right and remembering to center my body for balance.

At eighteen I'd been as reckless as I was now. Despite only having ridden a motorbike a few times, I'd not forgotten how thrilling it was. An old boyfriend had reluctantly agreed for me to take his bike out for a spin. I'd become so enamored with the rush I'd disappeared down Salisbury's country lanes for hours. When I'd finally returned with his bike I'd faced his wrath. I'd fallen hard for his bike but never him. Even then I knew I wanted to be a policewoman. I'd never seen myself doing anything else. I swallowed that memory down along with this self pity. There was no room for selfishness in this mission.

Navigating across The Mount's causeway, I was grateful the tide was out, but even more grateful for this second chance.

There was no time to wait for nightfall, and I feared Jadeon may question my plan and try to stop me. I had no choice but to do this on my own and I had to finish this fast. Too much time had already been lost.

The surge of adrenaline forging though my veins stayed with me all the way to London.

Within hours, I was back where all this had started: the Bainard Building.

Using the service entrance around the back, it had been easy to enter the office building and feign with a confident air that I worked here. No one bothered me. Security wasn't exactly tight. With Hauville gone and his wife distracted, the staff would no doubt feel a little lost, and with deliveries coming and going I went unnoticed.

Standing in Lord Hauville's office, I took in the room. There was that central desk with Hauville's computer, since returned from Scotland Yard's forensics after being stripped of all necessary evidence. That window I'd stepped out of to hide, precariously balancing on the ledge; teetering on the edge of reason.

That threat of a fall now had a new meaning.

I sensed that Lady Hauville had purchased that lamp in the corner. Its antique Victorian flair was a throwback to more conservative times. The tassels running around the base of the shade were so feminine, so gaudy. Lord Hauville hated it, yes, that was what I detected, and from the encircling energy he'd hardly spent any time in here.

Because this was not his office. It was *hers*.

Which meant that computer was also hers.

Like a transparent ghostly image, yet of a living person, I watched mesmerized as the residual fluctuation of Lady Hauville moved about the room and finally came to still by the window. Her apparition peered out at the city. Her angst reached me across the breadth of the room and I unraveled the emotions as they found me, felt her terrible aching over Olivia's diagnosis and her exasperation that her daughter was dying. Fear surged within her veins from the realization there was nothing she could do to save her daughter's life. Another wave brought the reality of her willingness to do anything to try.

Anything...

Returning to the storage room, I read what I could from its memory. That camera inside the fox had been placed there by Lady Hauville. Though I struggled to pull out of the ether her motivation for putting it there. There was just too much confusion. Scotland Yard's policemen coming and going had seemingly contaminated the essence of the memories.

With more questions than before, I made a discreet exit, retracing my steps out of the back of the building and quickly finding the Ducati where I'd parked it. My gut told me more answers could be found at The Royal London Hospital, where Lady Hauville held a consulting position.

Weaving through the busy streets, dodging cars, taxis, and double decker buses, I sped toward Whitechapel Road and one of London's oldest hospitals.

The stunning facade meshed old architecture with new. This hospital was also a teaching facility. Training nurses, midwives, doctors, and dentists to continue the tradition that impressively hailed all the way back to the year 1740. Even today it was reputed as one of the best facilities in the country, providing state-of the art care to patients. After safely parking the bike, I dodged an ambulance pulling away from the curb and made my way into the accident and emergency department.

The heavy aroma of bleach hit my nostrils, sending my nerves on edge. The waiting room was packed with casualties of one form or another—people all sitting upon plastic chairs. The uncomfortable kind. Restless, they waited to be ushered on in to the treatment area and, by the look of many of them, admitted overnight. They, like me, were not getting in there without the triage nurse's permission.

Sensing someone behind me, I turned and scanned the many faces.

Merging out of the crowd, Anaïs strode my way, a stunning gothic vision dressed in a black T-shirt, leather pants, and high platform boots.

I gave her a nod of appreciation. "Jadeon sent you?"

"Yes."

"Is he angry with me?"

"He understands." She shrugged. "I'm under strict orders to

summon him if needed."

"A hands off approach?" I asked, surprised.

"He's never far away, Ingrid, should we need him."

I chuckled. "The illusion of control."

"What do you need from me?"

"I have a hunch."

Anaïs took in the emergency room. "You're looking for Dr. Hauville?"

"I need to speak with her."

Her gaze found the door and it responded, clicking open and permitting our entry. She flashed a smile to the guard and his eyes glazed over; she'd successfully tranced him out. Usually I'd have expressed my disapproval, but not today.

Together we strolled down the white washed corridors, passing nurses, doctors, and technicians, and other hospital staff, all of them with somewhere to be five minutes ago. Anaïs drew the attention from the occasional passer-by, which kept their eyes off me. As I no longer existed, this was a good thing.

We lingered on the outskirts of an organized chaos exacerbated by constantly beeping machines, alarms, and call bells. The staff were right in the middle of shift change. Day staff chatted away in medical lingo, giving detailed reports on their patients to the night nurses and transferring care.

I approached the fifty-something female receptionist. "Can you page Dr. Hauville for me, please?"

"She's not here today," the receptionist said. "Can I take a message?" Though from her expression she didn't want to.

"Which way is her office?" I asked, holding up the beige folder I had found discarded. "Results she asked for STAT." It was of course empty, but she didn't need to know that.

The receptionist, who looked as busy as hell, soon spilled the location. "Down that hallway and third door on the left."

Within minutes, Anaïs and I had located her office. It was decked out in frugal NHS furniture; the small space of a busy doctor. The thin door did little to block out the noise outside. The medical textbooks lining the shelves reflected her specialty, interspersed with family photos here and there to lighten the mood. Her desk was stacked high with paperwork, forms, memorandums, and several medical journals. The lack of patient files proved she'd honored the confidentially she was bound by.

Anaïs guarded the door and I set to work at Dr. Hauville's computer. Taking a seat, I scanned the office for residual traces of movement. She hadn't been here in days so there wasn't a lot to go on. Just her moving around, her mood low, irritated.

After a few minutes, I found the post-it note where she had scribbled her computer access code. A series of numbers and letters both upper and lower case that anyone would be hard pushed to remember. I set to work hacking into her desktop.

Clicking away on the keyboard, I found my way in. Under the patient search icon I entered Beatrice Shaw. Her name didn't come up.

Unfazed, I used the trick that Nick Greene had showed me, accessing any digital evidence that revealed wiped files. Although not as talented as Nick when it came to computer forensics, I knew what to look for when recovering deleted data.

"You found something?" Anaïs said.

"Give me a second." I focused back in.

She joined me by the computer.

I found the ghost file. Anaïs leaned in close and together we read the report, scanning the digital file that had been removed from the medical records database.

"This is a report on a Jane Doe," I said. "Same time frame."

Beatrice had been in a serious car accident and brought here via ambulance. Medics had found her a mile from the accident, seriously injured. That was why Miller hadn't found a trace of her being rescued.

"But where did Beatrice go from here?" Anaïs said. "The morgue?"

The door opened.

A young nurse hesitated when she saw us. "What are you doing?" she said.

"We're techies." I raised my hand to counter her argument. "Dr. Hauville's computer crashed. Sorry we're late getting to it. IT is swamped."

Anaïs folded her arms defensively.

"There it is." I returned my attention to the screen. "The mother of all computer bugs. What the hell was Hauville doing downloading all this illegal software?" I said, exasperated.

Anaïs feigned worry. "Can you save her hard drive?"

I deftly slid the mouse around and clicked away on the keyboard. "Can you ask Dr. Hauville to return to her office? I have a few questions for her."

"She's not here today," the nurse said, frowning.

"No problem," I said. "We'll get this issue sorted by the time she's back." I smiled at the nurse. "Don't worry. No one need know about this."

"Are those contacts?" she asked me. "Your eyes are beautiful."

"Contacts," said Anaïs.

We sighed with relief when the nurse left.

"Dr. Hauville was Beatrice's physician," I read from the screen. "Beatrice's neck was broken and she sustained multiple fractures. Found unconscious."

Anaïs flinched. "She must have been so scared when she woke up."

I pointed. "She looked dead to them."

"As a fledgling she would have taken longer to come round."

"Just like the medics, the emergency staff thought they had a dead Jane Doe."

We read the report detailing the minimal care delivered to Beatrice. "Hauville was the doctor who pronounced her dead," I said. "That's interesting."

"The report ends ten minutes after she was brought in." Anaïs leaned in closer. "Hauville must have witnessed Beatrice's reawakening."

"Her full recovery." I stared up at Anaïs. "Right in front of Hauville's eyes."

"It must have looked like a miracle," Anaïs said.

"No. Hauville saw it for what it was. A supernatural event." Clicking around the screen, I found no discharge information. "No tests were ordered. No emergency transfer to ITU."

"And she made no attempt to document what she saw."

"But every attempt to hide it," I said. "Hauville deleted Beatrice's file."

"Why?"

I shot Anaïs a look. "Let's ask her, shall we?"

CHAPTER 28

The Hauville's secluded Windsor estate was off the beaten track. The last time I had visited here was with Helena, back when we'd believed our arrest warrant would deliver a result.

My throat tightened as thoughts of her surfaced again. Guilt, dragging behind it a whole host of other emotions, caused me to waver. This gut wrenching panic that I was striving to keep at bay threatened to rise to the surface and incapacitate me. I had to force myself to focus.

A Ford Explorer was parked outside the front of the house, hinting someone may be home, and hopefully that someone was Dr. Hauville. Other than that, the place looked deserted.

There was no answer when I knocked on the door.

From behind the house, Anaïs scaled the rear wall while I watched. It truly was a surreal moment, observing what was humanly impossible unfold before my eyes. Anaïs ascended swiftly up the brickwork, soon reaching what looked like a cracked open bedroom window. It kind of looked a little creepy. I wondered how long after a fledgling was turned they'd be able to move like that? Flying would take the kind of courage I wasn't sure I had.

I mean *what the fuck! Flying?*

Caressing my forehead, I tried to soothe this looming headache, soothe this angst that only taking action suppressed. My life was turned on its head. The idea that one day I'd be breaking and entering had never crossed my mind. Yes, I'd taken certain privileges during an investigation, but never had I foreseen I'd be pursuing the same activities I'd once arrested criminals for.

I was somewhere between needing to curl up into a ball and sob for a life that was no longer mine and grasping for the faith that my new life would have meaning. Maybe, just maybe, I'd have more freedom to do more good. I really needed to believe this.

Right now this hope was all I had to keep me going.

Anaïs appeared on the other side of the glass sliding door. She opened the catch and let me in. We made our way through the living room and searched room after room, hoping to find even the smallest clue that Beatrice or Helena had ever been here.

After a few minutes, Anaïs found me in the kitchen and watched with fascination. "You're picking up on something?" she said.

There was a shift in the energy in here. A potent sense of tension, and it wasn't just coming from us. Steadying my impatience and suppressing all my nervous energy from being holed up in a castle for days, I tried to relax a little. "I'm sensing the residual energy."

Her eyes widened.

"I'll explain later," I said.

"Any other super powers you want to tell me about?"

"So far just eyes that glow in the dark and this." I managed a nervous smile. "Do you sense Beatrice?"

"It's too foggy."

I leaned against the kitchen counter and continued to read the room.

Dr. Hauville making tea. Making dinner. Talking on the phone. Preparing a meal...no meals...for more than one.

A shudder of fear slithered up my spine, followed by a tidal wave of emotion. I wasn't sure if it was mine or hers, or Beatrice's. The fractious pulses of energy were difficult to distinguish, impossible to define. Another vision fluctuated. That of Dr. Hauville stomping across the room toward the pantry. Following her ghostly image, I opened the door. Her transparent imprint kept on going before disappearing through the back wall of the pantry. Scrape marks from a door opening and closing marked the tile floor. Though it wasn't immediately obvious, there was a door here.

Please let this be it...

The cold hit us as we descended the dark wooden steps. Another door greeted us at the end of the stairwell.

"Is this a bunker?" I whispered.

"Built during the war?" Anaïs said. "Oh God, no one would ever hear you if you were trapped down here."

Though no stranger to this kind of danger. I was reassured to have Anaïs with me.

"Someone's down here," Anaïs whispered. "A mortal."

The sweet, pungent scent of an air freshener drifted. The quietness was so exaggerated every noise we made echoed. Way down the corridor, the darkness lifted and shards of light burst from beneath a door.

With a nod from Anaïs, she confirmed that this was the room where she was picking up a mortal's presence. Though from the way she frowned she was sensing something else too.

"What is it?" I said.

"Not sure."

Cautiously, we entered.

Anaïs and I locked eyes, stunned...

There, lying beneath the covers of a duvet, was a pale child of no older than twelve. Her shallow breaths were ragged, and her face twisted in torment. A troubled sleep. This was the very same girl from the Hauville's family photo. Olivia, the daughter they were grieving over.

From the equipment, this would pass as a hospital room. A blood pressure machine flashed its last neon result. Her heart rate was dangerously low. An oxygen tank stood ready beside the bed, the 02 mask hanging over it. A blood transfusion hung from a pole beside her, delivering scarlet fluid into her left arm through a bright red tube. A breakfast tray positioned within reach was filled with cups of bright red jello. One of the cups was half eaten with a silver spoon sticking out.

"Is she a vampire?" I whispered to Anaïs.

"I don't know what she is," she said.

The hairs prickled on my forearms and the room felt cold.

Dr. Hauville was standing in the doorway. And she was

pointing a gun at us.

"We want to help you," I said. "Please, put the gun down, Dr. Hauville."

She narrowed her gaze. "I thought you were dead?"

"Is this Olivia?" I said.

"You're trespassing."

"Call the police then." Anaïs folded her arms across her chest.

I gestured to Anaïs as a warning. "Everything is going to be fine." I turned back to Dr. Hauville.

"I read you were killed in a fire?" she said.

"A misprint?" I said.

"Really. Then why was your obituary announced in The Sunday Times?"

My mind scattered into a thousand pieces. Wave after wave of emotion stretched the full length of the room. Fear. Hate. Remorse. Regret.

Olivia stirred, pulling me back into the room.

What the hell was Dr. Hauville doing here? What was she doing to her daughter?

A faint waft of fear slithered past me and I stepped back to avoid it, steadying my feet against the onslaught of transparent waves of emotions.

"Ingrid?" Anaïs threw a concerned look my way.

"I'm okay." I used the pole to steady myself. My hand fumbled for the IV bag, turning it to face me to see it better. There was no label.

"Let go of that," Dr. Hauville said.

"You're giving your daughter vampire blood?" Anaïs said.

Her stare shot from me and back to Anaïs. "How many other people know vampires exist?" She stepped forward. "Do you have any idea what this means?"

"You're not trying to turn her," Anaïs said.

"Just enough to keep her alive." Dr. Hauville held a crazed stare. "The implications are endless."

My gut wrenched with what she was putting Olivia through.

"Where's Beatrice?" Anaïs said.

Hauville looked stony-faced.

"Please," Anaïs said softly.

"Careful. The gun," I sent the mind message to Anaïs, hoping she'd not rile Hauville up and get us shot.

"Your daughter is a hybrid," Anaïs said.

"How do you know?" Dr. Hauville waved the gun at Anaïs. "You're a Gothica, aren't you? You dress like one."

Anaïs glared back at her.

"Please, Imogen." I motioned to the weapon. "We want to help you. We want to help Olivia. Put down the gun."

"You killed your husband?" Anaïs said, her advantage of delving into Dr. Hauville's thoughts both an advantage and a liability.

Her forefinger slid over to the trigger. "Rupert was willing to let her die." Her face turned to sorrow. "I had to choose between them."

The air down here was thin, suffocating so, and I hated this time we were wasting on hearing her confession, yet I knew it would lead us to the girls.

Dr. Hauville shrugged. "I just have to get the levels right and she'll be normal again." She sucked in her breath. "Olivia's alive and that's enough."

"Olivia drinks blood too?" Anaïs said.

Dr. Hauville stared off. And I stared at those cups of jello that weren't.

Whose blood?

"Beatrice came through your A & E," Anaïs said. "She was your patient."

Hauville nodded. "It was a busy night. We'd spent hours sobering up drunks and a few drug users. The nurses were run ragged. I was left alone with Beatrice to pronounce her dead." Dr. Hauville's face was a mixture of defiance and wonder. "I'd never seen anything like it. She was dead. No pulse. Beatrice shook violently and at first I thought she was seizing..."

"How did you realize Beatrice's blood would help your daughter?" I asked.

Dr. Hauville lowered her gaze. "I was preparing the paperwork to send her body to the morgue. She started breathing spontaneously. All her contusions dissipated before my eyes."

"And then you brought her here?" I said.

"I told her I was bringing her back to let her make a full

recovery. Beatrice liked that. I told her I had horses and she could ride them. At first she wanted to help Olivia, but after a few days she wanted to leave."

"You drugged her with laudanum?" I said.

Dr. Hauville looked surprised.

"And Eden?" I said. "What went wrong?"

"An accident," she said. "I was drawing her blood to feed it to Olivia..."

"You didn't realize she wasn't a vampire?" I said. "You drained her thinking she'd survive? Didn't you see her deteriorating?"

"Eden had that circled brand," Dr. Hauville said, looking confused. "Like Beatrice."

"They get the brand before they are turned," I said.

"I know that now," she said.

"When did you find out about your husband's illegal activity?"

"A month ago," she said. "At first the plan was to get him imprisoned so he wouldn't interfere here. Wouldn't stop me."

"The camera in that fox is yours?" I said.

"You found it then?" She looked puzzled. "You faked your death, inspector? Why?"

I waved off her question. "You made sure the police found the evidence that would convict your husband?" I said. "You uploaded the photo of Beatrice bound to a wall. You knew it would put all the attention on him."

"Yes, I set him up," she said. "Rupert cared more about that castle then our daughter. He sold counterfeit goods for years without me finding out. All our savings went on inheritance tax when his father died. We were close to bankruptcy. My salary with the NHS didn't help. He was trying to save us from financial ruin. Social embarrassment."

For the first time, I saw her waver.

Dr. Hauville continued, "When I found Rupert's secret room in the Bainard Building, I realized what he was up to. I begged him to stop. Told him it threatened what we were trying to do here with Olivia. He wouldn't listen. I assumed he'd go to prison for a few years. Give me the time I needed to perfect all this."

"What made you change your mind and kill him?" Anaïs

asked.

"He threatened to put a stop to what I was doing here."

"How did you kill him?" I asked softly.

"Laudanum overdose."

"Where's his body?" Anaïs asked.

"I buried him out there." Her gaze slid east of the house, her lips trembled.

"I'm so sorry, Imogen," I said, but I wasn't sorry for her. My sorrow was for Olivia and Beatrice and Helena, and the loss of Eden.

"Where's Helena?" I said softly. "She's not a vampire, Imogen."

Her eyes widened. "She has the mark too."

"She's not a Gothica," I said. "She got the brand to help find Beatrice."

Dr. Hauville frowned. "And Beatrice must feed."

Bile rose in my throat. "Is Helena still alive?"

"Mummy?" Olivia stirred, peeking above the bedsheet. "Who are these people, Mummy?"

"They're leaving now, darling," Dr. Hauville said.

"Can I have my drink now, Mummy?" Olivia said.

"In a moment, darling. Let me see these nice people out."

The child looked possessed, veins bulging, her glare full of fury. Those fangs bared and ready.

"In a moment, darling," Dr. Hauville said calmly, waving the gun at us. "Out."

Anaïs and I preceded Dr. Hauville out into the corridor.

Anaïs knocked the gun out of Hauville's hand, sending it flying, and she pressed her up against the wall, trying to control her flailing.

I picked up the gun and pointed it at Dr. Hauville. "Where are they?"

"I have to finish my work." She struggled against Anaïs' grip.

My hair was yanked painfully and I staggered back, feeling Olivia's fangs puncturing my throat. Struggling against the attack, I fell.

Anaïs dragged Olivia off and away from me. I felt a trickle of blood snaking down my neck. Olivia turned on Anaïs, screaming wildly, her eyes feral, her irises as black as night. Anaïs tried to hold her back, hold her off, but the child was strong.

I tried to help Anaïs.

Orpheus pushed me out of the way. Never had I been so happy to see him. He grabbed Olivia by the shoulders and yanked her off Anaïs. With his fangs bared, Orpheus' rage looked bestial. His strong hands squeezed the child's throat, choking the life out of her. Olivia flopped in his arms like a rag doll and slipped from his grasp. She lay still, *dead.*

Dr. Hauville flung herself at me, screaming, thrusting me against the wall. She held a pointed wooden dagger to my chest.

Another shot rang out.

Dr. Hauville's eyes widened and her face reddened and her cheeks puffed. She slumped to the ground beside me.

Jadeon had shot the fatal bullet. "Ingrid, are you all right?" He knelt beside me.

Olivia raised her head, her eyes blinking.

"Oh hell no," Orpheus said.

Olivia flew toward him like a wild phantom, her eyes full of fury, her fangs bared, her fingernails scratching him. Jadeon picked up the wooden stake from the floor, flew at her, and rammed the tip into Olivia's back. She gawped and slipped to the ground.

"That should work," Orpheus said calmly.

Fighting the dizziness, and this nauseating realization we'd killed a twelve-year-old, I tried and failed to get up. I was too weak to argue, and too stunned by a child lying dead mere feet away. Her mother too. A sob tore from me that I'd failed them. Not handled this right. Not gotten through to Imogen.

"Oh God..." The only person who knew where Beatrice and Helena were lay dead.

"They're here," Orpheus said, his glare directed into the dark.

Jadeon rose and offered me his hand. He pulled me to my feet. Half distracted, my stare found Olivia.

"She wasn't human," Jadeon said. "I know it doesn't make it any easier." He ran his hand through my hair, trying to comfort me.

"We have to find them," I said, shaking off this angst. I'd fucked up again.

Together, Jadeon, Orpheus, Anaïs and I went in search of them. Only this moment mattered. Everything that had gone before became a blur. Ignoring this trembling, feeling battered and bruised, I used the adrenaline surging through my veins to give me the strength to keep up with them.

My sigh of relief echoed.

Helena lay in the corner of a locked cell, curled up in a ball with her back to us. She was clean at least, clothed, seemingly well cared for, despite the cruelty of her capture. Jadeon easily broke the lock to her prison and quickly entered. He scooped her up in his arms, offering words of comfort that she was safe now.

From somewhere down the corridor came the cries of relief from Anaïs at finding Beatrice. Freedom for them was a few steps away and my heart finally eased a little.

Jadeon carried Helena out of the basement and up through the house and out into the night. I so wanted to embrace her, but she couldn't be allowed to see me. I couldn't burden her with the secret I was alive. Helena still had to learn of Riley's death and she'd already been through so much.

From the front lawn, we watched Orpheus leap behind the wheel of the Viper and set off fast with Helena lying in the back passenger seat. Wexham Park Hospital was only six miles away in Slough. They'd be there in minutes. I knew Helena would receive the care she needed. Her paleness indicated she'd need a blood transfusion within minutes of arriving.

It amazed me how I truly believed Orpheus could be trusted and that he'd do what needed to be done. He really was a changed man—*vampire*.

I could breathe again.

Anaïs refused to let Beatrice go. She sat upon the grassy bank holding her in her arms, rocking with her, refusing Jadeon's offer to help. There was something beautiful about the way Anaïs held Beatrice, her wrist pressed against her lover's mouth to nourish her as the laudanum wore off.

Standing beside Jadeon I waited, not rushing Anaïs' reunion with Beatrice, giving them both the time they needed.

"You really are an extraordinary woman," Jadeon said. "Do

you know that?"

I shook my head in disagreement. My heart ached that Olivia and her mother hadn't made it.

"Olivia would never have survived," he said.

"She was child."

"Her suffering was prolonged. Her death was inevitable."

"How do you cope with everything life throws at you?" I said. "For centuries without end?"

Jadeon wrapped his arm around my waist and pulled me to him in a hug. "You fall in love."

"You soothe my soul, Jadeon Artimas," I said. "I've lost count of the times you've saved me."

"You don't need the immortals. It is we who need you."

"Will there ever be a time when I'm welcome in your world?"

"You always find a way."

"When we were in the morgue, you told Riley that if you turned him he might lose his soul?"

Jadeon gave a slow, assured nod.

"You have a soul," I said. "I know you do. I feel its warmth, its vitality."

"There are times when I believe I do..."

"What?"

"Consider what I am."

"I love what you are." And I did. To me, Jadeon was the most beautiful man I'd ever met, and the threat of living without him was impossible to bear. It felt good to be in his arms again, and as I nestled into his chest I realized that wherever Jadeon was meant home.

"I love you, Ingrid."

"I know." I nuzzled in farther. "Meet me tomorrow night."

"Of course. Where?"

"The Athenaeum." I braced for his response.

Jadeon took in a deep, cleansing breath and reached into his jacket pocket. I recognized the Scirpus, the metal key. I'd left it at the flat that night when I'd gathered my belongings in a haze drenched panic.

Jadeon offered me the key. "Then you'll need this."

CHAPTER 29

Highgate Cemetery had this way of making death feel so romantic.

The grandness of the place, the way it elegantly paid homage to those who rested here, was truly inspiring. Tombstone after tombstone rose out of the ground with their dramatic statues watching over them. Some were of stone angels, others were animals, and there was even a life-size grand stone piano inscribed with the name Harry Thornton. The shrubbery provided a comforting green backdrop to the graveyard, interspersed with the loveliest flowers. Winding pathways proceeded in every direction, leading off to even more elaborately carved tombs.

The mood was calm. There was a residual imprint of mourners who'd strolled by a few hours ago, and remnants of their emotions mixed with the flotsam left behind by foreign tourists who'd come to admire how we honored our dead. This gift to read the history of a place had still not left me. I had mixed feelings about whether it ever would. The cool evening air filled my lungs and I breathed it in.

The stillness here gave me hope that one day I'd find it for myself. Despite all my suffering, peace lay on the other side of my struggle. My life would never be the same again and my mind went round and around in circles trying to come to terms with the fact.

I'd survived, unlike my dearest Riley.

This arched tombstone honored his life. He'd never have wanted anything decadent. The dates between his birth and death were cruelly short. My throat tightened as grief welled over losing him. Wiping away stray tears, my attention drifted to the plot beside his, as though he might care about such a thing. Mary-Anne Webster was buried next to him. A sixteen year-old, her tombstone dated June 12th, 1860. Jadeon had made sure that Riley's resting place was at least peaceful and in a quiet corner.

Jadeon had also told me that somewhere amongst all these tombstones lay mine. I wasn't ready to pay a visit, not yet. Seeing my name on a gravestone may very well have sent me spiraling. The wretchedness of finality.

I must have looked strange, this young woman standing at the graveside dressed in black leather trousers and a black silk shirt; high heeled books rounded out my homage to goth. An Edward the III sword was strapped to my back. I'd snuck back to Jadeon's flat, the one I'd once called home, and removed it from his spare bedroom, lifting it from the back wall with the reverence the weapon deserved.

Paradom had warned me *the bridge beneath your feet will crumble.*

And it crumbled still.

"It's unlike you to be morose." His tone was deep, cultured.

I turned to see Orpheus standing a few feet away, dressed warmly in a black woolen coat, his hands tucked into his pockets as though the cold might have any effect. He went to unbutton it but I raised my hand and gestured I didn't want it.

The pinch of cold was keeping me sharp, keeping me focused. "Orpheus, are you still following me?"

"I imagine you'd like that," he said. "What are you intending to do with that sword?"

I faced Riley's tombstone.

"I know a thing or two about revenge," he said. "It's never worth it."

"Surely the great Orpheus' heart hasn't softened?"

He arched a brow. "Jadeon will protect you to the end of the world. Which I suppose is what true love is all about."

I shuddered with the full impact of what I'd done to put Riley in harm's way. I'd visited that place, with all its secrets. If I didn't have such a respect for books, for history, I'd burn the bloody place down. Whatever was hidden in the Athenaeum wasn't worth Riley's death. Closing my eyes, I went within, though found no refuge.

Orpheus stepped forward to comfort me, but I motioned for him to keep his distance. I didn't deserve his sympathy.

"Let's go back to Cornwall," he said. "Sebastian will take good care of you."

"I don't need taking care of."

"You need time to heal, Ingrid."

"I'm not ready to go back."

"If you were mine—" He flashed the sharpest fangs. "I'd lock you away in that castle until you promised to comply."

I raised my chin, defiant. "You'd soon bore of me."

He glanced at the sword. "I doubt that."

"Well, if you'll excuse me, I have an appointment with the old guard."

He gave a nod, conceding that nothing could be done to stop me. "See you on the other side then."

"You doubt I'll survive this?"

"You'll be the first." With a tilt of his head, he conceded.

"I never did thank you," I said, "for keeping me alive all this time."

"I've grown rather fond of you."

"Does that make us friends?"

He gave a roguish smile and dematerialized as swiftly as he'd appeared. Autumn leaves tumbled in the place he'd stood.

Beneath this headstone rested a perfect man who had dedicated his life to science, to the betterment of mankind. He would be mourned for eternity.

I knelt before his grave. "Riley, I commit the rest of my life to doing good in your name. This I promise you."

The stillness paid homage to all he had given and all he had been.

Withdrawing from the graveyard under the cover of darkness, I headed out toward Pall Mall. Not being stopped by anyone, for the sword strapped to my back was both reassuring and alarming at the same time.

I headed on in.

Within the Athenaeum I surveyed the empty foyer, again admiring the immenseness. This grandeur that served to intimidate any visitor. But not me. Not now. And never again.

I soaked in the elegance, marveling at the marble flooring that I now felt worthy to walk upon. Sensing unseen eyes that traced my every move, I stood in the center and withdrew my sword from its sheath, the blade breathing its way to freedom. The scrape of metal against metal.

And I waited for him.

Even here in this vampire's lair, I sensed a residual trace of those who'd visited. Though unlike the mood that mortals left behind, I picked up on energy like no other. An unwavering confidence, a surety, a sensuous semblance that drifted by; a dark luring me into the very heart of the underworld. The Athenaeum was the center of the elder's domain.

Adrenaline forged through my veins, setting my nerves alight and heightening my senses. A shadow loomed in the distance and I readied myself, widening my gait for balance. He rose into the air and scurried along the frescoed ceiling, heading closer at an alarming speed. Turning, I traced his movements.

The monk leaped to the ground before me. His eyes burned with hate as he flipped back his hood. The only sound was that of my breath. The only sensation that of my racing heart.

He lunged at me.

I aimed the sword at his chest and he flew over me. Spinning around, sensing him behind me, I thrust my sword at his throat, but he dodged the strike and flew into the air and landed a few feet away.

He sent me hurtling. My head bashed against the stone staircase, dazing me, blurring my vision and sending a blinding pain into my skull. Clutching my sword before me, I braced for another attack.

He halted feet away. His grimace frozen. His eyes wide in terror.

The tip of a sword, though not mine, protruded from the front of his stomach, and blood poured from his mouth. He slumped to his knees. Jadeon stood behind him and withdrew his blade. Blood dripped from the end, staining the marble floor red.

"I'm not usually one to interfere," Jadeon said calmly. "But as it's you…"

He stood proudly, his blazing stare full of power, dashingly dressed in the finest waistcoat and black suit. His hair ruffled to perfection. His expression calm, it dissolved into a gentle smile. He oozed serenity, even with the monk crumpled at his feet.

The monk wasn't moving, but he was far from dead. Shocked, no doubt, at being impaled by Dominion himself. I pushed away, putting some distance between me and my attacker.

"Is that my sword?" Jadeon said.

"Might be."

"Thought I recognized it."

"I didn't need your help." I took in the deepest breath, wanting to believe that lie.

Jadeon raised a hand in the way of a command. Two other monks, their hoods covering their faces, trekked toward us. They grabbed their fallen colleague and dragged him away across the floor, his legs scraping behind him.

"What will happen to him?" I said.

"He disobeyed an order," Jadeon said.

"Will they kill him?"

"There will be a trial. So we'll see." He lowered his gaze and held out his hand, assisting me to my feet, his strength disarming.

I let go and raised my sword toward his chest. "It was you who poisoned me?"

Jadeon reached out and his fingers touched the tip of my sword. He lowered it. This was Dominion, the most powerful vampire that had ever walked the earth, and I'd just threatened him with my sword.

I'd threatened my lover. *Once lover.*

My lips trembled.

Jadeon responded calmly. "Blue illuminate would have killed you. I improvised. That is, Fabian Snowstrom concocted something for you that was a little more palatable."

"But you were angry with me for drinking it?"

"I was angry with you because you were determined to drink blue illuminate."

The sob caught in my throat. "What have you done to me?"

"You asked me to find a way, Ingrid." He lowered his gaze. "I did."

"What is happening to me?"

"An incantation reserved for kings who once ruled the earth. It made them legends. It was better than the alternative."

"Oh." I swallowed hard. "Is is permanent?"

"Yes."

I sucked in my breath, dazzled that I'd been left with this. The implications were far reaching. This gift. *This curse.*

"The alternative wasn't an option," he said. "I made a vow to protect you and I intend to keep it."

It crossed my mind how this gift would have been back when I was in the police. Only days had passed since my old life had bled away, but it felt longer.

"I was willing to die," I whispered it.

"Then you are ready."

Jadeon's aura exuded a supernatural force, as though he'd harnessed nature's power. Having been bequeathed this new sense to interpret energy fields emanating from each life force, I'd not felt it from him before. I wanted to throw myself into his arms, embrace him, but his sternness held me at bay. Now I understood why Orpheus and all other vampires respected him. The energy circulating him would have those around him on their knees.

Shaking my head in denial, trying to focus through this blur of radiating light that came off him, I tried to convince myself this wasn't happening. That this new found ability wouldn't endure a lifetime.

"Don't be frightened of it," he said. "It's always like this at first. That same intuition you've relied upon your whole life, that same inner feeling that has guided you during your darkest days, it's still there. It hasn't left you. In fact it's burning brighter than ever. Give yourself over to that trust, Ingrid. Surrender to this sorcery bestowed upon you."

"I'm ready."

He held out his hand. "The Athenaeum holds one of the greatest secrets of mankind. It's time we shared it with you."

A jolt of excitement ran up my spine. "But is it worth dying for?"

He gestured. "Yes."

We made our way through the foyer and onward, our silence

doing nothing to ease the tension between us. With a pull of the candle holder upon that familiar fireplace, the entryway to the lower chamber scraped open.

Within the grand library, the temperature dropped and blackness befell the enormous chamber. That faint scent of old books and burning wax permeated the air, instilling a sense of timeless knowledge yet to be discovered. This wonder of literary greatness would bring any awed scholar to their knees.

"Over there, we have books on every religion known to man." Jadeon swept his hand outward. "And over there are sacred texts strewn upon shelves, waiting for when the reader is ready to find them. As though the books themselves are living, breathing entities."

"What about Riley?"

"His memory will be honored."

"It's not enough."

"It rarely is." He lowered his gaze. "Heaven exists for men like him."

Taking in the view, the soft yellow lighting that bathed the library, I knew there was more to this place than books. Within the Athenaeum's walls lay a profound revelation that I only now felt ready for. "The spell Fabian cast on me made me worthy to stand here," I said in realization.

Jadeon gave the faintest smile. "The elders will only approve of you if you are befitting their world."

The magnitude of his disclosure left me stunned.

"To be one of us," he continued. "To serve alongside us, you must be considered a celestial being."

"One with a unique gift?"

It's too much...

"I'm here for you," he said softly. "I always will be."

I needed him to tell me I could stay, that he'd let me remain by his side as his friend, his lover. Whatever he wanted me to be.

He gave a slow, calm smile.

"Is that a yes?" I said.

"Take off your sword."

Lifting off the harness, I laid my weapon at the door.

He reached for my hand and took it in his. "Observe. Say nothing. Understand?"

"Yes."

The next room we entered seemed insignificant compared to the grandness of the library that we'd left behind. Jadeon gave a nod that this was what he wanted to show me. I was stunned by the simplicity of the area.

Leather couches were positioned here and there. The fireplace roared with fresh firewood, its smoke billowing up a chimney. The scent of pine and cigars lingered. Five men sat in well-worn armchairs, their ages stretching between twenty and sixty-years-old. Some of them were reading and others chatted amongst themselves. They regarded us briefly before their focus returned to their books, or their conversations, showing an easy comfort. Their irises had given away their immortality. Unlike the vampires who reigned above, these were easily more sedate. The atmosphere oozed calmness.

I tried to read from Jadeon what he was showing me. It all seemed so ordinary. A door opened behind us and a man of seventy or so entered. His flock of white hair and matching beard gave him a professorial air. He was dressed smartly in black trousers, a checkered shirt, and a suede jacket. His shocking brown irises gave away his immortality. He oozed an old-school charm. He could have strolled along the corridors of Cambridge University, or Oxford, or held a lecture at some other prestigious college and his students would be none the wiser.

The vampire took Jadeon's hands in his. "You've left it too long between visits," he said in a Scottish accent.

"Alecks, it's good to see you," Jadeon said.

"And who is this lovely lady?"

"Ingrid Jansen."

"Welcome Ingrid. We're delighted to have you visit us."

"It's good to be here," I said, wherever here was meant to be.

"So your death was faked too?"

My throat tightened and I gave a weak nod.

"You get used to it," Alecks said, turning to his friends. "We all did."

"They are waiting for her," Jadeon said, cutting this introduction painfully short.

They?

"Let's not leave too much time between visits," Alecks said, his face crinkling into a smile.

I followed Jadeon out. Hands shaking, not sure what that was all about, I reached for my sword and eased the harness back over my head, securing the weapon snug behind me. I trusted Jadeon with my life but felt safer with my weapon close to hand. He led me back through the library toward the exit.

Was this the secret? A bunch of old men sitting in an anteroom and smoking cigars? Studious men with a good deal of wisdom no doubt, but surely not the kind anyone should die for?

"Jadeon?"

"Nothing in life is ever as it seems," he said. "Dare to peer beyond the ordinary."

"Who was that man?"

His face lit up. "Dr. Graham Alexander Bell."

I took the deepest breath.

No, impossible...

Jadeon arched a brow. "The telephone."

The same Bell who invented..."

"Yes."

"You called him Alecks?" I said.

"That's his name."

The air felt thick, stuffy, just like the room we'd left behind, cloaked in too much cigar smoke.

"And the others?" I said.

"All of them chose immortality so that their genius would endure."

"They're all inventors?" This rush made my head spin. I needed to sit down. I needed to go back in there. "How many are there?"

Jadeon gave a mega-watt smile as that tough, masterful demeanor cracked a little.

I failed to hide my exhilaration.

"Many advances both in science and medicine have been discovered here and allowed their freedom in the world." He gave a nod, letting me know more would be revealed in time.

There were so many questions. A need to settle my rambling thoughts and think rationally about what this really meant. I turned away, needing to go back.

Though we walked the full distance of the library, I scarcely remembered it. My mind was too far away, trying to piece together the revelation that perhaps many of our greatest minds had chosen the pathway of immortality.

My heart raced with the thrill of it. "You offer these individuals the choice to become vampires?"

"Council members deem whom to approach. It's been done this way for centuries."

We made our way up the stone steps and out, along the foyer, toward an enormous double doorway, reaching at least twenty feet high and making it one of the most impressive entryways I'd ever seen.

Jadeon gestured to the door.

From inside my jacket pocket I removed the ornate key that Jadeon had handed me last night. "You gave me this?"

"No," he said.

My thumb caressed the metal ridges.

"Those who wait for you on the other side." He brushed a stray hair out of my eyes. "If you were ever to make it this far, Ingrid, they would consider you worthy to use it."

The key fit perfectly into the double doorway's lock. I took a moment to savor this. And then turned the key, its mechanism echoing. These endless possibilities beckoned.

Doors swung open before us and my heartbeat faltered.

Within this vast candlelit room, hundreds of immortals were gathered, all dressed in their finest regalia. Again their striking beauty awed me, all of them dressed decadently in velvets, and silks, and richly textured leathers, just as I'd seen when I'd first visited. I recognized the tall redhead who wore an outfit of armor. That stunning raven haired goddess who had eyed me suspiciously. Elaborate headdresses were worn by some, most were bejeweled in one way or another.

A pathway cleared down the center.

Jadeon swept his hand wide. "If you were to enter through these doors, you would enter as Bohemia."

The greatest joy swept over me. "Bohemia," I whispered.

"But you're not going in," he said flatly.

My gaze shot to the many beautiful faces, the glare of the irises holding me in a vice-like mystical grip. "Why?"

"Because—"

"I have as much a right to be here."

"That may be true—"

"I've more than earned my right to stand here. Go in there."

"Woman! Will you listen to me?"

"Okay," I relented, readying for whatever he was about to say and preparing for my comeback. Which would be right of course. My opinion would carry weight and have him seeing reason.

Jadeon reached into his inner jacket pocket and held out a small black velvet box.

"What is it?"

He eased open the lid, revealing a dazzling sapphire ring. I mean gorgeous. Like stunning and take your breath away kind of gorgeous.

My voice found me again. "Are you…?"

"Yes, I am."

"Is that…"

"An engagement ring." He beamed at me. "I thought we'd go out and celebrate. If you like?"

I flung myself into his arms and held him tightly.

"You haven't answered?" He hugged me.

"You have to say the words," I said, tears falling as I pulled back to look at his face. His gorgeous, handsome, perfect face as I looked into those dreamy eyes that held mine with all their mystical deliciousness.

"My, you really do have it bad," he said.

I thumped him.

Jadeon flashed a mega-watt smile. "Ingrid, will you marry me?"

"Yes, of course."

He held my shoulders. "Listen, my darling, I know what it is you have been through. I know what you have lost. I promise with every fiber of my being to give you the life of your dreams."

Trembling in the wake of all that had happened, my life no longer recognizable, I reached for him, needing to be closer.

"Hey," he soothed. "I'll always be right beside you, guiding you every step of the way." His gaze found the room of vampires, their faces staring back at us. "Ancient civilizations have risen and fallen. We are not perfect by any means, but we, they, have done what needed to be done in order to survive. There's too much at stake here. You see that now. Mistakes have been made and those who are guilty will be punished. We ask your forgiveness."

"They accept me then? Us?"

"Well, now that the risk of you arresting anyone has been eliminated."

"You sound like Orpheus."

"Careful."

"Sensitive subject?"

"Orpheus will never have you." He raised my chin with his fingertip. "I claim you. You're mine."

"I am yours."

"Paris sound okay to you?" he said. "For a honeymoon?"

I covered my face with my hands. He knew I'd always wanted to go with him.

"Well that went better than expected," he said.

"You didn't think I'd say yes?"

"Oh, I knew you'd say *yes*."

I thumped his chest playfully again.

Jadeon laughed and cupped my face with his hands, leaning in to kiss me leisurely, circling my tongue, not caring about these witnesses. My lips pressed against his, desiring this feeling of him being this close.

Saving me. Possessing me. Loving me.

Completing me.

ABOUT THE AUTHOR

USA Today bestselling author Vanessa Fewings writes both contemporary romance novels and dark erotic suspense.

vanessafewings.com

Made in the USA
Columbia, SC
05 October 2022

68849175R00162